COMPOUND FRACTURE

LETTER FROM THE AUTHOR

Hopefully, by the time this book goes to print, I'll have scrapped this letter and written a new one.

I mean it. I'm desperate to write a different intro to this thing. If I do write a new one, I'll write about how much I love West Virginia. I'll write about family reunions in the mountains, and steep switchback roads, and venison in the freezer, and my half-remembered Appalachian drawl and and and.

Instead, I have to write about how tough it is to be trans in America right now. By the time *Compound Fracture* is released, I'll be twenty-six years old, and I'll have seen bathroom bills, state-sponsored attempts to remove trans kids from supportive parents, crackdowns on gender-related care, and so much more. And if you're disabled on top of it? Christ.

I guess what I'm saying is, I'm sorry it's so difficult. We shouldn't have to fight so hard to exist. We deserve better.

But, of course, this is a book about fighting as hard as you can. So please note that we're going to deal with some difficult topics: graphic violence including police violence, transphobia, opioid use and withdrawal, and disturbing images. This is a book about an autistic, queer trans kid who loves his family and all the people who love him back . . . as well as all the people who want him dead. Actually, this book is kind of like moonshine. It's gonna burn like hell going down.

And, well, looks like this author's note is still here.

If I promise you that this book has a happy ending, does that make it better? Does that make any of it easier to swallow?

Yours,
Andrew

For my family.
This one is about you.

—A. J. W.

Published by Peachtree Teen
An imprint of PEACHTREE PUBLISHING COMPANY INC.
1700 Chattahoochee Avenue
Atlanta, Georgia 30318-2112
PeachtreeBooks.com

Text © 2024 by Andrew Joseph White
Jacket illustration © 2024 by Evangeline Gallagher

Edited by Ashley Hearn
Design and composition by Lily Steele

Printed and bound in July 2024 at Sheridan, Chelsea, MI, USA.
10 9 8 7 6 5 4 3 2 1
First Edition
ISBN: 978-1-68263-612-1

Library of Congress Cataloging-in-Publication Data

Names: White, Andrew Joseph, author.
Title: Compound fracture / Andrew Joseph White.
Description: First edition. | Atlanta, Georgia : Peachtree Teen, 2024. |
    Audience: Ages 14 and Up. | Audience: Grades 10–12. | Summary: After
    being nearly beaten to death for evidence he holds against the corrupt
    sheriff, sixteen-year-old transgender Miles joins his fellow townsfolk
    to end the blood feud and oppressive politics that plague his town.
Identifiers: LCCN 2024014907 | ISBN 9781682636121 (hardcover) | ISBN
    9781682637395 (ebook)
Subjects: CYAC: Transgender people—Fiction. | Vendetta—Fiction. |
    Corruption—Fiction. | City and town life—Fiction. | Appalachian
    Region—Fiction. | West Virginia—Fiction. | LCGFT: Thrillers (Fiction)
    | Novels.
Classification: LCC PZ7.1.W4418 Co 2024 | DDC [Fic]—dc23
LC record available at https://lccn.loc.gov/2024014907

ANDREW JOSEPH WHITE

COMPOUND FRACTURE

PEACHTREE
Teen

TWIST CREEK CALAMITY

Part of the West Virginia coal wars

*This article is about the 1917 strike. For the preceding mining accident, see **North Mountain Coal Company disaster of 1917**.*

Date	May 27 to June 4, 1917
Location	Twist Creek County, West Virginia
Resulted in	Law enforcement victory
• 40–50 killed • 200 arrested • Execution of strike leader Saint Abernethy	

The Twist Creek Calamity, or the McLachlan-Pearson labor riot of 1917, was a confrontation between striking coal miners and mine operators, the Baldwin-Felts Detective Agency, and law enforcement. Though the strike unofficially began on May 24, after the North Mountain Coal Company disaster of 1917, the kidnapping of Joseph Davenport by striker Saint Abernethy marked the official start of the incident. It is also one of the only confrontations of the coal wars to occur in the northern coalfields of West Virginia as opposed to farther south.

While one of the deadliest labor conflicts in American history, it is often overlooked due to a lack of reporting or firsthand accounts.

This article is a stub.

CHAPTER
ONE

When the sheriff of Twist Creek County—and all those other sons of bitches, the Baldwin-Felts agents and bloodthirsty strikebreakers—finally caught my great-great-grandfather and dragged his ass up from the mine to make a spectacle of his execution, they killed him by hammering a railroad spike through his mouth.

That's what they did to labor strikers a hundred years ago—machine guns, spare World War I munitions, railroad spikes. And I don't know if you've gone and picked up a railroad spike before, but they're big. Big enough that my great-great-grandfather must have choked on it. He must have gagged waiting for the hammer to come down. One time I opened Dad's toolbox and put a big rusty nail between my teeth and held it there, breathing around the metal, trying to imagine how it'd be to go and die like that.

Our family name is misspelled in the article, by the way. It's Abernathy. Not Abernethy.

CHAPTER TWO

Last week, I stole a fistful of old photos, made exactly three sets of copies at the school library, and put the originals safely back in Dad's lockbox. The originals are blurry, and the scanner made it worse, but it's enough. Twisted metal and out-of-focus fire, Mrs. O'Brien's charred corpse almost visible if you squint. I have one of the sets now: all the photos on the same piece of cheap printer paper, folded twice and jammed in my pocket.

But before I sneak out to the graduation party and make a mess of things, I check on my parents.

My dog, Lady, trails behind me as I slip out of my room. "Shh," I whisper, crinkling her ears. She huffs. "Don't fuck me on this."

Mom's in bed for once. She sleeps all curled up, knee to her chest and wrists tucked under her chin. I get that from her. She has the fan going too, full blast even though summer rarely gets warm enough to justify it, with the corner of grandma's quilt clutched tight in her hands. She deserves the rest. Nursing home's been running her ragged. I leave her be.

Dad, though, is passed out at his computer. The light of the screensaver makes the living room look strange; it washes out the camo-print blanket and reflects in the glass eyes of the deer head over the TV. I step carefully, avoiding the spots of the old floor that creak, and lean over my father to inspect the tangle of emails and printouts.

Election results map. West Virginia municipal guide, the *running for office* version. A bunch of email drafts, all unfinished, most to recipients I recognize but some I don't. Tylenol. Discarded cane under the desk. Lockbox of photos from the accident that I definitely didn't find the key for last week.

I should probably be excited he's gotten it in his head—seems like he's gonna run for a county seat again, if I'm reading all this right—but I just feel sick. After what happened last time, it's hard not to be scared.

But that's why I'm helping, right?

Quiet as I can, I gather the printouts in a folder and ease them into a drawer. Close the emails and PDFs. Wipe the browser history, scrub the downloads folder, clear the "Recent Items" section of the File Explorer. Lady sniffs the couch and watches me sideways, asking why the hell I'm sneaking around. Dad snores a little. In the blue light from the screen, the scars on his leg are paper white.

And then I stop. Maybe I could—

I pull out my phone and reopen my own email draft, a finger hovering above *send*.

I don't have to send this. Full honesty, I probably shouldn't. Mom and Dad have enough to deal with right now, because being poor means there's always something to deal with—endless medical bills, squirreling away cash to keep the heat on this winter, fronting house repairs because our landlord can't be bothered—and I've been putting this off for so long that, really, what's a few more weeks? Months?

But whatever. I'm already doing stupid shit tonight.

I hit *send*.

An email notification flashes on the desktop. Subject line: *Mom, Dad, I'm trans*. Body text: *I'd say there's something I have to tell you, but the subject line is kind of a spoiler . . .* etc. etc.

Dad should thank me. If I forgot to hide something, this should cause enough of a ruckus that Mom won't notice.

Still, before I leave, I double-check the desk and pour Dad a glass of water, because he always wakes up thirsty. The photocopies are heavy as buckshot in my pocket. The email notification on the desktop makes me itch.

Bite the bullet, Miles. Do it.

Lady sits in the kitchen, head cocked but silent. She knows when not to bark. Good girl. "Love you," I say over my shoulder to the quiet house.

✦

Twist Creek County High throws a graduation party every year, right on the riverbank at the bottom of the valley, a straight shot down the mountain from my house. It's a game, apparently, seeing what all you can sneak away for it. Red jugs of gasoline, coolers for the drinks, moonshine jars from the back of the freezer. Some parents have started staying up on the last day of school with flashlights, trying to bust it, but most roll their eyes and let it happen. Nothing else to be doing round here, and I figure they'd rather their kids do this than blow shit up with their dad's hunting rifle for fun.

I've never been to one before. Even if Mom and Dad weren't so paranoid about letting me out of their sight, and rightfully so, I don't do parties. Simple as that. Deer don't do hunting season, rats don't do traps, and I don't do parties. So I'm huddled behind the snack table, chewing on the shoelace I bought specifically for chewing on, scanning the party for trouble.

I don't got anxiety or nothing. No more than I need to stay in one piece around here, at least. I just—

I don't know. People are too much work, and I don't like most of them.

Anyway, I swear the whole student body of Twist Creek County High is here, throwing homework into the bonfire and drinking cheap beer, though we're a small school so that's only, what, two hundred people? Jared Fink—graduating senior, class clown, etc.—has CONGRATS CLASS OF 2017!!! painted on his chest. A gaggle of sophomore girls wade into the shallow water, and Skeeter's by the fire selling oxy at a markup only freshman are dumb enough to fall for. They'd get a better deal at the urgent care half an hour south. Doctor must be getting a nice kickback for all the scripts he shits out.

So of course, we've got everyone out on the riverbank except Cooper O'Brien, who is the only reason I'm here. Jesus Christ. It was risky as hell getting those photos to school. Putting them in the scanner and printing out the photocopies in public bordered on dangerous. I wouldn't have done it if I had a choice, but I didn't, because who the hell has a personal printer? Nobody we trust, that's for sure.

And if Cooper don't show, I'm gonna be pissed. He said he'd be here.

"Hey, Sadie!"

The name hits like an ax. *Sadie.* I yank the shoelace from my mouth and Kara Simmonds comes up to the table with an awkward smile like she's trying her best to be friendly. I don't know why she's trying. It ain't like I'm friendly back. But I spent a semester doing her homework in exchange for gas money, so she thinks we're good. Guess being the smart kid overrides both my family reputation and the fact that I growled at people in elementary school.

"Breanna's over there," Kara says to me, crouching to inspect the dwindling selection of stolen drinks sweating in the cooler. "If you wanted to talk to her."

I know. Breanna's by the fallen tree with the rest of the school's resident queers. Not that we got a ton, but still. A he/they lesbian, the girl that defected from the popular crowd when her ex outed her, some boy who has a crush on the football captain. The usual. I keep my distance from them, though. They have it hard enough without me.

"Why would I want to talk to Breanna," I say.

Kara straightens up with a jar of strawberry moonshine in hand. "You ain't into girls?"

"Kara."

"Oh my god. You're straight? Really?"

I know the short hair and cut-up *John Brown Did Nothing Wrong* t-shirt would set off even the shittiest gaydar, but Kara's got no idea what she's on about. "You seen Cooper?"

"I—you're into *guys*? No way."

"Where is he."

She unscrews the jar of moonshine and takes a sip. I can smell the Sharpie smell of homebrewed corn liquor from here. "This tastes like ass. Anyway, I don't know. Let's find out."

She takes a breath and hollers, *"O'Brien!"*

I recoil. Half the party turns to face us and I'm gonna break out into hives. Why would she do that? "Kara, what the fuck—"

But, from across the party, Cooper bellows, *"What?"*

Instantly my stomach uncurls from its knot. Thank Christ. He's here.

Kara winks at me. Again, like we're friendly. "Found him." Then she raises the moonshine. "C'mere! Sadie Abernathy wants to talk to you! Did you know she's straight?"

There's a small crackle of laughter, and then attention on us dissipates—a joke at the Abernathys' expense, fine, there's better things to do—but Cooper cuts through the crowd, nursing a Bud Light and wearing his John Deere hat backwards.

"Hey now," he says. "You don't gotta be yelling that everywhere."

Cooper O'Brien. Brand new graduate of Twist Creek High. Twice my size and three times as shiny, all torn-off sleeves and sanded jeans, finishing off the can and crunching it in his fist. His dad technically manages the Sunoco stations in Twist Creek, but after the accident, his dad got sick—that's what we call it around here, *sick*—so now Cooper keeps them all running the best he can. Maybe it'll get easier now that he don't got school to worry about no more.

We were best friends before the accident. These days, we're . . . something? We're friendly, sure, but we don't talk as much, not like we used to. Things got tough and we grew up quick and, well.

"You hear me, Kara?" Cooper says, flicking the can into the limp garbage bag between us. "That's her business, not yours."

Kara blushes. Cooper's got that effect on people. "Thought you'd want to know. Just don't drink everything before my brother gets here." She shoots me a look I think is supposed to be conspiratorial, like she's done me some grand favor. "Later, you two."

And then it's just us.

Cooper folds his arms at me with a snort. "You don't do parties."

To preface, it ain't my fault I'm bad with people. Or more accurately, you can't say I haven't tried. I spent so many years *trying*. Mom taught me how to smile and make eye contact, or fake it if I had to. I watched my classmates and memorized how they talked to each other, even built a book of scripts in my head: express this emotion this way, that emotion that way, on and on. And sure, I figure everyone has to do all that, but Jesus, ain't it exhausting? Ain't it hard remembering to smile and say the right thing and look everyone in the eye?

These days, I save the effort for the people that matter. Like my teachers, or my boss. If it means I'm an antisocial asshole to everyone else, I'll take it. At least I'm an anti-social asshole that don't break down in tears every day after school.

Cooper, though? It's not as hard with Cooper. I don't have to try so hard with him.

I think I have a crush on him, but I'm not sure.

"Parties are loud," I say, putting the shoelace back in my mouth. "And boring."

"I mean," Cooper says, "of course they're gonna be boring when you don't drink and also have no friends."

"Fuck off."

Cooper laughs. "Yeah, yeah, fuck off, I know. What's the special occasion?"

I can't say, *I found photos of the accident that killed your mom, you know, the ones my dad lied about having, and we both know he lied for a good reason and I really shouldn't have taken these out of the house but I found them, look, we have proof.*

"I, um," I manage, pulling out the paper. "Here."

I press the folded sheet into his hand.

"Okay," he says slowly. "This ain't—"

I don't wanna hear whatever he thinks this might be. No matter what he guesses, it'll be worse than what's really there. "Open it."

He does.

He goes still.

"What is this?" he chokes. He slams the paper closed and glances nervously over his shoulder. "Jesus Christ, Sadie. What are you doing?"

"I found them last week," I say, winding the shoelace around my fingers until it starts to cut off circulation. "Dad had them. He's been hiding them from Sheriff Davies."

"Of *course* he's hiding them from Davies." Cooper shoves the paper into his pocket and grabs me, pulls me out from behind the table, drags me towards him. I let him. I'm too shocked to do anything else. "We ain't talking about this here. Come on."

Cooper leads me through the mess of people, through classmates that pity me, don't talk to me, try not to look in my direction. Cooper may have managed to salvage a reputation in Twist Creek, but I haven't. Even if I had the social skills for it—I'm an Abernathy. That's how it works. I keep my eyes down until we're at the riverbank, outside the jurisdiction of the bonfire, until it's just the rumble of the river and the distant mutter of the radio.

Here, Cooper takes a deep breath.

I can see why someone would have a crush on him, why I probably do. The moonlight catching the edge of his wavy hair, the scar on his cheek from a bike accident. And sure, maybe it's because he's the only person I'm capable of holding a conversation with these days, but that's how it's supposed to work, right? That's how it goes?

Not that it matters. Because I'm a boy. I'm not out yet, but that changes tomorrow. So.

"I thought you might want it," I say, so he can't get a word in before me. My hands wind the shoelace around my wrist, unwind it, wind it up again. "Proof, I mean."

"Proof of what?" Cooper says. "We have a death certificate and a gravestone. I don't know what else you need."

I grit my teeth. Yes, Mrs. O'Brien has been dead for years. Mr. O'Brien can't leave his apartment half the time, Dad don't walk right no more, and last I heard Dallas Foster had recovered from the burns—a miracle if you ask me—but now Dallas is in Charleston and lost our numbers and we don't talk no more. But that's not what this is about.

"Just," I say, "look at the pictures."

"I did."

I pull the photocopies from his pocket— "Jesus!" Cooper says—and slap them into his hand. Ain't enough light to see by, so I hold up my phone to use the lock screen as a lamp.

"There. Look."

Cooper sucks in air through his teeth and takes the photocopies. He's shaking.

Dad took these photos as the car burned, seconds after he'd pulled himself off the twisted crunch of metal that'd sliced him open a dozen times from hip to calf. Bleeding out on a cliffside in the middle of the night, trying to save a child seconds from burning to death, holding back a friend whose wife had immolated in the back seat. In the second photo, there's the edge of Mrs. O'Brien's body, slumped over, swallowed by flames.

Dad took the pictures because Sheriff Davies was there. At the top of the cliff. By the wrecked guardrail.

Because Sheriff Davies ran them off the road.

And in these photos, in the firelight, you can see him.

"There he is," I whisper. "We got *photos*. We got *proof*. That he did it." Cooper's throat bobs and his fingers dent the paper. "And—I don't know. We could do something with this, right? If you want to give it to your dad? I think Dallas's brother and sister-in-law came back to Pearson too, bought out some old building, and if . . ." I nod back through the trees, up to town. "If we want to give it to some grown-ups. See what they can do."

"Sister-in-law?" Cooper asks, even though he's barely there. Just staring at his mom in those pictures. "Ms. Amber?"

"Yeah."

He breathes in shakily. "You think they could do something?"

I don't say, *I think Dad wants to run for county commission again, and maybe some blackmail is in order, to keep the sheriff away from him.* I don't say, *I think it'd help your dad if he puts himself towards something again, if he wants to get involved too.* I don't say, *I know this is dangerous, but we have to try.*

"I think so," I say. "We can't recall the election, but we can make his life hell."

Did you know that Sheriff Davies's great-grandfather is the one that hammered the railroad spike into Saint Abernathy's mouth?

Cooper slowly takes the photocopies. Folds them. Tries to breathe.

I lean forward, holding my shoelace tight.

What are you thinking, O'Brien?

And then feet crash through the underbrush and I jerk away from Cooper like he burns, because the sheriff's son is standing on the riverbank with his friends and laughing, "Shit, sorry, didn't mean to interrupt the lovebirds."

CHAPTER THREE

Freshman year, Noah Davies and his friends—Eddie Ruckle and Paul Miller—killed Nancy Adams's dog because Noah asked her to homecoming and, wouldn't you know it, the bitch said *no*.

Eddie filmed it the same way he filmed his little stepsister in the shower that one time: breathing hard, struggling to keep the subject in frame. Noah had a Milk-Bone in one hand and a hunting knife in the other. Paul held the dog down while it screamed. And the morning Nancy found the corpse on her front porch, you could hear her clear across the holler. I thought it was a cougar, or another car crash. For a moment, eating breakfast hunched over the kitchen sink, I could have been convinced the world was ending.

The video got posted wherever it'd do the most collateral damage. Facebook, forums, group chats. The kids in Twist Creek County have a fight-or-flight response to the sound of shoes squeaking on wet grass. As for Nancy, she left town the next week. Rumor says Noah cornered her in a bathroom, said he'd do the same to her if she didn't shape up, and she decided running was a better option.

That's how it goes around here. Eddie is a wet-rat-looking son of a bitch, a bestgore.com fanboy if I've ever seen one. Paul never says much, always hangs back, but his family runs a wild game processing business that'll take any animal out of season as long as you pay the right price. Then Noah—well, Noah's gonna be a cop when he graduates. Get elected sheriff when his dad can't keep up the gig, because that's how it works.

I remember, distantly, that Twist Creek County don't got ambulances no more. You gotta call EMTs down from Maryland these days.

"For what it's worth," Noah says, stepping towards us and fully out of the distant light of the bonfire, "y'all make a cute couple."

"We're not—" I start.

Cooper interrupts. "What do you want?"

It ain't biologically possible, but I swear Noah's eyes catch the moonlight and shine like a coyote. He's grinning and showing all this teeth. "Thought I heard something, so figured I'd check up on everybody." Noah gestures at Cooper. Eddie and Paul follow his finger, two pairs of eyes snapping into place. "What's that you got there?"

Cooper puts the photocopies in his pocket. "Some old homework. Was gonna burn it." Good move. We can afford to lose a set if it means avoiding suspicion. "Got distracted is all."

For some reason, Eddie finds this hilarious. "By Abernathy? Really?" He lurches forward, peering over Noah's shoulder. "Nothing much to look at if you ask me. Those ain't tits, those are mosquito bites."

"Shut the fuck up," Cooper says.

I don't like when Eddie looks at me. Like he's trying to find the best place to split me open, like I'm that dog. Or at least, he's looking for the best angle to watch from.

"All right boys, all right," Noah says. "No need for this. Just doing my rounds, not trying to start fights." *Rounds*, like he's already a cop. He's always done this; sticking his nose where it don't belong, hissing like a snake in a burrow. Eddie groans. Paul says nothing. He ain't even paying attention to us, instead looking into the woods, the sort of thing Mamaw and Papaw told me never to do around here. Noah continues, "Glad to hear you're good, O'Brien. Abernathy? You good?"

Stop talking to me. "I'm good."

Does he feel the weight of it every time we cross paths? A hundred years of bloodshed? Dad, left to bleed out on the side of the road. Papaw's brother shot dead in his truck forty years ago and Papaw tracking down Davies's uncle to do the same. My great-grandmother Lucille locking her daddy's killer in the old post office and burning it down. The railroad spike through Saint Abernathy's mouth.

Does he feel it too, or is this all some game to him?

"I was, uh," I say, "about to head out."

Noah says, "Wait. Before you do." He clicks his tongue to make sure my attention is solidly on him, but how could it be anywhere else? "I heard Mr. Abernathy swung by town hall a few days ago. Asked some questions. Any clue why?"

I have the sudden urge to vomit, but what comes out is, "No idea. Tax bill, probably."

Noah hums. "Shame y'all are so behind on those."

"Yeah, well, the accident kinda put us out an income, so." That's only half a lie—Uncle Rodney has Dad working under the table at the garage, but it barely covers groceries. These days it's mainly Mom at the nursing home and my dishwashing gig at Big Kelly's. "Can only do so much."

Noah nods as if in sympathy. "It'll do that. Get on, then. And make it quick. Don't want a little girl in the woods alone for too long after dark."

Little girl. It stings.

"Want me to come with you?" Cooper asks.

I glance between Cooper and the boys. I don't want to be alone, but I also don't want Noah to think we're doing anything we shouldn't. "I'll be fine."

"Be safe," Eddie giggles, giving me a little wave.

Cooper swallows hard. He don't like this. I don't like it either, but I force a smile and tap my pocket. Think about the photos, O'Brien. Show your dad. It's been five years since our parents tried to save Twist Creek County, I know, but five years is enough time to do it better this go-round.

Just let me get back home in one piece—and past my parents, because lord knows if they find out I ran into Noah Davies at a late-night party, I'm in deep shit.

I give them all a nod in goodbye, because maybe being polite will keep me a little safer, and slip past the tree line.

Navigating the woods ain't too hard. All I have to do is keep going straight and I'll hit the road eventually; that road will be McLachlan's Main Street, and home's right up the mountain from there. I can see a streetlight or two through the trees if I really try. Cooper, Dallas, and I used to play down here all the time.

Still. I can't breathe until the boys are out of earshot. My mouth is dry and my skin is too tight. I swear to god, even the air around Noah and them is rotten. I unwind the shoelace from my wrist, where it's left an indent in the skin, and jam it back in my mouth, teeth grinding against the one plastic aglet I ain't ripped off already. Sure, it's a little gross, but I wash it every few days, and it's better than picking at my scalp. I do that when I'm stressed. Chew on stuff or tear up my skin until it bleeds. It's a compulsion. It calms me down, I think.

The plastic gives way, cracking in my mouth. I grab a branch and haul myself up over a dirt ledge.

I pause here. Lean against a tree, squeeze my eyes shut and try to breathe. The shoelace dangles from my mouth. My chest hurts and my head might as well be stuffed with cotton, my stomach turning. Breathe, Miles. C'mon.

It messes with you, growing up like this. Knowing someone wants to hurt you for the hell of it. My parents tried to keep the feud from me because they're good parents—like they tried to hide the money troubles, and the year Dad couldn't get off OxyContin, and the gun hidden in the safe under the nightstand. But it's harder to hide the rules. Don't go nowhere without an adult, even if Cooper or Dallas are there. If we call the house, you better be there to pick up. Stay away from the Davieses. Stay away from Ruckle and Miller. Keep your eyes down, don't cause trouble, and above all, don't get in grown folks' business, because grown folks' business gets people hurt.

Only problem is, Mom and Dad raised a smart kid. I figured it out. I have pictures of our family going back a hundred years, copies of every birth certificate and land deed and newspaper clipping. I have Dad's medical bills and the photos he thinks he locked up for good. I have the papers from when he and Mrs. O'Brien filed to run for county commission, when Ms. Amber ran for county assessor, when Mr. O'Brien ran for sheriff. I know every damn thing about this family and everyone that's ever touched it.

And you think I stopped there? I printed out a copy of *The Communist Manifesto* five pages at a time on the school computers. I devoured Kropotkin and Engels, every preserved piece of John Brown's work. Did you know West Virginia broke off from Virginia in refusal to join the Confederacy? Did you know socialists armed the miners of Twist Creek County?

That's what I call myself. A socialist. Because my great-great-grandfather was, and he was a socialist for a damn reason.

I have to keep going. Get out of these trees, get home to Lady. Ugh, I really should've let her come with me. I'll let her sleep in my bed tonight so I'm not alone, and then I just have to wait for morning. For my parents to find the email. We'll see where we go from there.

But I pick up my head, and in front of me—

A light flicks on.

It's so bright it hurts. I instinctively close my eyes against it, stopping in my tracks to hold up a hand. My first thought is almost nonsense: Is someone spotlighting deer? So close to town, so far out of season?

But then: "Hey, Sadie."

My vision clears as I get used to the light, blinking desperately to make sense of what's in front of me.

Eddie's there. Between the trees. A flashlight in one hand and his phone in the other—horizontal, like he's recording.

He's recording.

I take one step back. Another. My heel hits the ledge I'd climbed over, dirt raining down. How did he get ahead of me? "Eddie. I don't—" My voice cracks. Usually when I put emotion into my voice, I'm doing it on purpose, I'm actively putting it on to get a point across, but these words shatter before I can stop them. "Cooper and me, we weren't doing nothing, I swear. We were talking about graduation. Turn that off. Please."

Behind Eddie, something moves. I make out Noah's face. Paul's.

"Weren't doing nothing," Noah repeats slowly. He pulls a piece of paper from his pocket, unfolding it carefully. "You know, I *was* gonna ignore all that commie shit you were reading at school, because really, what's a girl like you gonna do? But . . ."

He whistles and holds up a set of photocopies.

"Gotta admit," he says, "these ain't doing you any favors."

Oh.

Where did he get those? There were three copies before I left the house, so he couldn't have broken in and stolen one. Did he take it from Cooper? But Cooper didn't text me, or yell for me, or anything like that. Was Noah in the library when I made them, sneaking in behind me to print out a copy for himself? Has he been *following* me?

"I'm not—" I stammer. "It's—"

But there's no way to deny what those photos are of.

"Poor thing," Eddie giggles. His voice is wet and high. "If it makes you feel better, we're giving you a head start. Ain't no fun if it's just a slaughter."

My brain is almost calm as it sorts through everything I'm not gonna get to see tomorrow. Lady. Mom and Dad. Mamaw and Papaw. I left that coming-out email on the desktop, and now they're going to have to read it without me. I shouldn't have sent it. *I'm not the child you thought I was, sorry I died in the woods at a party.* At least I said I love you before I left the house? At least I signed the email with a heart emoji, so they know?

For the first time tonight, Paul speaks, and all he says is, "Run."

There's no time to argue. No time to plead or beg. A deer can't negotiate with a bullet once it's been fired.

I run.

CHAPTER
FOUR

i don't remember what they did.

CHAPTER
FiVE

Only that there was a lot of blood, and all of it was mine.

CHAPTER SiX

Then nothing.

CHAPTER SEVEN

A moment later—or maybe it's only a moment to me, god knows how long it's really been, I don't know I don't know—I'm awake and screaming.

It hurts. My throat is swollen shut like there's a railroad spike jammed in my mouth and I taste copper and there's something in my arm. I want it out. I grab it. Rip it free. Blood spills out from a vein, sputters towards my wrist as I sit up, grab my face, find bandages and sharp spikes of pain. There's a shrieking *beep beep beep* and it keeps getting faster. I can't breathe. I can't—

Hands grab my shoulders and push me against cheap sheets. Hold me down. I push back but they shove desperately, pleading. *Please.*

I stop. Drag down a single breath. Beg my lungs to work again.

Distantly, the working sounds of a hospital. Everything I memorized after the accident. An EKG. The rustling of notes and paper. Someone's voice rising out in the hall. And the smell: disinfectant, bleach, alcohol. The overwhelming medical cleanliness that reminds me of visiting Mom at work, the nursing home scent clinging to her scrubs.

And wheezing. The wet, fleshy churn-sound of choking.

I force my eyes to focus. To make sense of the blurry mess in front of me. Because there's a man—not a nurse, not Dad, a man in a stained shirt and red fabric around his neck—holding me down. Looming over my hospital bed. Lean and sharp-mouthed, almost cruel-looking. There's dirty blond hair hanging over his eyes and coal dust in the lines of his face.

No, that's not right. The mines ain't operated in Twist Creek County for decades. But he's here and he's struggling to breathe just like me. Wheezing desperately.

I'm not scared, because I know him.

I want to say it. *I know you. I know you from somewhere. Who are you?*

Before I manage to ask, a nurse bursts into the room. "Oh shit," she says. She grabs my arm. I realize I ripped out my IV. The medical tape hangs limply in the crook of my elbow, the plastic tubing lying coiled in my bedsheets. I'm suddenly woozy. My own IV? I did that? *"She's awake!"*

I try to point to him, ask why this man is here, who he is, but he's gone.

CHAPTER EiGHT

Mom and Dad hover by my bed—Mom sipping her coffee slow to give her hands something to do, Dad bracing himself on her chair because he refuses to use his cane—while the doctor does whatever doctors do after someone barely survives getting beaten to death. She's in a rush, because of course she is. Southern Memorial Hospital is understaffed. There's a scare piece in the local paper, *Southern Memorial at Risk of Closing*, every month at this point. I won't believe it until I see the doors boarded up.

The doctor makes one last note and tucks the clipboard under her arm. "She's fine. Be back in a bit. And get that IV back in, Christ."

The nurse winces as the doctor leaves. "Sorry."

"I can do the IV," Mom says. "If you're busy."

"You will *not*."

It takes a minute to recognize her, but my nurse is Amanda. She used to work with Mom at the nursing home before she got her degree. We like Amanda—she's a tall, shrewd-faced woman who despises small talk and tells us things to our faces.

She picks up my (cleaned and bandaged) arm with a well-meaning glare.

"And you, missy," she says, "are not going to rip this out again. You're in bad enough shape as it is."

She's right. My entire head is swollen and thick; when I touch my face, it's all bandages and splints. Several of my fingers are taped together and my arms are a scatterplot of bruises, scrapes, gauze. I think the nail of my pinkie finger is—is it gone? My chest hurts every time I breathe in. *Everything* hurts.

And I'm seeing things too. Maybe I have a concussion to boot, some kind of traumatic brain injury.

"I won't," I say, and Amanda laughs as she readies the replacement IV.

From the corner of my eye, I see Dad cringe at the needle. He never likes to look at people, but now he's staring blatantly at the ground, fidgeting with the drawstring of his pants.

"Dad," I say carefully. "You ain't gotta be here for this."

Dad slouches. "I'm fine."

The accident changed him. When I compare him to the diagnostic criteria for PTSD in the DSM-5 which I've done at least twice, he hits all the beats. He's not nearly as bad as he used to be, but bad enough: refusing to drive, struggling to sleep, flinching like a frightened rabbit if you burn something in the kitchen. This is the first time he's been inside a hospital in years and he's clutching Mom's shirt like a lifeline. He's playing it off as his hip being bad, but I can tell the difference. It's in how he distributes his weight.

It's weird to call it an "accident," but that's what Davies calls it, so it's the word we have to use.

"You're not fine," I say. Mom sighs. "Go outside. You're about to puke."

Amanda hesitates with the IV cannula in hand. Dad glances from Mom to me, then grabs my head in his big hand. He presses his mouth to my forehead carefully, to avoid whatever's going on up there. Stitches? I don't know. It's clumsy, and he hits something that hurts, but I don't care. I slump awkwardly against him. He smells like the same brand of aftershave he's used since I was four.

And then, I remember: *the email.*

The coming-out email. The damn thing I left on the computer for them to find in the morning. They have to have read it, right? Or did they miss it in the confusion, when they learned something happened to me?

"Can't get anything over on you, can I?" Dad says, wholly ignorant of the crisis I'm swallowing down. "Love you."

"Love you," I say. My voice is perfectly level. I have emotions, obviously, but sometimes it's a bit of work to show them, and right now it's best if I don't.

Dad limps out of the hospital room. He thinks I can't see it when he scrubs a hand over his face, looking as haggard as he did the day after the accident. I huddle against the flat pillow. I want my shoelace. Maybe I should ask for it back, if they have it. If I didn't drop it on the forest floor. In the meantime, I fidget with the plastic bracelet around my wrist, the one with my legal (incorrect) name and identification barcode.

Amanda shoots Mom a glance over the hospital bed once Dad is out of earshot. "I'm gonna get him using that cane one way or another."

"Good luck," Mom says.

"His hip's *fucked*." Amanda offers me a flat smile. "Pardon my French."

"I don't give a shit," I say. That gets Mom to laugh. "Can you do my IV already?"

Amanda says, "As you wish," and takes my hand to put the IV in my wrist, since apparently I busted the vein in the crook of my arm. I wince as she pushes the needle in. "You gave us a hell of a scare, you know."

With most people, that sort of statement means they're trying to get an apology, but I'm not going to apologize for almost dying, and also I don't think Amanda would be so indirect. I sniff and a shock of pain shoots up my face. "What's the damage? Can I see my chart?"

Amanda gives me a look. "Honey—"

I realize I forgot to be polite. "Please."

Amanda turns to Mom for direction. I know what the answer's gonna be before she so much as moves. We're the same kind of person. We need all the information, and we need it upfront.

Mom waves her consent.

"Right," Amanda says, turning my electronic health record towards her. "The O'Brien boy brought you in"— *Cooper?*—"and you were real bad. In shock, losing more blood than I thought we could replace. Fractured ribs, internal hemorrhaging, broken orbital socket, broken nose, broken fingers. Thought you had a skull fracture too, but it was just a flesh wound, thank god." Another flat smile. "Plus a hundred little contusions and more bruises than you can shake a stick at. What a way to start summer vacation."

I run my tongue over my front teeth and find a piece of enamel missing, right at the front. I'd forgotten that the party was only hours after class let out for the summer. There'd been no signing yearbooks or hanging out in the gym for me. I'd spent my last day of junior year swiping cupcakes from my auto shop classroom and helping the librarian sort books.

"But I ain't dying?" I say.

"You ain't dying," Amanda confirms. "Not anymore."

Amanda does her job: checks my vitals, changes my bandages, shows me where I've been hurt. She says I've been in and out for a day or so, but it's no surprise I can't remember it. She lets me touch the stitches on the shaved part of my scalp and carefully pulls aside my hospital gown to show me where surgeons cut me open. Apparently one of my ribs punctured something, requiring an emergency operation. I try to imagine myself in the operating room, cracked open so they can yank a jagged piece of bone from my lung, or—what else would a rib hit? My liver? "Not much we can do for the bones themselves," she admits.

"We put them back in place with some nice pieces of metal, though. You'll be setting off detectors for the rest of your life."

All of that, I take fine. The boot-shaped bruises on my stomach and legs, fine. The medical bills I'm definitely racking up, fine. It's fine. But a sick thought crawls up the back of my throat.

I glance up at Amanda. "Was I . . . ?"

I can't say the words, but I don't have to. Beside me, Mom makes a broken noise. I don't know if—if something like that happened. No matter how much I try to recall, it's like my head is stuffed full of gauze. Just dark leaves and the taste of metal in my mouth.

Amanda goes pale. "Did you remember something?"

"No," I admit. "But . . ."

"We can run a kit if you want."

Mom cuts in. "Those are so invasive."

And they cost money. I think. I'm not sure.

"We don't have to," I say quickly. "It's fine. Can I—can I talk to my mom?"

Amanda nods, changing the topic as deftly as a nurse is trained to. "Of course. Press this button if you need me. And here's your painkillers. Don't be a martyr about it, okay? If it hurts, take them."

She places a single pill, which I immediately recognize as OxyContin, in a cup by the side of my bed, along with a glass of water. When she scans my ID barcode to add the cost of it to my patient record—at a 500 percent markup—she winces in apology, and then she's gone.

I push the pill towards Mom. "It's, um."

Mom pulls a face. There are bags under her eyes, and her nose is bright red despite the stoic set to her mouth. You can use her hair as a barometer for how bad a situation's gotten—it's fallen out of its bun and she ain't bothered to fix it, which hasn't happened since Dad was in the hospital. She don't look people in the eye, the same way I don't, the same way Dad don't. Mom has a trick, though. She watches people's mouths when they speak, or a little spot at the corner of their eye. It's close enough to eye contact that most people can't tell the difference. Now that I know, I can tell when she's doing it to me, but that's fine because I'm doing the same.

Mom takes the cup, inspects the pill, hands it back. "I'll keep an eye on you. We know what not to do this time."

She's technically right, but it seems optimistic. I swallow the painkiller anyway and show my tongue to prove it went down; a holdover from elementary school, when I'd spit out any medicine they tried to give me.

"Guess they couldn't hook me up to a morphine drip," I say.

"That's for people who are dying," Mom says, even though I don't think that's right. "I would ask how you're doing, but that feels mean."

"I'm as good as I can be, considering."

She splutters a laugh. Despite the fact that she's a mess, she's doing her best to stay as poised as possible. That's Mom for you. She ain't from around here—she grew up in Maryland—but she's as tough and strong as any mountain woman. She has to be, marrying an Abernathy the way she did.

"What happened?" Mom says.

I don't answer. No response seems right. When I think about it for too long, I want to collapse into a heap of tears and panic, but my sense of decorum constantly outweighs what I actually want. The idea of losing it is embarrassing, so I simply don't.

"Was it the sheriff?" Mom asks.

"No," I say, and it's the truth. It wasn't him, technically. "And I don't need Dad thinking it was. Okay? It wasn't him."

It don't seem like she believes me, but she says, "Okay."

I don't want to talk about this no more. I grasp for straws—*How's Lady? How's Cooper, or Mamaw and Papaw? Have you seen a strange man who can't talk?*—and land on . . .

"Did you get the email?" I ask.

Mom makes a forcibly nonchalant noise. "Email?"

It's clear she knows what I mean, but I play along with the feigned ignorance because it's the expected thing to do. "The one I sent before." My head wobbles vaguely, implying the obvious. "You know."

Mom takes a deep breath.

She hesitates.

"That's not," she starts, then reconsiders. "I mean, yes. We got it."

I can't pinpoint her tone. "Oh."

"And we read it. While you were in surgery."

The email was a long one. A good one, if you ask me, with a curated list of hyperlinks and an extensive FAQ section. Yes, I know I'm a boy, I figured it out late last year; no, I'm not a masculine woman, I already tried that; yes, I'm nervous too. An email seemed like the easiest way to do it. I've always preferred writing things to saying them out loud. I wanted to head off every question, provide every detail ahead of time, in hopes that this would be as simple as possible.

"It's a lot to take in," Mom says.

"I know," I say. "I said that. In the email. This is a lot, and you don't gotta get it right away—"

"And I don't think it's a conversation we're ready to have right now."

My stomach drops. "Mom."

"A lot of bad shit just happened, and it's a lot to process. I'd rather us take it one thing at a time." There's no smile on her face, no softness at all. She's approaching this like I'm an argumentative resident at the nursing home, like I'm Marie Jo insisting she don't need a shower. "There's a lot we'll have to talk about."

"There's nothing to talk about," I whisper. "I said everything already."

I don't talk back to my parents. They're reasonable people, and we're all the same kind of *off*, so we work together real well. We don't raise our voices. We rarely butt heads. I've never been grounded, and any harsh words are immediately followed with an apology and a hug. We trip each other up sometimes, sure, because every family does sometimes, but it's never a big thing. I ain't good with people, but my parents are *my* people.

So this—this don't sit right.

"I'm a boy," I say. "That's it."

Mom says, firmly, "Sadie."

Like she's trying to shake some sense into me. Like if she don't say my name, she'll lose it forever.

"Once you get home," she continues, "we can talk about it. But not right now. Not after what—"

I can't listen to this. Before she can finish, I jam my finger into the nurse call button. "I need to go to the bathroom."

✦

Mom goes to work. She's already taken too much time off, and I inherited her tendency to walk away from emotional conversations instead of facing them head-on—it's kind of our thing—so Amanda helps me to the bathroom because "If you slip and eat shit, I will *not* have it be my fault."

So there I am, in front of the bathroom mirror in my papery hospital gown, holding on to the IV pole and turning the ID bracelet around and around my wrist.

The way Amanda was talking, I knew it was bad, but . . .

My face is swollen with bruises, purple and green and black, a mess of butterfly bandages and the yellow stain of medical iodine. One of my eyes sits lower in its socket now, unsupported by the broken bone. My nose is held in place with splints, and my tongue probes the broken corner of my tooth. A strip's been shaved out of my hair to make room for the stitches running from my forehead up, up, up.

Gotta admit, it's hard to look like a straight-A, keep-it-together daughter when you're a smear of roadkill held together with gauze and surgical tape.

It's hard to look like anything, really.

My body gives me five second's warning by flooding my mouth with saliva, and I lurch over the sink just in time, dry heaving until a single trail of acidic empty-stomach bile falls into the porcelain. I spit twice, rinse out my mouth, and scrape my scabbed lips with a rough paper towel.

The worst part is that we knew this was gonna happen eventually. My parents could try all they wanted—pulling me out of classes I shared with Noah or his friends, refusing to let me ride the school bus, never letting me out of their sight—but it wasn't going to last. This was always going to trickle down to me.

But I thought I'd be ready for it. I thought I'd have time to get a little older. I thought I was getting ahead of the curve by doing . . . whatever I was doing at the party. It feels pathetic now. What were a bunch of photos going to do against Davies? Jesus.

When I straighten up, pressing a hand to my cramping stomach muscles, the man is there. In the mirror. Over my shoulder. Watching me.

I yelp, clutching the pole of my IV. His eyes are red-rimmed, clothes torn, fingers curled into claws. And there's a bandana around his neck. He must have used it to clean blood off himself. The stains have dried brown.

He wasn't there, and then he was. Amanda's waiting outside, blocking the door. And his clothes, his haircut—they're a whole era out of date. Several eras. He reminds me of all the archival photos of Twist Creek County's mining years, the black-and-white and sepia times.

I gasp down air. "Who the fuck are you?"

He can't answer. Only chokes. Like there's something lodged in his throat he can't get out.

The bandana is what gets me. A redneck. That's where the term comes from, you know. Sure, that thing about the sunburned back of the neck, that had been true once—politically, a long time ago, a poor white man with nothing much to his name—but we took it back. For a glorious moment, it meant a union man, wearing red around his neck to show loyalty to the people. It didn't matter who you were; if you wore red, you were one of us.

Funny how much we've lost. How much has been taken from us. *Redneck* conjures images of crude, unwashed white trash, and the color . . . I mean, it's hard not to flinch at red baseball caps these days.

This man, whoever he is, is one of us.

"Sadie?" Amanda calls from the other side of the bathroom door. "You all right in there?"

I turn to glance at the door, even though she's not there. "What? Yeah. I'm fine."

And he's gone. Again.

I know you.

Who are you?

✦

I open the bathroom door and Amanda is waiting. "Hand," she says sternly.

"I can walk to the bed," I protest.

Amanda ain't having it. "If your momma ain't here, I'll mother you for her."

And then, a new voice. One that makes my heart stop.

"Your nurse is being awful nice, Miss Abernathy," Sheriff Davies says, taking off his sunglasses and perching them on top of his head. "You best not be giving her trouble."

CHAPTER NINE

There's something wrong with Sheriff Davies. You can't look at him too long, the same way you can't look at that video of Nancy's dog without getting sick. It's the uncanny valley. His clothes are always too perfect and he's always smiling too wide and he don't blink enough, just kind of tracks you across the room like a fox watching chickens through the fence.

He's there in the doorway with his hands behind his back. Standing the same way he did in those photos.

Amanda says firmly, "Sadie's not taking visitors. She needs her rest."

"Oh, I understand," Sheriff Davies says. He steps inside and closes the door to my room behind him. Amanda's hand tightens on my arm. "Really, I do. I want to make this as quick as possible—no reason for me to get in the way of healing." He cocks his head at me. "Go on, tell your nurse you'll be okay."

My fingers are hooked through the ID bracelet like I'm going to snap it off my wrist. I can't be alone with him. Not after what he did to my family, not after what his son did to me.

But you don't say no to Sheriff Davies.

"I'll be okay," I say. And I will be, I think. He won't do anything to me here, not with so many other people in the building. Sheriff Davies is smarter than that. "It's fine."

Amanda grits her teeth. "Right." She helps me back into bed and puts the oxygen monitor back on my finger, hooks me up to all the machines again. Maybe so she can tell if any of my vitals suddenly spike. Or stop. She's taking her sweet time too, trying to find everything she can to do to stall—checking my IV fluid, readjusting my blanket—but it's not enough.

"Any time now, Miss Bailey," Sheriff Davies hums.

Amanda swallows hard. It ain't like Sheriff Davies holds a grudge against any other family but mine, but we all know he won't hesitate to hurt anyone if they end up in his way. Amanda's fingers jitter. "You call me whenever you need me, okay?"

And then she's gone, again, and I'm alone with Noah's dad.

He won't hurt me here. He can't.

Sheriff Davies walks around my little hospital room, peers out the window, rubs the material of the curtain like it's new to him. The room ain't much. Southern Memorial can't afford much. There's another bed across the room; not being used, thank god. I think I'd lose it if there was another person in here with me. He inspects the computer too, like he wants the gritty details of what his son did to me.

There's no way he don't know what Noah did. Noah strikes me as the kind of person to come home bragging about this.

"Well," Sheriff Davies says, "this is a right mess of a situation you've got yourself in." That's one way to put it. "How're you feeling?"

"Like I got some strong painkillers in my system," I reply. I'm proud of myself for this move: frontloading the information so anything I say wrong can be waved away. *She's on meds, you can't take her seriously.* "Could be worse."

"Looks like it hurts." He comes over to sit in the chair by my bedside, makes himself comfortable. "Heard about all this through the grapevine, you know. Thought your parents would've come right to me. That's what a sheriff's for, right?"

"They were stressed out, I guess." I forget myself. "Sir."

He hears *sir* and his smile cracks wider.

"Of course. So I'm here to take care of you. Take a statement, make sure whoever did this is brought to justice." But there's a moment where he thinks. He leans in a little bit to get a better view of the line of stitches over my scalp. "Though you did take a good hit to the head. Didn't you?"

"I did."

"So it'd be a miracle if you remember who did it."

Deep breath. "Would be, wouldn't it."

"Do you?"

This is how it goes. If I remember, there will be consequences. Maybe he'll report Dad's job to the IRS. Maybe
he'll get Mom fired from the nursing home or find an
excuse to condemn our rental. Maybe my dog will end up
gutted too. And nothing will happen to Noah, and nobody
will say anything, and it will just repeat all over again.

It don't matter if I *actually* remember. This is a pact. A
mutual understanding, if you will. The two of us deciding
on the truth of the situation, regardless of the reality of it.

I wonder if this is the same kind of deal Sheriff Davies
cut with Dad in his hospital room.

"Like you said," I mumble. "Hit my head. Can't remember
shit."

Sheriff Davies reaches for me. Takes my arm. Presses
his thumb into the bandage where I ripped out my IV.

He says, "And you'll lose those photos, won't you?"

The burned-down theater, where Davies's ancestor
executed mine, is still standing in McLachlan. It's at the
end of Main Street, a blackened health hazard. One of
the few surviving reminders of the Twist Creek Calamity.
Grass creeps up between collapsed walls and iron beams,
flowering into wheat-like things every summer. I give it
another few years before the rotting stage finally gives way
and all that's left is charred brick.

There's been a few movements to try and get it
demolished—saying it's an eyesore, someone's gonna get
themselves hurt—but they always fail. There's two reasons
for that. The first one I agree with: the burned-down
theater is our past. There ain't a lot of recorded history

about the Twist Creek Calamity, given that the Davieses got a reputation for killing journalists and burning court transcripts. It's what little we have. There's nothing wrong with wanting to remember.

But it's also still there because Sheriff Davies wants it to be. Because the ruins remind us of what his family did to us once. What he'll do to us again, if Twist Creek steps out of line.

A psychological warfare kind of situation.

When Sheriff Davies smiles at me, the air smells like the ruins after a hard rain.

I say, "Yes, sir."

And then he's up. He's putting his sunglasses back on and straightening his shirt. "Good girl. You take care of yourself, Miss Abernathy. You and your folks."

You want to hear something funny?

The Davieses and the Baldwin-Felts agents and the strikebreakers did all that work to stamp out the labor uprisings in the coal mines, only for every vein in the county to dry up a few decades later, leaving our families wrung out and poor and, in a cruel twist of fate, still dying of black lung.

CHAPTER
TEN

Four days: that's how long it takes for the doctor to decide there's no surgery complications or sneaky head trauma, like blood or spinal fluid filling up my skull.

It's a bad few days. I don't bring up that I'm seeing things. Dad tries to take Lady to my room, but the front desk won't let him, so he has to leave her in the car with Mom while he brings in my pillow. It's as old as I am and stained a gross yellow under the case, but I can't sleep without it. Plus, I get my shoelace back, which I tie around my wrist so I can't lose it again. The food sucks, though. Amanda loses her mind after the third day— "No more plain pasta," she begs. "Will you eat a peanut butter sandwich? If you tell me what brand of peanut butter you'll eat, I'll go to the dollar store and buy it right now." The only time my stomach ain't growling is when Mamaw and Papaw visit, because Papaw brings a two-pound milkshake. That's how he shows affection.

"What—?" Papaw starts, eyeing the extent of my injuries.

Mamaw shakes her head.

Cooper texts to check in on me too. He's busy with work, and Mr. O'Brien ain't doing good, so the hour's drive to the hospital ain't feasible, but this is the first time we've spoken regularly in a while. We're falling back into an old rhythm. It's nice.

Miles

jfc my earbuds got busted too

this is the worst thing that's ever happened to me

Cooper

Why are you still up. SLEEP Abernathy it's LATE.

Miles

theres nothing to do but sleep!!!

and the TV is eight dollars a day!! i don't got TV money!!!!

The day I'm allowed to leave, I only look vaguely better. The swelling's gone down, the iodine stains are fading, the bruises have begun to drain from dark purple to reddish green. I'm taking painkillers like clockwork, even though the sight of the pills makes me queasy: *God this is expensive* and *Please don't let my nervous system get used to this*. The doctor compliments how well I'm healing as I change into outside clothes, but I'm not. I'm just good at gritting my teeth so nobody starts fussing.

When a good chunk of your emotions are expressed manually—when you have to actively decide to frown, or grimace, or whatever's expected at the moment—there's hardly any point in expressing the negative ones. Showing pain or exhaustion *on purpose* feels manipulative. I tend to wait until my nervous system breaks under the pressure and acts of its own accord. Absolves me of the guilt, you know.

If I had to guess, I'd say that's why I don't react when Amanda settles me in a wheelchair—no matter how much I insist I don't need one—and he's there again. Watching. Like he's waiting for something.

I don't startle, and I ain't afraid. I lean forward on my knees and try to memorize his face. He tilts his head curiously. Studies me in return.

We recognize each other.

I know him—I know I do. He's one of us. He has to be.

◆

Mom gets antsy during the discharge procedures. She's late for work, and the hospital is a good bit from the house, not even counting the time it'll take her to actually get to the nursing home. She nearly snaps at Amanda— "I can remove the stitches myself," she says, "so no, I won't schedule a follow-up." —and her foot jiggles impatiently as she waits. She always gets on Dad and me for bouncing our legs, but she does it too. I chew on my shoelace, a bag of personal belongings and my pillow in my lap, and try not to fidget in the wheelchair I don't need.

I'm being sent home with a lot of pills. Painkillers. Antibiotics. Decongestants, which are apparently needed for orbital fractures. Some other stuff I don't recognize.

"Dear," Amanda says to Mom, a vague chiding note to her voice as the receptionist clicks away at her computer, "they'll understand." I don't know if that's true. Pretty sure that if the nursing home needed to drop employees, they'd flinch away from an Abernathy first. "Can Jeffery come pick her up, or . . . ?"

Mom's expression turns even more sour, if that was possible. "He doesn't drive."

But then someone cuts in. "I can get Sadie home, if you want."

Walking in through the unwashed glass doors of Southern Memorial Hospital is Cooper O'Brien. Shirt sleeves gone, jeans frayed, work keys hanging out of the pocket.

The boy who dragged me here.

"Cooper?" Mom says, a bit confused.

He gives her a polite nod. "Mrs. Abernathy. I was coming down to catch up with Sadie, finally got some time off, but"—His eyes slide to me. I swallow hard. Did he show his dad the photos? What's going on in his head?— "guess she's up and about. We were getting worried is all."

"I'm fine," I say.

"Like hell," Cooper shoots back. Amanda snorts. "Seriously, though. If your momma needs to get to work, I have the rest of the day off. I can take you home. As long as that's all right with . . ." He turns his puppy-dog eyes on Mom and Amanda. "With y'all."

Nobody can resist Cooper. He never even has to pull the dead mom card; he's a golden retriever in a human body. A retriever with teeth, sure, but big and sweet enough you don't notice.

"We don't like sending nobody off with someone who ain't next of kin," Amanda muses, "but we can make an exception. Linda, you fine with that?"

Mom thinks about it. We're a paranoid family, but the stress of keeping her boss happy must override whatever she's paranoid about, because she nods.

"I'll have to be. Thank you, Cooper." Mom grabs her purse and kisses my forehead. "Sadie, I'll call Mamaw and Papaw to keep an eye on you before Dad gets home. Be safe."

I sigh. Of course she's still calling me Sadie.

Cooper looks me up and down just like he did at the party, his expression laced with a tinge of pity. I pop the shoelace out of my mouth so my glare has more impact.

He says, "You look like hell."

"Can we just go?"

Amanda is too tired to fight me on the wheelchair, so Cooper takes my things and helps me out to the parking lot. Cooper's truck is a fifteen-year-old shitbox gas-guzzler he inherited from a cousin who died in Iraq, complete with a bald eagle figurine hanging from the rearview mirror. I breathe in the early June air, pull my arm from Cooper's, and walk to the edge of the lot.

"Hey now," Cooper says. "Careful."

Southern Memorial Hospital is situated at the top of a hill, the edge of the lot dropping into a valley of trees and lakes and a quaint mountain town. The sun is shining. There's a light breeze. I close my eyes and take a long, deep breath of air that ain't contaminated with bleach and antiseptic smell, that's just the rustle of trees instead of electronic beeping and churning HVAC. God, I missed the outside.

Maybe my brain will work better out here. Or maybe I should've told the doctor about the man in my room.

Behind me, Cooper unlocks the truck. "Apologies in advance, by the way. AC's broke, and the shocks ain't doing real well, so it might be a bumpy ride. You holding up okay?" He keeps talking as he packs my things in the truck but I'm too tired to pay attention. "I hope you ain't mad that I didn't call an ambulance. But, you know, they never showed up last time I called them for Dad, so I figured I'd drive you myself. Thank god I had a tarp, or the bloodstains never would've come out of my seat."

A pause or something, I'm not sure.

Cooper clicks his tongue. "You listening to me? Sadie?"

Through the exhaustion and painkiller haze, I only manage to cue into that last word.

Sadie.

The pathetic well of rage that hits my chest at that word, *Sadie*, don't even make sense. What am I so mad for? It ain't like Cooper is using the wrong name on purpose, not like Mom is. Instead, I'm pissed at myself for keeping it a secret for so long, for being too scared to say something. And I'm *still* scared. But I can't handle being called that one more time, not when so many other things are going wrong. I need somebody to acknowledge it, accept it, so I don't feel like I'm losing my mind more than I already am, because apparently I'm *seeing things* now.

I turn around and say it before I can chicken out. "My name ain't *Sadie*."

Cooper stares. He has no idea what's going on, because why would he? "Hell are you talking about?"

"It's Miles. I'm trans." The words are strange coming out of my mouth, like it's absurd that five syllables could carry so much weight. This is why I wrote a coming-out letter: I'm bad at it when it has to happen out loud. Though, how much does Cooper know about trans people? I backtrack. "You know, like—do you know who Chelsea Manning is? That, but the other direction."

Cooper says, "Dude, I know what a trans person is. Why is she your example?" I'm about to counter, *Because obviously she's a hero*, when it sinks in for him what I actually said. He blinks in surprise. "Wait. Oh shit. Really?"

I have no idea what to make of that response.

"Not," he stumbles, "not that I'm surprised. I mean, I guess I'm surprised, but I ain't totally blindsided?"

"You aren't," I say flatly. It was supposed to come out a question, but I can't fathom the effort to make the word curl up at the end.

He gestures vaguely. "I mean, I could've guessed something was up with you, but I figured I'd let you tell me eventually. The, uh, haircut was kind of a giveaway. And the clothes." Then Cooper winces as if he ain't totally sold on the next thing he plans to say. "Wait, if you're a guy, are you a straight guy? I've never understood that part."

I groan. I genuinely have no idea if I'm gay or bi or what. "Don't call me a heterosexual, O'Brien."

That actually gets a laugh out of him. "Right. Well, uh. Miles, then? That's your name?"

"Yeah."

"Cool. Get in the damn truck. I gotta get you home."

An awkward giggle escapes my throat as I turn the shoelace around my wrist. What do you mean, it was that easy? No pushing back, no telling me how hard this will be for him. Just my new name, easy as that. Cooper offers a smile and his eyes crinkle a little at the corners, and I notice because that's the sort of thing I'm supposed to notice.

✦

If you grow up in West Virginia, there's mainly two ways to think about the place.

The first is you hate it and want to get out as soon as possible. This is the option that liberals love; they devour voyeuristic think pieces about Trump Country and our obsession with voting against our own best interests, titter condescendingly about how anybody with potential would never stay here long. And yeah, sure, a lot of people here are conservative assholes carrying Confederate flags. Sometimes our water ends up full of chemicals and our schools are struggling and our healthcare infrastructure sucks. So from an objective standpoint, I get it.

But I'm the second. The only way you'll get me to leave this state is in a body bag. For all its problems, it's mine. For all the overdose deaths, environmental disasters, and reactionary politics, West Virginia is *mine*. The Twist Creek Calamity is mine, the highest rate of trans kids in America is mine, the population crunched under the boot of a right-wing government are mine. Even if I don't like people, you know, it's hard not to give a shit about *people* as a whole.

I hate being sentimental, but I'm glad I survived to come back home.

Take that, Davies.

Cooper takes us onto US 50, which cuts through another run-down town boasting signs for black lung programs and dialysis clinics before we end up on the long stretch of road back to Twist Creek County. We don't talk. Cooper turns on the radio, glances at me to make sure it's acceptable, and lets me rest. I hold my pillow to my chest—its name is Squishy Pillow, but I don't advertise that—and try to sleep.

It must work, because Cooper hums as we cross the county line. "Here," he says gently. I blink, almost rubbing my eyes before remembering how painful it'll be to touch them. The pale roads are crowded by guardrails and sharp cliffsides, trees hanging over us protectively. Everything is a switchback, and half the turns would make a city driver pop a bone in their jaw. It wouldn't have been hard for Davies to knock Dad's car off the road.

"You get some rest?" Cooper asks.

I nod.

Cooper glances at me as he takes a sharp left to town. Left to McLachlan, right to Pearson, the only two cities in Twist Creek. Even though they're only cities on a technicality.

"I, uh," he says. "I'm sorry I didn't come visit sooner. Dad ain't doing well, and—"

I cut him off. "You dragged my ass to the hospital, so you're off the hook." He snorts. "I appreciate it."

"You would've bled out if I hadn't done something. No thanks necessary."

I mull that over for a second, trying to decide if I want to know the answer to my next question. "Was it bad?"

Cooper says, "I thought you were dead."

I put the shoelace back in my mouth, absently peeling the plastic off the cracked aglet. Back when we were friends in elementary, middle school—and Dallas was there too, all that time ago—he never made fun of me for chewing on my hair or sucking on the drawstrings of my sweatshirts, not like most people did.

"I swear I tried to distract them," he continues. "Keep them from following you, I don't know. Guess it didn't work. And they took off when I showed up, just left you there. Could've sworn you weren't breathing. It was . . ." He trails off. "Yeah, it was bad."

The image pops into my head unbidden. Cooper pulling my limp body off the forest floor, getting blood all over his hands and jeans, desperately holding his fingers to my throat to check for a pulse. I swerve to another topic, like Mom walking out of the hospital room. "Has Noah said anything?"

"No. The sheriff swung by work to thank me for my help in making sure you were okay, but you know how he is."

My stomach drops. "Davies talked to you too?"

Cooper spreads the fingers on one of his hands without letting go of the wheel: *calm down*, it reads. "I didn't tell him a damn thing. What'd you say?"

"Told him I got hit in the head. Memory's shaky, you know. It's—" I turn my gaze out the window. "Maybe we should both lose those photos. If we don't want to get hurt."

Cooper knows the deals Sheriff Davies makes across hospital beds. The inside of the truck goes silent.

I didn't think this was how the summer before senior year was going to go. I thought I'd be helping Dad with whatever campaign he's trying to pull off, working at Big Kelly's, filling out name-change paperwork, stuff like that. Normal stuff. Or as normal as we can get around here. Cooper and I should be talking about his last year of school, what he wants to do now that he's graduated. Not reassuring each other that our lies to law enforcement lined up.

"I know we ain't talked all that much since the accident," I start.

"It's fine," Cooper says.

"Didn't mean to drag you back in like this."

Cooper sniffs and stares out the windshield. Davies has been leaving him and his dad alone since the crash. He was supposed to have a choice—those photos were supposed to give him a *choice*. But saving me? That's put a target on his back all over again.

"Yeah. Well," he says, "I wasn't gonna leave you there."

Finally, we hit McLachlan. Cooper drives down Main Street, with its one-room post office and tiny pizza parlor, the storefront that used to be a grocery store but ain't no more, the laundromat with half its windows boarded up. The burned-down theater sits menacingly a few buildings down. Once we turn off Main Street, the sidewalks disappear and cars end up parked in the yard since nobody's got a driveway. Every house has a pile of random junk on the porch: rakes and shovels and busted furniture, sometimes a treadmill or broken water heater. There's a Confederate flag at the end of the road too. High on a flagpole for everyone to see. Half the houses still have Trump signs, even though the election ended months ago. Someone put one in our yard last year and Dad ripped it up, dumped the scraps in the road.

My family has lived in McLachlan for a hundred years, and I love it more than anything, but it's a mess.

Cooper comes to a stop in front of my house. I fumble with the door but refuse to let him help me, yanking it open and hopping down to the ground.

We rent our house from Mom's uncle, some asshole from Maryland who sends me twenty bucks every year for my birthday, and the place is in bad shape. The deck is rotting, and half the windows are visibly warped. The side door don't even close all the way no more, so Dad boarded it shut. I'd say rent is dirt cheap, since it got bought on foreclosure and all, but dirt cheap is still too much for us sometimes.

I hear my dog barking inside.

"Lady!" I call, forgetting Squishy Pillow in Cooper's truck as I stumble up the rickety stairs. I grab the key from under the mat as Lady bays forlornly. "Hi, baby, I'm home!"

I unlock the door and Lady slams out onto the porch, jamming her big head against my stomach and wagging her tail so hard she's about to shake out of her skin. Oh thank god, she's okay. I know if something happened to her, my parents would've *said*, but Christ, it's impossible not to think about what Noah and those boys did to Nancy's dog. I can't keep myself upright anymore. I collapse onto the porch as she pushes her whole body on top of me, whining and nudging my face.

"I missed you too!" I say as she tries to lick my mouth. *She's okay, she's okay.* "Christ, you're on my rib!"

Lady is a black mouth cur I got from one of Papaw's hunting buddies a few years ago. I trained her myself. She does the usual dog stuff—tracking, guarding, all that— since she gets loud and a little destructive if I don't give her enough to do. But she does more than that. She puts herself between me and other people, so I always have breathing room, and lays on my feet if she thinks my heartrate is getting too quick. She's a living thing to be around when *people* are too much. I think she can tell I have a hard time every now and then, even when nobody else can.

Once she's done reassuring herself that I'm alive, she flops onto the porch, tail thumping the wood. My ribs hurt like a bitch and my face stings, but I don't care. I'm home. I sigh and lean against the railing.

Cooper comes up the stairs, holding Squishy Pillow and my bag. "Forgot this."

"Oh." I take the pillow from him, and he reaches down to scratch Lady behind the ear. "Thanks. You, uh, don't have to stay or nothing. Mamaw and Papaw will be here soon."

Cooper shakes his head. "I have the day off."

"I'm probably just gonna sleep."

"That's fine."

When I don't respond, he crouches beside me, forearms resting on his knees. I can't even make myself fake the eye contact like Mom tells me to. I stare at the tan line on his wrist, the outline of a watch he's not wearing right now.

"They tried to kill you," he says. "Okay? They tried to kill you, and the sheriff threatened you into shutting up, and I'm sorry if it sucks, but you absolutely *cannot* defend yourself. Even if you hadn't almost *died*, Christ, you wouldn't have a chance." He's right. I'm five-two on a good day and built like barbed wire. "No way in hell I'm leaving you alone."

My voice cracks when I speak. "Even after . . . ?"

It's not that we stopped talking entirely after the accident. We went to Mrs. O'Brien's funeral. We spent a lot of time in the hospital with Dallas. But Mr. O'Brien got *sick*, and Dad got *sick*, and we were all hurting, and, well. I couldn't blame Cooper if he can't look at me without thinking my dad was the one that started it.

CHAPTER ELEVEN

Cooper and I sit on the porch—cups of Kool-Aid on the steps, bag of barbeque chips leaning against Cooper's leg, my head on Lady's side—until Mamaw and Papaw make it down. They live in rural Twist Creek, half an hour out. They claim it's because of traffic, but it's really because, you know, a Davies killed Papaw's brother and everything. Best to stay out of town.

"Oh, Cooper!" Mamaw says, slightly surprised as she steps out of the Jeep. "Sugar, how long you been here?"

"Not too long," Cooper says. He gets up to leave, patting my shoulder as he goes. "Take care of her for me, all right? Later."

I'm glad he called me *her* to Mamaw and Papaw—I ain't ready for that conversation yet—but I wish he'd checked or something.

Mamaw ushers me inside. Home is all wood walls and vinyl floors, deer heads and hand-me-downs. Dad leaves his tools everywhere, and Mom has the clothes rack in the bathtub since the dryer broke last month. And then there's my things: pencils from homework I don't have to do no more, worn-down books I've scoured from resell sites. I pick one up as we come in. It's about failures of American foreign policy. I don't agree with the author's political leanings—he's too middle-of-the-road for my taste—but the interviews are smart.

Mamaw, all stick-thin and leathery skin, makes me lay down on the couch with a quilt like I have the flu. Lady jumps up to sit on my legs, and nobody tells her to get down. Papaw sits in the armchair in silence. He puts on the hunting channel.

"They find who did it?" Papaw drawls eventually, hands folded across his big belly.

I glance at him. His nose twitches over his mustache. We both know who did it, but it's an easy translation to what he really means. *Did you lie to the sheriff? Did you cut a deal too?*

"No," I say, which means *Yes, of course I did.*

"Roger," Mamaw says, "let her rest."

I try to read—I'm at the part of the book describing American war crimes in Vietnam, which has always been a pet subject of mine—but can't keep my eyes open. When I wake up some time later, Dad is home, and everyone is talking softly, and Papaw says something about his twelve gauge. "There ain't one son of a bitch that can talk his way out of a slug."

◆

That night, I can't relax until I take my stapled-together copy of *The Communist Manifesto* and the two extra sets of photocopies and my torn-up *John Brown Did Nothing Wrong* shirt and anything else that looks vaguely leftist and hide them between my bookshelf and the wall. I cram a blanket over the mess and fall back on my haunches and realize I'm breathing hard and shaking.

All that commie shit.

Piss off.

◆

In the stress of healing, the social consequences of some horrible action or another, it's easy to let things slip through the cracks.

Like the man with the red bandana.

It's just that I'm always tired and nobody ever leaves me alone. Mom, Dad, Mamaw, Papaw, Cooper, sometimes Amanda, sometimes Uncle Rodney and his wife, Jill. But it's only the people willing to risk getting close to us, which means it's family and not much else. Even Uncle Rodney and Aunt Jill don't stay long. Uncle Rodney nervously watches the driveway as if waiting for Sheriff Davies to show up. I promise to entertain the constant *Are you okay, do you need anything* as long as I can, but before the end of the second day I snap and shut myself in my room.

But being alone is bad too. At least when I'm around people, my head is too busy with eye contact rules and facial expressions and scrambled attempts at conversation to think too hard about what happened. Alone, I can't shut it out, no matter how many times I reorganize my bookshelf or watch the same YouTube essay on repeat. There's a video sitting on Eddie's phone of me half-dead, and he's probably passing it around the boys and jerking off to it or something. Plus, there's the medical bill Mom and Dad will get in the next few weeks. Our insurance won't do a damned thing, so I'm planning to get the billing center phone number from Amanda to haggle it down to something that won't bankrupt us.

And then the trans thing. When Dad talks about me, he stumbles over his sentences, tripping on my name or avoiding it entirely. Mom says *Sadie* and *she* with a cold finality, so long as I'm not in the room. When I am, she gets quiet, like she's been caught doing something she knows she shouldn't be. I start knocking on walls before I enter a room so I don't have to overhear them.

It's easiest when Cooper's here. He swings by after work as much as he can, even though he's exhausted, and we sit on the back porch: him with a root beer, me with an ice pop and my shoelace, Lady with her head on her paws. I don't tell him that I miss when we were younger, before the accident, walking home from school together every day, but I think he knows.

Another thing to point out is that I don't know how crushes are supposed to work. Back when I was still trying too hard—when I made myself sick with exhaustion trying to understand people, devouring every possible script in hopes that it'd get easier somehow—I dedicated a few months to reading cheesy teen romances, in case I ever needed a baseline to work from. None of them made any sense to me, though. I didn't want to be anyone's girlfriend; then once I realized I'm a boy, I wasn't sold on being a boyfriend either. The physical part of it sounds like fun, but the rest? I don't get the appeal. Still, I memorized the symptoms. It's all stereotypical. Butterflies in the stomach, an adrenaline rush at the idea of whoever, getting nervous and stammering, that sort of thing.

I dunno. That sounds like a fear response to me.

"How you feeling?" Cooper asks over his bottle of root beer, once it's been a few days at home.

"Fine?" I'm bad at answering that question. Feelings are weird and slippery. When I'm deciding how to react to something, there's a good chance I'll pick what I think I'm *supposed* to feel because I have no idea what's actually going on in my head. "Tired. Kinda like someone beat the shit out of me."

"I mean." Cooper shrugs.

I laugh dryly. It was bad enough going about my daily life before this, wondering if I'd bump into Sheriff Davies or Noah and get myself into trouble. But now? We may have a shared agreement that I don't remember who did it, but still. I don't know if they meant for me to survive, and I ain't eager to find out.

✦

Almost two weeks after the graduation party, it's mid-June. The surgical wound across my ribs has stopped weeping into its gauze, and Mom is fixing to take out my scalp stitches like she promised. Mamaw is making a late lunch in the kitchen while I sit on the edge of the tub, Lady snoring on my feet. Mom's already boiled the tweezers and scissors and she's rubbing them down with alcohol pads now. The smell makes my head hurt. I stare into the small hand mirror I grabbed to watch.

"Is the, uh, whole orbital fracture thing going to be a problem?" I say, turning my head to get a better angle. My eyeball still sits odd in my face, and it hurts a little when I blink.

"What?" Mom says. She puts up her hair and tugs at the shirt she uses for house repairs and DIY medical procedures; it's from an old West Virginia University children's hospital fundraiser, Mountaineer colors and everything. She's never gone to med school, but she has Amanda on speed dial and that's good enough. "Your eye? It won't need surgery, if that's what you're asking." She pauses. "Are you having vision problems?"

"I don't think so."

"Then it's fine."

That is to be interpreted as: *insurance won't cover enough of the procedure, and you won't die without it.* I can respect that.

She washes the top of my head, puts on her gloves, and sets to work. Tweezer to lift the suture knot away from the skin, scissors to cut, then pull out. The *snip* of the scissors is loud against my skull.

In the kitchen, Mamaw clears her throat loud, which reminds me.

"So," I say carefully, only slightly frustrated that I washed my shoelace recently and it's drying in my room instead of tied around my wrist, where it should be. "Did you tell Mamaw and Papaw about . . ."

Mom sighs above me, dropping the stitch into the paper towel in the sink. "The email?"

"Yeah."

"No, I didn't." She takes out another stitch. "I don't think it's fair to them to hear it from me. If you want them to know, you should be the one to tell them."

I stare at the mirror, watching Mom's latex-covered fingers try to find the best angle for the next knot sewn into my skin. "I dunno, I'm still recovering from a near-death experience. You could probably do the hard work for me right now."

Mom's hands flop to her sides. "Jesus."

What? I'm right. She's a parent—it's her job to help with the scary stuff, ain't it? Especially with something as big as this? But when neither of us say anything for a few seconds, both of us vaguely embarrassed by our reactions, Mom just gets back to work. *Snip*, pull, *snip*, pull.

There's a whole spectrum of reactions to coming out. Getting kicked out is one extreme—being accepted wholeheartedly is the other. But in the middle, there's this. The awkwardness, the refusals to acknowledge, the uncomfortable weirdness of turning away. In the stories I've read online, parents seem obsessed with performing their grief about a child's transition. *Don't you know how hard this is for us?* And you know what, fine! Have feelings about it! There are a lot of things to have feelings about when your kid is trans! But don't have them *at* me.

The stitches end an inch past my hairline, and when Mom pulls the last one, she drops the scissors and tweezers in the sink and yanks off her gloves.

"I don't know how they'll react," she says, wrapping the stitches up because they're technically a biohazard. "But they're older. You can't get upset if they don't understand."

"I ain't gonna be upset."

"And like I said—"

"It's a lot to take in," I interrupt because I know where this is going, "and we're dealing with a bunch of shit, I know."

Mom rocks back a little to look at me. I can't figure out her expression, like usual.

So I move to another topic. "My boss texted me. Asked if I wanted her to mail my paycheck." I pull out my phone to give my hands something to do. As nervous as I am about going outside, I have to leave the house or I'm going to lose it. Besides, I need to talk to Big Kelly about when I can get back to work. If money wasn't already tight . . . "Told her I'd come down."

Mom shakes her head. "She can mail it."

"I'm going down."

"I'll come with you."

"Go tell Mamaw I'm a boy, and you can come with me."

That gets Mom to deflate. "Seriously?"

I get up from the bathtub. Lady snuffles, picking her head up off the floor. I hate pulling stuff like that, but sometimes you have to. "I'll be safe."

Mom grinds her teeth for a second, then says, "If it starts to hurt, or you think you aren't gonna be able to make it back, you call me. All right? Mamaw and I will come pick you up."

"All right," I say. "Love you."

"Love you too," Mom says quietly.

CHAPTER TWELVE

I started working at Big Kelly's last year, right before I turned sixteen. Embarrassingly late for a first job around here. I had some good excuses for why I was unemployed, at first: no driver's license, no time for Mom to ferry me around and, you know, jobs are tight when we're all hoarding a few to make rent.

But the real reason is that I was scared. Every time Mom suggested I put together a résumé, I either stopped talking or started crying. I know I was a brat about it. It's just that the idea of going to a new place, full of new people and new expectations, was terrifying to the point of nausea. Weren't things already hard enough, with school and Dad and everything else? Why did I have to do this too?

Eventually, our landlord raised the rent, so I sucked it up to take a job washing dishes at Big Kelly's. Starting off was a nightmare. Not because of the scalding dishwater or thick, humid kitchen air—coming home blistered and sweating through my clothes was no problem. The real issue was the people. The other dishie thought it was funny to pick on me, I'd get snapped at for incomprehensible mistakes, and suddenly I was being held to rules nobody would or even could explain. It got so bad I stormed out in the middle of a shift and burst into tears right outside the back door.

Kelly didn't fire me, though. We stayed out there for an hour while I calmed down, me clutching a glass of water while she smoked a cigarette, and made a deal: If I agreed to give it at least another two weeks, she'd help me out. She'd make sure instructions were clearer, tell the mean older waitresses to lay off, and laminate an employee manual and put it by my station so I always had the rules on hand. She even explained things nobody had bothered to explain before. *I know it's repetitive, but if you don't say hello every day, you come off rude. Nobody cares about the difference between an explanation and an excuse. And if someone points something out, they probably want you to do something about it.*

("Didn't your momma or daddy teach you these things?" Kelly said to me, and I'd replied, "We say what we mean in my house. None of this beat-around-the-bush shit." That'd gotten her to laugh.)

These days, I like my job. I got it down to a science. I eat leftovers brought back on the plates, run maintenance on the industrial washer, and glare at anyone that steps too close to my corner of the kitchen. It's hot and muggy and loud, and sometimes I pull eleven-hour shifts on the weekend, but it's good. Repetitive and menial. I like it.

God knows when I'll be able to get back to it.

I park my old car in the rear lot of Big Kelly's by the dumpster corral and sit there uselessly, picking at my shoelace. Don't even have the presence of mind to tie it into a knot or wrap it around my fingers. This is the farthest I've been from the house since I got out of the hospital. The lot is empty and isolated, and the security camera back here's been busted for a year, so if anything happened to me, nobody would see it. I wouldn't be so lucky a second time.

Jesus. I wasn't followed here, and I know that. But the paranoia is killing me. I don't get how I managed to pretend this would wait until I was eighteen. Is that really how I thought it worked? That any of this would wait for some flimsy idea of the age of majority, some arbitrary line in the sand?

Dude, get out of the car. It's fine.

One more breath, one more moment to collect myself, and then I'm out and muscling my way in through the heavy back door. Into the cluttered hall to the kitchen. Past the dry storage and the cooler. Even though we're in a lull between lunch and dinner, it don't mean that Big Kelly's ain't hectic. Before I'm in the kitchen, I hear it. A cook is yelling at a waitress, *"When I say hot, I fucking mean hot"*—someone has Metallica playing on their phone, tinny like they've jammed it into a container as a make-shift speaker—dirty cups hit a metal counter—silverware clatters, the industrial fans whir, a plate drops and breaks. *"Shit!"* It smells like french fries and ranch dressing and soap. The underside of my neck is instantly damp.

One last turn, and I step into the kitchen. The fans hit full blast. The noise is overwhelming and sharp. I reach for my earbuds, but they ain't there, because I didn't bring them. Because I'm not working today. Right.

The first person to see me is the other dishie, Daryl Chavis. He's twice my age, and I spend most of my shift rewashing the dishes he sent out with pieces of food still stuck to them. He makes a surprised noise and drops the dish hose dangling from the ceiling, letting it slap against the cinder block wall. "Sadie! They weren't kidding!"

The entire kitchen grinds to a halt. Two cooks, a hostess, and three servers peer up from their stations, plates in hand and food sizzling on the grill.

I don't like having everyone's attention on me. It makes me itch.

"Did someone hit you with their car?" Daryl says.

Joanna, a waitress in the same grade as me, whirls on him. "Oh my *god*."

"It's fine," I mutter, even though it's satisfying when someone snaps at him. He's tried to hit on me a few times. I think. I can never tell. "Is Kelly in her office?"

One of the cooks points towards the shoddy back room. "Doing the books."

I go over to the dish pit to grab my stuff: my water bottle, the notepad I use to mark off hours during longer shifts. Daryl watches me the whole time, saying stuff like, "Your eye looks real bad, don't it?" I ignore him.

True to the cook's word, Kelly has taken shelter behind the janky office door, hunched over piles of paperwork and a computer as old as I am. She is in fact big, tall and thick with a shaggy wolf cut that makes her ambiguously queer, not that she's ever told anybody one way or the other. There's no AC in the office, so she's got three mini-fans at her desk. I clear my throat to be heard over the whir.

"If you need something to do," she barks, "the grease trap smells like something pissed in it."

"Nah."

Kelly looks up. Somehow, the boxes of files and bags of washed aprons, all the schedules taped to the walls, her expression when she sees me—they all make her tiny in comparison. She's not supposed to be tiny.

Kelly says, "Christ, I could've driven the check on up myself if you wanted me to."

I'm sick of people reacting like this when they see me. "I needed out of the house."

She hesitates for a moment before reaching into her pile of stuff. Disconnected computer mice, dead pens, one of the few Hillary 2016 flags scattered across the county. Almost 70 percent of the state voted red last year, almost 85 percent of the county, and she's one of the few that didn't. I wonder if it lines up with her being one of the few people around here willing to give me a job, with my last name and all. Kelly swears and mutters as my eyes drift around the room.

"I know it's here somewhere," she says.

I tap the shoelace against my lips since I make a point not to chew on it at work. "Take your time."

My gaze lands on the schedule. My name's been taken off, replaced with the word TRAINEE.

"Figured I'd be back by the end of the month," I say. "Or, at least, I thought. Wanted to talk to you about that, actually." I flick my hand at the printout so she knows what I'm talking about. "Really need to hire someone in the meantime?"

Kelly yanks out a set of envelopes. "There they are. What was that? About the—" She pauses, sees my hand near the schedule. Her face tries to settle on an expression, but can't find one. "Oh. Sadie, I don't . . ." She sighs. "It ain't right to make you work. After everything? You're just a kid." She shakes her head. "You're on leave until the end of the summer."

What? No. She can't do that. There are medical bills to cover now, and the way inflation's going, the rent might get raised again, and Mom had to take time off to care for me, and we absolutely cannot, in any way, shape, or form, afford this.

I need this job.

All I say is, "Oh. Okay."

"Here." Kelly hands me the envelopes. "Final paycheck, for now, with a small bonus from an event we did last week. Plus a get-well card. Sorry we couldn't get it to you while you were in the hospital."

I nod quickly. "Thank you." I know my voice is coming out flat, but I'm too overwhelmed to force it into any other shape. "I appreciate it."

"Of course, sweetie." Kelly offers a sad smile. "Now get on home."

I leave quick as I can, ducking into the back hall with the envelopes against my chest.

But I ain't going home yet. I stop in front of the back door—the noise of the kitchen is muted here, the humidity less intense—and stuff my usual paycheck envelope into my back pocket. I know what that one is. Whatever. It's the second one that confuses me. It's purple, with *Sadie* written on it in script. I put the shoelace in my mouth to keep my teeth from grinding together and rip it open.

You're one tough cookie! The front of the card features a little pastry held together with a Band-Aid; the inside, a bunch of get-well-soon messages. *Take it easy, we'll miss you*; *I hope they catch the bastard*. The usual. And, tucked safely inside, is a Shop 'n Save gift card.

Two hundred dollars.

If we really stretch, that's groceries for a month. Two hundred more dollars we can put towards something that ain't feeding ourselves.

This is how it's supposed to go. Right? If someone in your community gets hurt, you help. You make things easier for them. Come on, I'm a socialist, that's the entire point of my politics. But it's hard to undo all the rot, the guilt eating at your brain. Saying you're being pitied, you can't take care of yourself, you need to pull yourself up by your bootstraps.

I focus on the shoelace and try to look at this objectively. I'm sixteen, almost seventeen, still legally a child. People are supposed to be taking care of me. This is what small-town America is supposed to be like, when your family history ain't turned you into an outcast. This is kindness, not pity. It's okay.

None of it works, though. I put my bruised wrist in my mouth and bite until the chipped tooth leaves a dark red welt in the skin.

Sheriff Davies did this to me. To us. It ain't supposed to go like this. It ain't right.

The heavy metal slab of a back door swings open.

Shit. I sniffle, swallowing hard to keep my voice from croaking. "Sorry," I say because that's what's expected, and because if one more person treats me like I'm a kicked puppy, I might lose it. "Just heading out."

But I see them and I freeze. The person in front of me freezes too, halfway through the door, where it swings back and hits him hard in the arm.

Eddie Ruckle.

In the doorway. With non-slip shoes and a nametag reading TRAINEE.

I've never been this close to Eddie, not that I can remember. He's frail and lanky, not a scrap of muscle on the bone, with chewed-on nails and a mouth that's always in the shape of a smile even when he ain't smiling.

His nostrils flare. Something like uncertainty flickers across his face.

"Sadie," he says. "That, uh, looks bad." He giggles nervously. "Heard what happened. Real sorry."

Even through the oxy, I can feel my ruined rib, my broken fingers, the vague throbbing under my eye. Over his shoulder, the back lot is empty, only my car and his bike leaning against the dumpster corral. Behind me, the kitchen churns and burns like it always does. Clattering, shouting.

All it'd take is for me to turn and run back to safety. A few steps and I'd be surrounded by men twice my size and security cameras that work. I could find another job once I heal, probably. I could back away and leave and it'd be okay.

But I don't.

Because my great-great-grandfather tortured strike-breakers, and my great-grandmother burned her sheriff alive, and Papaw shot a man right on his front porch, and I'm pissed.

I grab the heavy metal door, wrench it back, and smash it into Eddie's face.

Eddie's nose breaks with a wet *crunch*. He stumbles back, feet dragging in the gravel lot. His nose is suddenly flat and gushing blood. Looks like it was pasted cockeyed onto his face.

I breathe deep, without pain, for the first time in weeks.

"*Fuck!*" he shrieks, grabbing his face. "What the fuck is—" He coughs, trying to get his balance. Blood splatters over his lips. I step outside with him and shut the door to keep his screaming from reaching everyone else. Can't have that. "What the fuck is wrong with you, bitch?"

My heart thumps hard in my throat. I'm shaking but my voice is calm. "What'd you do with the video?"

Eddie gets it. It clicks. Panic flushes over him. He's started to cry from pain, which, yeah, that happens when it hurts.

"I—" He shakes his head pathetically. "It wasn't my idea. Noah told me to do it, swear to god. You know how he is." He tries to laugh, show he don't mean no harm, but

I take another step forward and he yelps. "Swear to god! Thought he was just fucking with you! I didn't know what he was gonna do, swear it."

I don't care what he thought was happening. "What did you do with the video?" I ask again, slower this time so he can understand. "Show it to Sheriff Davies? Or did you jack off to it first? You like stuff like that, don't you, Ruckle?"

"Christ," Eddie keeps saying, holding his nose, "Christ."

Another step. He coughs again, trying to get the blood out of his mouth. It's hanging over his lip in a wet glob.

"Noah wanted to show it to his dad!" he says. "Okay? He made me record it. I told him it was a bad idea, but, you know how he is, he don't like being told no."

I breathe in.

"Please," he whispers. "I need to get to work."

He ain't going nowhere with his nose like that, except to the bathroom to wash off the mess and maybe set it himself. Don't know if the Ruckle family's got broken-nose money.

"Sheriff Davies's seen it?" I say.

Eddie nods weakly. "Noah made me send it."

For a moment, I consider holding out my hand for his phone. Making him send me the video too, so I know exactly what they did to me. So I have something to fill the gap in my memory, stitch together the pieces I've managed to hold on to.

But I don't need to. The medical bills are proof enough, a road map of what they did.

Gravel crunches under Eddie's feet. His shadow, stretching out awkwardly behind him, almost brushes the concrete wheel stop. I put a hand on the back of my neck and squeeze until the bruises ache.

"Let me go," he says suddenly, "or I'll tell Noah you remember."

My blood runs cold.

He nods a few times as if gathering the courage to say what comes next. "You told Davies you didn't remember. What happens if I said you lied? He knows your daddy's working, right? What'll happen if that gets out?" He sniffles. Attempts to stand his ground. "What happens if he decides to do something about those photos?"

The photos I agreed to lose. Of Sheriff Davies by the guardrail, police lights off, watching the car burn and Dallas sob and Mr. O'Brien scream before he radioed the accident in to dispatch. Just because he wanted to watch them all suffer. When you're dying, every minute is a lifetime. Every minute is a dead body.

This son of a bitch.

I lunge for him. I don't know what I want to do—jam my fingers into the wrecked mess of his nose, grab his phone to shatter it, something, anything—

But he jerks away from me.

And slips on the gravel.

And falls.

His head hits the concrete wheel stop. The sound is hollow. *Thunk*.

Eddie Ruckle stops moving.

CHAPTER
THiRTEEN

I stare at Eddie—unmoving, on the ground, head propped up on the too-hard pillow of the wheel stop.

"Hey," I whisper, like he's just messing with me, or asleep. "*Hey.*"

Nothing. Blood leaks sluggishly from the back of his head. When the wind blows, the trees above us move, casting dapples of light across his pale face. It's a beautiful day, and his expression is weirdly neutral. Like he don't know how to feel about falling. Like he ain't sure if it hurt or not.

"Eddie?"

Silence.

His eyes don't blink.

His chest don't move.

Did I—?

No. No, absolutely not. I stumble to the ground, grab his head, pick it up off the curb to show him that it's not that bad, see? It was a fall. People don't die from *falling*. We're tougher than that around here.

But the back of his head has crunched in the slightest bit. It's not a big open wound, a crack, a split, like what's in my own head. When I grab his throat to find a pulse, there's nothing. I hold a finger under his nose to check for breathing, and there's nothing there either.

Shit. Shit, shit, shit. I jolt to my feet and back away from him, obsessively wiping my hands on my shirt even though I didn't actually get any blood on them.

Did I—?

I scan the parking lot in a panic. There's nobody. Just me and Eddie and the broken security camera. My ears are ringing and I keep forgetting how to breathe. Keep having to gasp, operating manually, reminding myself to blink and open my lungs.

I killed Eddie Ruckle.

No, I didn't. He slipped and fell. He hit his head. It was an accident. I didn't try to kill him, I didn't *mean* to.

But he's dead.

And I'm an Abernathy. I'm an Abernathy, and this looks like retaliation. This looks like revenge. This looks like the uneasy post-accident lull in the blood feud roaring back in full force.

An engine growls, and I jerk up my head to see a truck tearing down the road through the trees, completely ignorant to what's happening a few dozen yards away.

I can't do *nothing*. I can't leave Eddie here. I clamp my hands over my mouth, shoelace dangling limply from my wrist, and try to steady myself. Okay. I've touched dead things before. Papaw's a hunter. And sure, I ain't, but he used to take me out with him in the cold early mornings, show me how to field dress a kill, and this can't be that much different. Dead meat's all the same.

I grab Eddie under the arms, letting his bloody head loll across my shirt because it's better than dragging it across the gravel, and pull him to the dumpster corral. I have to hold him up with one arm while I wrestle the latch open and tug hard when his jeans catch on the jagged wood. It's nasty in here. The two dumpsters are half-open and baking in the summer sun. Smells like rotten food. Flies buzz. Corpses are heavier than they've got any right to be. I slam the rickety wood door shut.

Take stock of your options, Miles. Can't call Mom or Dad. Can't do that to them, can't put them through that after they've been through so much. Papaw would help me if I told him what I'd done, and he'd keep his mouth shut— Papaw's killed before, we all know he has, we just don't talk about it, why would we?—but when I drop Eddie onto the ground and pull out my phone, I can't make myself do it.

My reflection in the black of the phone screen is wild. Eyes wide. Nostrils flaring.

Eddie's dead.

I tell my family, and this gets big. I get caught, this gets bigger. It's been bad after the accident, it's been so, so bad, but in the grand scheme of what it's been like for my family for the past century, it's been goddamn peachy. This is throwing gasoline on a fire. And if Sheriff Davies knows about the pictures, that means anything I do wouldn't only hit my family, it'd hit Cooper's, and Dallas's folks just moved back into town so it'd hit them too, and *Christ*, I didn't mean to do this, I swear.

But I know someone who's already in as deep as I am.

I call Cooper.

I hate phone calls. Every time Mom tells me to make one—she says I ain't ever gonna learn if I don't do it—I have to write out a little script with what I want to say. Gotta practice so I get it right. I don't have time for that now. I put the phone to my ear and try not to vomit. Try not to look at Eddie's body.

It rings once. Twice. Cooper's probably at work, he's probably busy. I bite down on my knuckle because the shoelace won't be enough, I need the shock of the pain. He'll pick up. He has to.

Something moves in the corner of my eye.

And there he is. Again.

The man with the red bandana around his neck, coal dust under his fingernails, and old torn clothes. He couldn't even be thirty. Lithe, soft-jawed except where the mandible is clearly broken, shirt sagging around the stomach.

He opens his mouth and it's full of blood.

I scream. "*Fuck!*"

"Hey!" On the phone. The ringing's stopped. Cooper's picked up. "Sadie—shit, sorry, Miles—that you? You okay?"

I don't have the wherewithal to register the slipup of my name. "I—" *I've been seeing someone and I know him, I know him I swear to god I know him*, but I don't say that, because he's gone *again*, and I'm gasping for air and my rib hurts so, so bad that I almost can't say anything at all. I wrap an arm around myself and suck in air through my nose.

I'm seeing things. I'm literally hallucinating from stress. I have brain damage. Did the doctor at Southern Memorial not catch this? Should I have said something? I should have said something.

"Miles?" Cooper says, more worried this time. "What's wrong?"

I answer, "I killed Eddie."

Cooper coughs. "You *what*?"

"No." I shake my head, jam my tongue into the gap left in my broken tooth. I'm going to be sick. "I didn't kill him. We were talking—arguing—" On the other side of the line, I hear Cooper get up, something clattering. "And he fell. Hit his head. Stopped moving. He's dead."

"Okay," Cooper says. "Okay." He shouts at someone—"I need to duck out, you good until Jay gets here?"—and says, "All right, let me clock out and I'll be right there. Where are you?"

"Big Kelly's. Around back. I'm. Uh. With the dumpsters."

"Give me fifteen minutes. You gonna be okay until then?"

Not if I keep seeing things that ain't real. "I think. You got an extra shirt? There's blood on mine."

"Yeah, I have a shirt. Keep your cool, all right? Keep it together." A bell jingles and Cooper's side of the line is suddenly crunchy with wind. "How you feeling?"

"I don't know."

"You don't know?" Cooper says. I don't respond to that, but Cooper keeps talking. "I'm gonna stay on the line with you. It's okay."

"Okay."

How *do* I feel, though?

The sense that I did a bad thing just . . . ain't there. I don't give a shit that I hurt Eddie. To tell the truth, when it comes to him, there is not one shred of emotion in my heart.

It's what his corpse *means*. For my family. For Cooper's. For Dallas's, if we're not careful. It wouldn't be fair for me to drag the Fosters back in, not after everything, not after I already did it to Cooper.

"You're taking this real well," I manage into the phone.

Cooper lets out what's probably a laugh. "Well," he says—almost slowly, like he's being careful too— "You did Twist Creek County a favor, didn't you?"

✦

Cooper, apparently, knows how to deal with bad messes. He walks into the dumpster corral, hands me a clean shirt, thunks a jug of bleach onto the ground, and leans against the door. Hangs up the phone.

Says, "Jesus."

I tug on the shoelace clamped between my teeth, resisting the urge to itch my healing nose. I keep staring at the corner of this little room, where the man with the red bandana was standing, waiting for him to come back like I can catch him and show him to Cooper: *Am I losing it? Can you see him too?* Cooper's truck idles right outside the corral, engine rumbling.

"I think he pissed himself," I say.

"People do that when they die."

I knew that. I make Cooper turn around so I can change my shirt, and we bag it up for disposal. Not in the dumpster. We'll probably burn it, Cooper says.

The past fifteen minutes were some of the worst of my life.

I say, "If Davies finds out—"

"Then we're all dead," Cooper finishes for me. "Good thing he ain't gonna find out, then."

He has a plan. After I tell him that the security camera is broken, he pulls out a blue tarp, the kind usually used for hauling leaves, the one he used to insulate his truck seats when he pulled my bleeding body out of the brush. We roll up Eddie's body before wrapping it in bungie cords. I keep watch and scrub the wheel stop with bleach while Cooper lifts Eddie into the bed of his truck, then ties the bed cover in place. He moves Eddie's body like it's nothing.

"I can't get it all out," I say quietly, looking at the wheel-stop concrete. The blood is mostly gone, but it's all I can see: the tiny little specks settled into the porous material.

"It's fine," Cooper says. He grabs me by the shoulder, pulls me back towards the truck. "And don't touch his bike, neither. Not worth it. Let's go, we can talk on the drive, let's go."

I get in Cooper's truck. The eagle ornament hanging from the rearview mirror has turned so it's looking directly out the back window. It was watching us the whole time.

I don't move.

"Talk to me," Cooper says as we pull onto the road.

I'm not sure what I'm going to say until I open my mouth. "Mom's gonna be worried if I'm not home soon." I pull out my phone again. "I'll, uh, say I'm hanging out with you."

"Alibi," Cooper says with a nod. "Good. The guys at work think Dad's having some issues. Combine that, say you're keeping an eye on me."

Right.

Miles

hi mom!! ran into cooper, his dad's not doing well so

think i'm gonna hang out, keep an eye on him

cooper, i mean

Mom has read receipts on, because of course she does, and she sees it immediately. Her response don't take much longer.

Mom

Okay. You're not doing well either so don't push yourself.

I flatten myself against the seat and try to unknot the shoelace from around my wrist. My hands are shaking so bad I can't manage it.

Cooper says, "So. Body disposal. Could leave it out in the woods, let the coyotes get it, but there's a chance they'd drag part of him into town." He reaches down to the center console to grab a toothpick and offers it to me. I take it so I can chew on something tougher, since I destroyed the shoelace aglet back at the party. He takes a toothpick too. "There's a pig farm about an hour out, if you have the stomach to get rid of the teeth."

He's taking this *so* well. Maybe he's so used to cleaning up after his dad that my mess ain't much more; maybe he knows that keeping me safe is the only thing keeping him safe too.

You did Twist Creek County a favor, didn't you?

"Is the teeth thing real?" I ask.

"You wanna risk it?"

No, I don't. I put the toothpick in my mouth and almost immediately bite it in half.

I say, "The mines."

Cooper perks up. "The mines?"

The mines from the Twist Creek Calamity, right south of McLachlan. "I think we could do it." They're not strip mines, not like a lot of modern mines where you cut apart a mountain layer by layer until it's a hole in the ground; it's a slope mine, with an opening in the side of the earth going farther down, down, down. I pull up all the old documents I have saved on my phone, start to sort through them. "Only if you want to risk it. It's bad in there."

"There still a way in?"

The file I need, an old map marked up by government contractors, is a low-quality photo of a low-quality scan, but it serves its purpose. It's from some university archive in Morgantown, and I had to ask five librarians to get a copy last year. Nearly threatened to file a Freedom of Information Act request before I got my hands on it.

I say, "As long as you're willing to trespass."

"We take him in and hide him?" Cooper thinks for a second. "Could make it look like he got trapped. But then why would his bike still be at Big Kelly's—?"

"There's a winze." Cooper makes a confused noise; I translate. It's right on the map, marked with grease pencil a hundred years ago. "A sub-shaft. We could throw him down. Won't have to make it look like anything."

It takes a beat for Cooper to respond. He drums his fingers on the steering wheel.

He says, "If you can get us there."

CHAPTER
FOURTEEN

W e park the truck on the side of the dirt path, deep in the
wooded mountains—an offshoot of the road that snakes
out of McLachlan and across the Twist Creek Bridge. Where
the miners would have walked every day, where it's so disused
and overgrown you can't see between the trees. You'd think
kids would come out here all the time to cause trouble, but it
ain't like that. There's too much blood poisoning the dirt.

I've only been here once. After the accident. Papaw
took me to the entrance of the mine, the *adit* it's called, to
explain why Davies hates our family so much. What we
did to each other, what he did to us.

I've wanted to come back since. Just never had the
stomach.

We leave Eddie in the truck as we walk to the mine
entrance.

The shade of the trees is a blessing; the boxers I ordered
online stick to my legs and my sports bra keeps riding

up. It rarely gets above eighty degrees in the summer, so it's got to be stress sweat. I pick the band away from my back as I crouch in front of the entrance. There's a metal grate covering the adit—a gaping hole in the rock covered by iron bars—and I run my hands over it, trying to find where it comes loose. Papaw showed me. I know it's somewhere.

I have to pull down one of the rocks, but part of the grate pops free. I huff under the weight of it.

"Here." Cooper comes up behind me, takes it out of my hands, and hefts to the side, where it hits the rocks with a clang. "You'd think they'd do more than cover it with some metal. Collapse the entrance, something."

I nod to the warning sign right inside the bars: DANGER: RISK OF CAVE-IN. "Figure they expect it to go on its own." Cooper snorts, and I rock back on my heels a little bit, peering down into the dark gullet. It's all stagnant water, cobwebs, some leaves that blew in. Papaw didn't take me more than a few yards deep. I've never seen any farther. "Probably ain't worth the money."

Imagine spending hours down there. Ducking your head, splitting your hands, and breathing in coal dust, day after day. Knowing your boss would let you die for an extra dollar in his pocket.

Cooper goes back to the truck and pulls Eddie's wrapped-up body from the bed, drags it up to the entrance, and crawls through the hole in the iron bars. He looks like a prisoner. "Okay, push him towards me, I'll drag him through."

I shove Eddie's feet—or his head?—into Cooper's hands, where he pulls the body through all the way, and I follow. My hands and knees turn brown with dirt and rotted underbrush. Cooper is busy getting up, trying to figure out how to stand so he don't hit his head, wrapping one of the bungee cords around his wrist to make it easier to drag. I make the mine map my lock screen. Service falters, splutters, manages to hold out for a second before finally giving up.

But first, a flashlight. I pop it open on my phone and shine it down the throat of the mine. It's all lined with wooden beams and aching rock. I think a possum freezes in the light.

The mine's darkness overtakes the flashlight easily. It disappears into nothing only a few yards down.

"You know where you're going," Cooper says, gesturing me forward, even though that's only correct on a technicality. I know where we're going only slightly more than he does. "Lead the way."

The world is strange underground. It's cold, and muted, and distinctly unreal. It amplifies the dripping of condensation but muffles the sound of our footsteps.

After a minute of dragging quiet, Cooper says, "Is it really that bad of a cave-in risk?"

"A cave-in's what started all this mess, and I can't imagine it's gotten any better since then." I flick my phone's light across the walls so I don't miss none of the twists or turns. The map says it's a straight shot to the sub-shaft, but these old maps ain't real reliable. None of the supports or passageways, bearing scars of cost-cutting measures, feel safe. "Coal operators thought it'd be a bright idea to sink a sub-shaft right at the end of some big room. The miners said it was too dangerous. It'd weaken the mine structure, put them more at risk of cave-ins if not cause one outright. But of course, the operators told them to piss off and blew it up anyway."

Cooper snorts. "Figures."

"I mean, it was worse than that. They'd sent in a bunch of the guys that'd kicked up the biggest fuss and set off the blast while they were in there." I've never been a God-fearing person, but talking about the Twist Creek County mine disaster of 1917 and the calamity that followed while so, so deep in the mine? This is what praying in St. Peter's Basilica must be like. "Thought they'd teach them a lesson, scare them or something. But it actually did cause a collapse, and a bunch of them died, and . . ." I shrug. "You know how it goes from there."

"A riot," Cooper finishes.

"Exactly." I'm about to continue, give some wider context, because I'm never really sure how much anyone actually knows about the calamity—we ain't taught about it, and it's a touchy subject around here—but I stop. Too many memories of being told I was talking too much. I suddenly can't figure out if Cooper's responses sounded bored or not.

The air smells wet and old, more and more the deeper we go, like the same air's been trapped down here a hundred years. Cooper shudders in the dark, but I don't.

I imagine my great-great-grandfather down here with a rifle, nudging a coal baron's son in the knobs of his spine, snarling, *Move*.

"I hate this," Cooper mutters.

"Scared?"

"You ain't?"

I almost reply—*of cave-ins, maybe, but not of the dark*—but there he is again.

The man.

At the end of the tunnel. The flashlight illuminates him all wrong, throwing shadows where there ain't supposed to be shadows.

I stop. He's wheezing again, showing all his little teeth. His cracked lips are pulled tight in pain.

Cooper says, "You good?"

"You—" I glance behind me, to Cooper. He don't see him? Oh, I'm for sure losing it. The realization that I'm seeing things is surprisingly calming. What's one more problem at this point, right? What more is there to panic about? "Yeah. I'm good."

The man gestures for me to follow, and I do.

"This way," I say to Cooper.

The man leads the way to the winze. The tunnel opens up to a large room, or at least larger in comparison to how tight the tunnels have been, with enough space to stand up straight and stretch. My phone's flashlight catches the curve of the rock, the wooden beams holding it all upright, the scattered pieces of history: an ax, a glove, a bullet casing. A few lanterns, some with ancient candles and some that would have burned oil. It's all smothered in dust. And at the back of the room is the hole.

The man is gone again, but I've come to expect it at this point. I walk up to the haphazard barrier—long chunks of wood fashioned into a makeshift fence, held together with rope and rusty nails. Part of it has broken already, leaving behind a jagged point sticking straight up, a make-shift spear.

It's snared a red bandana.

I pluck it carefully from the splinter. The fabric has gone soft from years, maybe decades, of abandonment.

"This it?" Cooper says.

"This is it." I pack the bandana in my pocket and shine the flashlight down the hole. Nothing. I kick a rock over the edge and listen, listen, listen—*thump*. It hits the bottom some undefined distance away. "We're good."

Cooper grunts, drags Eddie over, and shoves him grace-lessly over the side.

We wait for him to hit the bottom. It's a muted noise. I think I expected it to be wetter, like the sound of a broken bone, but that never comes.

I killed Eddie Ruckle.

We hid the body.

We are in such deep shit.

CHAPTER FIFTEEN

We cover our tracks. We throw the bag with my bloody shirt down the winze. We put the metal grate back over the adit. We swing by Big Kelly's to get my car and go exactly where we're supposed to be, like nothing happened at all.

Cooper lives down the mountain from me, in one of the apartments above the lackluster shops of McLachlan's Main Street. We park in front of the shitty pizza parlor, and he leads me up the narrow stairs between the new post office and some derelict, unused space. There's bones and sticks scattered across the steps, bikes and shoes and cups. Since the town's on an incline, the apartment door is built into the back of the second floor.

Cooper can't stand still. He has a hard time getting the key in the lock to the apartment.

"Dad?" he calls, forcing the door open when it sticks. "You home?"

Cooper's place is the same as the last time I saw it a few years ago, just significantly messier. Checkered vinyl flooring and dust bunnies. Undone dishes. A TV or radio, something, playing quietly across the apartment. The curtains are drawn and it's dark. All of the permanent light fixtures have their light bulbs removed, leaving only a smattering of lamps.

"Hold on," Cooper says, and flits off to check on his father.

I wait in the cramped living room and stare at the stacks of *Nat Geo* on the table. Some of these issues are from the eighties: "Soviets in Space" and stuff like that.

Cooper comes back in a second. "Dad fell asleep watching TV. Still breathing. We're good."

Still breathing is the best we're gonna get out of Mr. O'Brien today, it seems. What's that statistic, there's four hundred opioid pills per person in the state? It ain't like we can be disappointed in him neither. Most people would be in his situation, after what happened. Dad was in the same boat once.

Mom promised she wouldn't let that happen to me, but—

Ain't this sort of thing genetic?

I look around the house. The bags under Cooper's eyes. His torn-up cuticles.

I make the split-second decision to stop taking my pain-killers cold turkey.

"Can I take a shower?" I ask. "I feel gross."

"What? Yeah." He grabs a towel off the drying rack in the kitchen. "You know where the bathroom is."

I do. I shut myself in the tiny, cluttered room—it's all plastic storage totes and hard-water stains—and try not to make eye contact with myself in the mirror.

I hate showers. Well, no, I hate bathing in general. For a while, I faked bathing as often as I could get away with it. I'd sit on the bath mat with a book and let the water run without actually getting in, hoping that the sound would convince my parents I'd cleaned myself, even though I *clearly* hadn't. Even these days, I put it off as long as I can, waiting until my hair is visibly greasy and dry shampoo won't cut it no more. Same thing with brushing my teeth. I used to get the bristles wet and pretend. I swear to god, it was more work to *fake* all this than to actually do it. It's gross and embarrassing, I know, but I . . . I hate it.

Apparently touching a corpse overrides that.

I get in the shower, scrub as fast as I can, and get out, swearing as I scrape myself dry. It's humid as hell and there's no bathroom fan, so I have to stand on my tiptoes to crack the tiny window above the showerhead. This sucks. I can't stand being wet.

I'm practically dressed—cargo shorts and sports bra, gritting my teeth against the texture of polyester against damp skin—when Cooper knocks on the door. "You good in there?"

"Yeah," I call as I towel a few stray drops off the back of my neck. In the grand scheme of things, him seeing me half-dressed is not the worst thing that's happened today. "You can come in if you want."

Cooper opens the door and stutters for a second. "Oh. You're, uh, still—"

"You're fine," I say, and he collects himself, coming in and shutting the door. He's trying to be polite with his eyes but clearly can't figure out what that would entail. I ask, "Everything good out there?"

"Dad left some bills out," Cooper mutters. "It's whatever." He must decide that looking away from me is ruder than not, because his gaze finally settles on me. His face screws up. "They really did a number on you, huh?"

In just the sports bra, he can see everything from the waist up. The faded bruises around my ribs to the surgical site that's barely safe to bathe with, all the lingering scrapes and discoloration. I've healed pretty okay, all things considered. I'll never be the same, not with my missing fingernails and crooked nose and lopsided eyes, but everything's stitching together fine on an anatomical level.

"The hair is the worst part," I say, picking at it. "Feel like—" I gesture vaguely at the missing stripe. "This all makes it more obvious. Calls it out."

"I have some clippers?" Cooper says. "If you want it all gone."

I inspect myself in the stained mirror. My hair used to be a pixie cut, but it overgrew because I didn't have the time or money to visit the hairdresser in Pearson, and also because Mom didn't react great when I cut it all off last year. Now it's too long on the back of my neck and keeps sticking out around the ears.

I let out a long, exhausted breath.

"Think it'd be kind of boyish," Cooper adds.

So that's what we do. I towel off my hair, and Cooper has me lean over the edge of the tub while he shears my head as close to the scalp as the machine will let him. His left hand holds my head still as he works. I close my eyes and focus on the metal skimming against my skull. The humidity of the bathroom, the cool porcelain of the tub, the fibers of the damp bath mat digging into my knees.

Cooper says, "Eddie deserved it."

I don't think we're allowed to be passing judgement on that—there's no point, the guy's already dead—but maybe it's something Cooper needs to say to justify all this. Maybe I should agree for the same reason.

"Remember when he filmed his stepsister in the shower?" I mumble into my arm.

"She was thirteen, wasn't she?"

"Yeah."

Another swipe of the razor. Another chunk of my hair falls into the tub. I reach down to grab it and press the light brown strands between my fingers. Mamaw always called it *cinnamon brown*, said it reminded her of my dad when he was younger.

"Remember," Cooper says, "when Travis Snyder lost his job and Paul snitched to the game warden that he'd been hunting out of season?"

That one was particularly brutal, because a lot of people hunt out of season to feed their families, when it comes down to it; the game warden is in Davies's pocket, though, so he'll always look the other way until someone needs their life ruined.

"Mr. Snyder got prison time for that," I say as a way to confirm that yes, I do remember. "He out yet?"

Cooper shrugs. "Think he's got a few more weeks. Claire told me they're moving once he is. Not worth it to stay round here no more."

That's fair. Most people who end up on Twist Creek's bad side just leave. I get it, but at the same time, it's kind of cowardly if you ask me. Or I'm too stubborn to up and leave.

I say, "Remember when Noah nearly killed that kid in the locker room?"

Cooper's laugh comes out bitter. "I was two shower stalls down."

"Really?"

"Heard the guy's arm break."

I wonder if it sounded the same as my nose.

Neither of us have to say anything about Sheriff Davies. There is nothing to remember, because it's not allowed to be a memory yet. You can't reminisce over a scar if it's still an open wound.

Cooper turns off the razor. I sit up, run my hands over my prickly head and meet his eyes for the first time. I don't like eye contact. It's aggressive, like I'm some kind of feral dog that takes it as a threat. So I only manage it for a moment. But when I do, he's watching me too, and his expression—it's somewhere between sad, and furious, and something else.

Something . . . softer? I can't tell.

He leans forward, awkwardly crouching in the tub. I can count the pale freckles on his suntanned cheekbones, see the flecks of gold in his brown eyes. The knees of his pants are getting wet.

"They're all pieces of shit," Cooper says.

I nod. "Yeah."

"And we don't deserve what they did to us."

Not what happened to Cooper's parents, not what happened to Dallas, not what happened to me. Not this— this *cascade* of tragedies. And certainly not what's gonna happen to us if Noah or Sheriff Davies finds out what we did to Eddie.

Cooper moves closer. Again.

I don't back away.

His lips brush mine, and then he's kissing me.

Remember all those books I read? The romances I tried to use as road maps, a clinical list of how things work? They ain't prepared me for this. For someone to touch you when you're raw like an exposed nerve, when you're still shaky from the adrenaline high, when you can still taste the air of the mineshaft. When you don't feel all that much different from a dead body yourself.

I told him I'm a boy.

I told him I killed Eddie Ruckle.

I told him I get it if he thinks everything is my family's fault.

It don't make sense, but I ain't gonna say no, no matter how confused I am. This is what I wanted. Right? Sitting on the porch with him, ignoring each other in the halls at school, hesitating at the door of the Sunoco every time I came around with a handful of change for gas. This is what I wanted.

My heart is beating out of my throat, *bum-bum-bum* like a deer that's noticed a hunter in the trees.

How are you feeling?

I don't know.

He pulls away. I suck in a deep breath, try to get a lungful of air that ain't just him. How am I supposed to respond to that? Is there any right way?

Cooper says, soft and so, so slow, "We've already killed one of them. What's a few more?"

CHAPTER SIXTEEN

What's a few more.

CHAPTER
SEVENTEEN

"Wait." Cooper catches me by the arm as I'm about to storm out of the apartment, drags me back, puts all his grip strength right in a yellow bruise. "Jesus Christ, *wait.*"

"Don't—" I yank away from him and hit the kitchen counter. I'm trying to keep my voice down because Mr. O'Brien is sleeping, but it still comes out as a yelp. "Don't touch me."

He takes his hand from me. Steps back. Breathes hard.

I claw for something to say and come up empty. Usually when I talk to people, I have some script to work from, some idea of the correct thing to regurgitate on command, copying my parents or classmates or a book. Not now.

What's a few more.

Finally, I snap, "You're fucked." I don't want to be here. I want to go home. "Fuck off. No."

Cooper looks at me like I'm the one being ridiculous. "Don't tell me you ain't thought about it. Getting rid of them for good."

"Stop."

Of course I've thought about it. When somebody ruins your life, it's hard not to think about ruining it back. Hoping there'd be a hunting accident, a fight gone wrong, something, anything. And sure, when I realized Eddie was dead, I felt nothing for him. If I felt anything, I think, I felt, *Thank god.* I felt, *There's one less of them now.* I felt, *Davies is going to kill me for this, but at least that stepsister of his is a little safer now, and thank god thank god there's one less of them now.*

But this ain't some action movie, and it sure as hell ain't the nineteen hundreds no more. Things don't work like they did when the feud started. It's different now. Can't get away with things the way you used to. Me and Cooper have been lucky so far, and who knows how long that'll last.

Besides. No way in hell I'm going to do anything else to put my family in danger. Not any more than I already have.

"What I'm going to do," I say, "is go home and tell my parents I've been put on leave from Big Kelly's, and spend the rest of the summer keeping my head down." My throat tightens like I'm gonna throw up. "If you're gonna do something stupid, you do *not* drag me into it."

Cooper scoffs. Reaches into his pocket. Pulls out the photocopies.

"I thought you were an Abernathy," he says.

This son of a bitch. I recoil. "Put that away."

"What were you talking about down there? Ruining Davies's life?"

"Yeah, well, that was before—" I can't say it out loud. "Jesus Christ, put that *away*."

But he's unfolding the paper. There they are, the photos I snuck out of Dad's lockbox. I groan, squeeze my eyes shut. It was never a good idea. I never should have done this. What did I ever think I was going to do with some goddamn *pictures*?

"He took my mom," Cooper says. "And he's taken a hell of a lot from you too."

It's hard to say that Sheriff Davies took anything. Safety, security, peace of mind—he didn't take it. I never had it in the first place.

Cooper says, "It's only right we take from him."

Take? I shake my head, my hands fluttering as I try to figure out what to do with them. The shoelace dangles. "Sure. Like we're going to be able to do anything to him. Or Noah. Or any of them." For some reason, my next words come out in a harsh laugh. This is such an unhinged idea that it borders on hysterical. Us? Against them? "And for what? We get revenge for *me*? As if we can actually—"

I'm giggling now. Pressing my hands into my face, more and more pressure until it hurts. Cooper grits his teeth. I swear I can hear it.

"What are we gonna do about it, huh?" I ask. "I'm a dishwasher who ain't even out of school, and you're some gas station manager! Fuck off!"

I gasp for air. Refuse to let myself get louder. Swallow it all down.

"It ain't gonna fix shit," I say. Quiet now. "It'll be the same thing as the last hundred years."

Hundred years seems to take Cooper off guard. Did he forget this ain't new to me? He straightens up a little, face blank, and I can't help but wonder if this has somehow managed to write itself into my genes. Epigenetics, you know, stress messing with your DNA and getting passed down in your cells. If you took a blood draw from me, could you see all this in there if you searched hard enough?

Cooper says, "So you're scared? Is that it?"

Of course I'm scared. I look at Mom and Dad and Mamaw and Papaw every day and they're scared too.

He don't get to say that to me.

When I leave, I try not to slam the door behind me. Mr. O'Brien is still sleeping.

CHAPTER EiGHTEEN

When I get home, I don't go inside for a while. I park behind Mom's old Subaru and cut the engine and take the bandana out of my pocket. Unfold it, fold it again. Unfold, fold. It's so old that it's gone impossibly soft, the edges fraying like the shoelace I've torn apart. The color hasn't faded in the dark. It smells like dust and damp air.

Eddie's dead.

Cooper wants to kill Paul and Noah too.

✦

Mom and Dad are in the kitchen when I shove in through the front door. Lady scrabbles across the room and jams her big head into my belly, and I've never been more glad to see anyone in my life. I am never going anywhere without her ever again.

I scratch her ears and pull the gift card out of my pocket to toss it on the counter.

"From Kelly," I say. "Grocery money."

Mom goes, "That's sweet of her," and then, "Hope Mr. O'Brien's doing okay, poor thing," and then she notices.

"Your hair," she whispers.

Dad leans against the kitchen counter, absently rubbing his bad hip. "Geez," he says, though he don't sound real surprised. "Awful short."

I don't have the energy for this. "Shaved it at Cooper's. His dad's fine. Kelly's got me laid off for the rest of the summer. I'm going to take a nap."

Mom and Dad say nothing. I brush past them into the back hall, putting a hand out behind me so Lady knows to follow.

✦

Because I have always been a very mature and responsible daughter, my painkillers have not been locked up. I grab the little bottle from the medicine cabinet, dump the OxyContin in the toilet, and flush while Lady whines outside the bathroom door.

CHAPTER
NiNETEEN

I don't plan on taking a nap, though. As Lady hops up
on my bed, standing there awkwardly like she's waiting
for me to follow, I open the bottom drawer of my dresser
and push aside a layer of old clothes. Church clothes, nice
blouses, camisoles, training bras.

Underneath are a set of photo albums and document
binders.

I'm careful with these. I lower the blinds to cut out UV
light and only use archival supplies, no matter that the cost
makes me wince. Not everything in here is old enough to
warrant it, obviously—a lot of what I've collected are scans,
printouts, whatever—but enough of it is. Family photos
found in Mamaw and Papaw's attic, newspaper clippings
so faded they're hard to read, handwritten letters in that
old-timey script. All sepia, yellowed, wrinkled with time.

I know who that man is. The man that stood there in the
dark mine, over my hospital bed, beside Eddie's dead body.

If he's anywhere, he'll be here.

Carefully opening the photo album, I pause to bask in how organized this is. I refuse to write on the photos themselves; each item is cataloged by date, subject, and anything else I know, all painstakingly recorded on a notecard. Take the first photo, for instance. *Sept 1971. Blackwater Falls, family trip. Left to right: Rodney Abernathy, Roger Abernathy, Robert "Bobby" Abernathy. Taken the week before Bobby's murder.* Papaw has a full head of hair, and Uncle Rodney is four, I think, clinging to Bobby's arm. Dad hadn't been born yet.

The man is not Bobby. Bobby is thick around the middle, big like Papaw. None of the sharp edges I'm looking for.

There are photos of Dad with Cooper's parents and Ms. Amber Foster, who wasn't a Foster at the time because she hadn't married Dallas's brother yet. Me and Cooper and Dallas playing in the backyard. Mom and Mamaw shucking corn on the porch. These photos have nothing to do with the feud, but I wanted to collect them anyway, prove we're more than just that.

Next, a set of accident photos. Hopefully I'll get to put the originals in here one day.

And then, farther back. Lucille, my great-grandmother, Papaw's mom. She never married, but she had two boys and loved them to the ends of the earth, even when she got shipped off to prison. Went to church every Sunday and burned a Davies alive. There are a lot of newspaper clippings of her. When she died in the seventies—half her life spent locked up in the Pence Springs women's prison—Sheriff

Davies's father celebrated with an opinion piece in the local paper, saying we were finally free of a menace. She's tall, with thin hair and a thinner face, but it can't be her.

I turn the page.

Finally, Saint Abernathy.

There aren't many photos of him. There's this one, and one more of his dead body nailed to the wooden stage floor of the burned-down theater. I try not to spend too much time with that one. But this one. Him, holding his baby daughter in front of a company house, with a bandana around his neck and a tall, bearded man at his side.

I pull the bandana from my pocket and lay it out carefully on my desk.

1916? Left to right: Saint Abernathy, Lucille Abernathy, unknown miner.

The sunken eyes, sharp nose, smooth jaw.

The same pattern on the bandana.

It's him.

✦

My great-great-grandfather, Saint Abernathy, had no official age when he was executed, but if I had to pick a number, I'd say his early thirties. The mines age you, the coal dust settling permanently into the creases of the face, so you always have to knock a few years off the guess.

He was a member of the illegal North Mountain Coal Company union and a card-carrying socialist. From the oral histories I recovered from a mining museum a few counties south—nothing's more American than scattering the history of a young revolutionary in an attempt to obscure it for good—he was also a mean son of a bitch. He yelled at the coal operators and threw glass bottles at cops, and the only person he ever said a kind word to was Lucille, which she wouldn't have been able to remember because he was executed when she was two.

There are some things about him I ain't been able to put together quite right. Nothing suspicious, because historical records get lost all the time, and when you're poor you might never have a record at all, but still, annoying. There's no birth certificate, no parents' names, no history before he started working for the coal company. No hint of who Lucille's mother might have been, neither.

But all of this started with him. And he's here.

I sit back and study the photo, monochrome and grainy, the white of the paper turned yellow with time. Saint has a sharp nose, dark eyes, a mouth that seems permanently set into a thin line. Small hands. Rough hands. Lucille takes after him, if you ask me.

And who is that, I want to ask him, as if pointing to the dark-haired miner by his side. *Can I commit the cardinal sin of historians and ask if y'all were gay?*

Then I pick up the bandana again. It's a hundred years old, if not more, with an awkward tear in the corner where it'd caught.

I don't believe in ghosts. Or anything else for that matter. Appalachia is a superstitious place, which makes sense—when foxes and cougars scream, it sounds like people. It's easy to think there's monsters in the woods when the woods are more than happy to let you die. But I don't believe in none of that, or ghosts, or God, because if I ain't got proof, I ain't budging. And why the hell do you need to worry about demons and devils when you got the Davieses to worry about?

But Saint Abernathy's dead, and I've been seeing him for weeks.

This is too much for one day. I'm going to bed.

CHAPTER TWENTY

In bed, with Lady sleeping at my feet and the sheet pulled over my head to block out the afternoon light, I google "opioid withdrawal," then close the tab because I don't want to see the results.

I don't come down for dinner, either. I wrap the shoelace around my fingers and press the rough fabric to my lips.

✦

Part of me wants to believe I hadn't been taking the pain-killers long enough to get hit by withdrawal, but the other part wants to be realistic. The nausea wakes me from a dead sleep. At first, hunched over the toilet at four in the morning, I think it's the guilt coming in, painful as a new tooth erupting from the gums. But sweat sticks my shirt to my back and my heart beats hard in my throat, lodged right where the nausea's settled like I'm trying to puke it up, and I spent enough time taking care of Dad to know what this is.

Lady knows too. She presses her nose to my arm and whines.

"I know," I whisper. "I know."

I put my fingers to my neck to count my pulse. Have to restart a few times cause I keep losing my place.

One hundred and twenty beats per minute.

Oh, I was for *sure* dependent on those painkillers.

I wait until both my parents are at work—grabbing the bucket from under the sink in case I get sick hiding under the covers—before stripping to my boxers and laying on the cool bathroom floor. Eyes squeezed shut, head pounding, three glasses of water on the ground next to me to keep it from getting worse.

Lady lies next to me in silence. There's a scar on her shoulder where a bear took a swipe at her last year. I trace it and she sighs like this is some great imposition, or like she's much older than she is.

It's okay. I can handle this. If I survived the woods, I can get through this.

My phone buzzes.

Cooper

Noah dropped by. Asked if I'd seen Eddie anywhere, told him to piss off. You okay?

I let my hand flop against the bathroom floor. I don't want to answer him. If he does something he shouldn't, like go after Paul or Noah, then I want my name far away from his.

But he helped get rid of the body. This is my fault. I can't ignore him.

Miles

i'm fine

he didn't do anything did he??

Cooper

No thank god. And hey. I'm sorry about yesterday.

I don't respond to that, but after a few minutes, he texts again.

Can we talk?

I hope my silence is enough of an answer.

What's a few more?

I didn't mean to kill Eddie. I wanted to hurt him, of course I did; it was only fair considering what he did to me. But kill him?

It don't matter if I didn't mean to. He's dead.

Coughing against the nausea, I get up off the floor, stick my head under the bathtub faucet, and turn the water on full blast. It hits the back of my skull hard as a brick. I gasp and splutter, the cold porcelain of the tub pressing hard into my ribs. Lady sits up and whines, pawing at my leg.

I wish I could tell my parents. Text them or send an email the way I did with my coming-out letter. *Noah and his friends tried to kill me in the woods, Sheriff Davies threatened me, I killed Eddie, Cooper and I hid the body and now he wants to kill the rest of them, I'm seeing Saint Abernathy, I'm pissed off and scared and confused and I don't know what to do.*

What? No, I don't feel bad about it. Not for Eddie. I feel like a bait dog in a fighting ring.

But if I do tell them? Mom will lose her mind. Dad will get himself hurt worse than he already has. Swear to god, Uncle Rodney would disown us, Papaw don't need another reason to burn down Davies's house, and Mamaw's trying so hard to keep it all together.

I turn off the water and gag helplessly into the bathtub.

I can't say a damn thing.

✦

Google search: "how long does oxycodone withdrawal last"

Result: "Symptoms will be at their worst seventy-two hours after the final dose, and can last for up to a week."

Prognosis: I'm gonna chew off my leg like an animal in a trap.

CHAPTER
TWENTY-ONE

It works in my favor that I've always been a recluse. I respond to hard times by going quiet and retreating from the world until it no longer makes me sick—stepping away, keeping my head down, doing anything to lay low. If my parents want to think I'm upset about getting laid off, I'll let them. Someone got fired at the nursing home, so Mom's too stressed out to pay attention and Dad's trying to give me space. Good. Leave me alone.

Plus, I can grit my teeth through a lot of hurt. I've spent my life refusing pain meds, binding broken toes with duct tape, and taking pet store antibiotics to fight off UTIs; this is a field medicine household, where you grit your teeth and bear it. I'm okay with that. I deal with pain far better than mild discomfort, after all. My broken nose has been easier to handle than a too-tight dress shoe.

But if this keeps up any longer, something is going to crack.

Which is why, when Lady jumps on my bed to start barking out the window, I nearly lose my shit.

"Shut up," I wheeze, grabbing her by the collar and dragging her back. It's one in the morning on day three of symptoms and I can't sleep and everything I do makes me want to puke. Since Eddie died, I've managed to keep down maybe a few protein bars and a glass of chocolate milk. My teeth chatter and I'm freezing. "Shut up, *stop*."

The start of a growl rumbles in her chest, and it ain't at me.

I struggle for air—*be quiet please please please*—and fumble open the window, wrestling to jam the paint stirrer stick under it to keep it ajar. My hands are shaking. "Look," I say. "Look. There's nothing out there." Just darkness and a few flecks of light higher up on the mountain, the neighbors' windows. "Stop."

Except I'm a liar. Because Saint Abernathy is in the backyard.

A summer breeze blows in through the window, chilling the layer of sweat soaking my throat. Crickets chirp. An owl calls. Lady lets out one more quiet noise: *Uff.* Her ears are held back tight to her skull.

Of course it's him. The bandana, the hardened hands, the old clothes smeared with dirt. It never could have been anyone but him. Was that what he wore when he died? Was he executed in an old linen shirt and scuffed pants?

He sees me and raises a single hand in greeting.

He's here. He's here again. My great-great-grandfather. The reason for all of this, and the person I admire most in the world.

It ain't that I envy his martyrdom. He didn't even get to be a true martyr at all. The strikebreakers and coal operators did everything they could to wipe him off the face of the earth. But, god, how could I not idolize him? A union man, a mean son of a bitch who did everything he could to make things better for his people, even if it didn't really work out in the end. He's done more than anyone could dream of. More than I've ever done reading alone in my room.

I need to tell him. I have to let him know.

"Wait," I whisper to him, begging that he hears me. "Wait wait wait."

I slip off the bed, grab my shoes, yank them on. My head screams when I move too fast, then my stomach turns and I have to grab the back of my desk chair, double over, clamp a hand over my mouth to keep from getting sick. Breathe in slow through my nose. Out through my mouth. Don't move. Wait for the wave to pass, slowly, until I can get a real lungful of air again—and then I'm grabbing the bandana to shove in my pocket, and I'm grabbing the photo album from my desk, and I'm taking Lady by the collar to get her through the back door.

Saint Abernathy don't disappear this time. In the grass, in the dark, I get right up close to him—close enough I can make out his scars, his unwashed hair, the bags under his eyes. The smears of blood at the corner of his mouth. The lines of muscles in his throat that're constantly clenched, the way mine must look when I'm trying not to gag.

Is that because of the railroad spike? It has to be. A hundred years with that thing stuck in your throat, filling your mouth to shut you up, I can't imagine.

The first thing I think to say, through the haze of pain and sick, is, "I thought about naming myself after you."

That takes him off guard. He blinks at me.

"Figured it'd be too dangerous, though." It's a struggle to get the words out, but I have to say them. "Might as well put a sign on my back saying, 'Hey, remember how y'all killed that guy a hundred years ago?' Because I do. And, you know, target's big enough as it is." I think I'm rocking back and forth a little bit. It holds the nausea at bay if I keep moving. "Probably safer to make Saint my middle name, but can't have the sheriff catching wind of that neither. Anyway, I wanted you to know that. I wanted—I wanted to do that for you."

I hesitate. The night is beautiful, and here I am with sweat stains under my arms and eyes bloodshot from exhaustion.

"Wait," I say. "Sorry. Sorry." I hold out the bandana. "Is this yours?"

Saint Abernathy laughs. It only lasts for a moment, because he immediately chokes on the spike. He clutches his throat, tries to recover, leans back and stares at the sky with tears glimmering in his rotting eyes. The moonlight settles on him all wrong, but it turns him into a painting.

Slowly, he recovers. He smiles and reaches out to take my wrist as if to say, *Of course it's mine.* He ain't warm, and he don't got a whole lot of grip strength, what with being dead and all, but I feel him. I don't know what to do with that information. This ain't a brain injury. This can't be a side effect of the withdrawal. Right? No way this is my brain short-circuiting, building something out of nothing, right?

The decision I come to is that it don't matter. When he starts to walk down to Main Street, Lady and I follow.

It's quiet in McLachlan now. I wipe my nose on my sleeve, try to keep my vision focused through the pounding headache. There are two weak lights on the other side of the street and not much else. If you head out of town to the east, eventually you'll hit Route 48/Corridor H, and then the Virginia border. To the west, that'll take you to the bridge over Twist Creek, past the path to the mine, and into Pearson, which contains both the only McDonald's in the county and Twist Creek's only stoplight. Lady's ears have perked up, her head on a swivel. I hold the photo album closer to my chest.

The last time I was out at night—

I try not to think about that.

We stop in front of the theater ruins. Saint stands at the edge of the overgrown grass, his hands casually in his pockets, surveying the destruction left behind in the wake of his death. Nobody goes past the grass. Not because there might be rattlesnakes or upset rats or nothing. It's just disrespectful. I'm too off-kilter to stay on my feet, so I sit on the sidewalk instead. Lady stands beside me, on guard.

"I'm sorry not a lot of people remember you," I whisper. Saint's gaunt face slides back to me. "But we do. I do." I try to smile but it comes out wobbly and nauseous. "You deserve better than that. At least the mine's closed. But I figure you know that already."

He nods. There's probably nothing he don't know already. The North Mountain Coal Company left Twist Creek behind a long time ago, back when Lucille was in prison. It bailed before it got cannibalized by some other mining company, the strip-mining operations popular down south, the kind that cut off mountain caps and dig out the sides of cliffs.

I'm fiddling with the cover of the photo album, and then the bandana, and then the shoelace. My fingers can't sit still.

"Were you there when they—" I stumble a little. "When those boys—"

Saint nods again.

The album's decorative pleather cover is starting to peel; I try to flatten it back out. Fidgeting, rocking, like I always do, like I've tried to stop myself from doing. I remember a comment from one of my parents—Mom or Dad, I can't remember—laughing on the back porch while I played in the yard. *Keep that up and we'll have to explain to our neighbors that our daughter is special.* Remembering that makes me feel gross, but there's no point in being upset. They didn't mean anything by it. I make myself stop moving and breathe carefully to control the nausea instead. It's hard to be mad at them for anything when they've always done their best, and when we have so many other things to worry about. Like those boys.

But then I realize, if he's been here the whole time—

Then he knows I'm trans.

"Probably not the descendent you were expecting," I mumble.

He gives me a sideways look, very *The hell are you on about?* That expression must be in our genetics somewhere.

Before I can respond—with what, I'm not sure—he crouches beside me. I can smell the damp air of the mines on him. It's nothing like the ancient rot of Sheriff Davies. It's comforting, even if it is what I imagine my grave would smell like one day.

He undoes the first few buttons on his shirt and pushes aside his collar until he's revealed part of his shoulder, a few inches of chest. There's no skin, though. It's some stitched-together garment, awkward but solidly made, pieced together from . . . what, linen and some tough fabric?

Oh. I'd recognize one of those anywhere. And it stings, because even I don't have one of these yet. I haven't ordered one online because I couldn't bring myself to, because I was nervous, and now my ribs won't be able to handle one for god knows how long.

It's a chest binder.

The withdrawal must be messing with me, because there's no way—there's no way. But it makes sense if you put the pieces together. The lack of records, the lack of history, his appearance out of thin air. He transitioned and made himself out of nothing. Whoever he'd been before, he'd destroyed them perfectly, and now all that exists is Saint.

Suddenly, I want to cry. Usually when people like Saint Abernathy die, they're violated. Their bodies are put on display. Ask me what happened to James Barry, what happened to Billy Tipton, what happened to all the poor bastards who ended up with an *F* on their death certificate. But Saint avoided it. Even when he died at the hands of one of the cruelest men West Virginia has ever seen, he made it to the other side unscathed.

I whisper, "You too?"

He taps the photo album. I flip it open, using my phone flashlight to navigate to the page I know he wants. The photo of him and Lucille and that miner. The one with the dark hair. I turn it so he can see.

"There," I say, and my voice comes out weak. I don't know if my hands are shaking from the withdrawal or nerves. "There's the three of you."

Saint presses his fingers to the plastic sheet keeping the picture safe. I look for proof that his weight is indenting the material, but I ain't sure if I see anything. The pad of his thumb lingers over Lucille's face, then the miner's, tracing the images of them slow. It must have been so long since he's seen them.

What he's implying is clear as day—to me, at least. There was no mother. Lucille Abernathy had two fathers.

"What happened to him?" I ask, studying the other miner's stern mouth.

Saint sighs. Gets up. Buttons his shirt again. His eyes slide, slowly, to the road to Pearson: right past the Twist Creek Bridge, the path that leads to the mine.

And then he's walking into the grass.

I close the photo album and hold it tight. He's running his hand through the grass, only some of which bends for him, until he reaches the wooden beams, the rotting stage.

So much has changed since he was alive. Ain't any mines in Twist Creek County no more, and no unions neither. No history beyond what little we've managed to scrape up in secret. Used to be that socialists were a real political party, and now you can't even say the word without being told you're an anti-American far-left fuck. (I mean, I am, but I don't appreciate the tone.) Democrats think we're all Trump-drunk illiterate hillbillies, self-sabotaging, too stupid or too proud to accept the help we clearly need; Republicans point at our poverty and dying communities and remind us that liberals don't care about us, which is funny because neither do they. Big-city Democrats need someone to feel superior to and Republicans need a voter base. That's how it works.

And if you're my dad, or the O'Briens, or Ms. Amber Foster, and you get it in your head that you can try to make things better—really, honestly better—you end up like us.

Saint climbs up on stage. The main character of a play, a tragic hero standing at the very spot of his murder. He's stunning. I push myself to my feet and, for the first time in my life, walk through the grass of the ruins to follow him. My feet disturb gnats and moths and little rodents. Lady presses herself close, careful not to let me stumble. My headache clenches so hard my vision darkens at the edges, but I don't stop.

Saint crosses the stage slowly, searching through the wreckage.

I want to be Saint when I grow up. Which is a funny thing to think, because I'm already almost grown, in the grand scheme of it all. I think I get to consider myself grown now that this has happened.

He finds what he's looking for. Bends down. Reaches between two rotted beams strewn across the stage and picks up a rusted hunk of metal.

A railroad spike.

I don't know if it's *the* railroad spike, but it don't matter. It's the principle of it. Saint comes to the end of the stage and hands it down to me. It's heavy, gone flaky from decades of neglect. Pieces of rust come off in my palm.

My first instinct is to drop it. I shouldn't be touching this. It means too much; it's an artifact meant to be preserved in a museum, held only with archival gloves. It's what *killed* him. My teeth are chattering with chills, muscles tightening painfully across my bruised back.

"What?" I say. "What do you want?"

But he's gone again, and it's just me in the grass. Lady whines. A trickle of sweat falls down my temple.

Why would he bring me here? Why would he show me who he is, only to disappear?

I thought you were an Abernathy.

I'm not gonna protect my family by hiding in my room for the rest of the summer, for the rest of my life. That ain't what Saint did. That ain't how the world works. The only thing that *works* is making it clear: If Sheriff Davies is going to hurt my family, fine. We're going to hurt his. Because that's what we do.

It's only right.

"Okay," I say, voice cracking under the weight of it. "Okay."

✦

Miles

okay

fine

i'm in

Cooper

Atta boy. Knew you'd come around.

CHAPTER
TWENTY-TWO

I ease open the front door, lifting up the handle so the hinges don't squeal, but there's no point since Dad's in the kitchen.

I stop in the doorway. Lady, blessedly ignorant, trots through the threshold and over to Dad, tail wagging.

Dad picks his big head out of his hand and pushes aside the handgun he'd laid out on the counter, reaching down to pet her ears. I try to swallow past the cotton in my throat. He bought that gun after the accident. Ain't like he carries it everywhere, just keeps it in the safe under the nightstand, but the fact that we need it is bad enough. It's a Glock 19 that Uncle Rodney sold to him for three hundred bucks. It's always loaded.

"Hi," I whisper.

Dad pinches the bridge of his nose. "Shut the door," he says.

I do. Behind him, the weak light above the sink flickers. It makes a droning noise. I don't like it.

"I'm okay," I preempt, even though I'm visibly not. With my bloodshot eyes and the photo album in my arms and the shoelace I'm putting between my teeth. "I was . . ."

Dad waits for me to finish.

"Taking a walk," I say. "Couldn't sleep. Haven't been, uh. Feeling good."

"Noticed that." Dad's tone is beyond me—concerned, frustrated, disappointed, I don't know. "Near enough gave me a heart attack when I got up to check on you."

"You been checking on me?"

Dad scratches his beard. I imagine him opening my door a crack every night, peering in, making sure I'm still breathing, like a new parent worried about a baby. "And the dog was gone too. I know you're a good kid, but Christ, after everything . . ." He's exhausted, but he always is; with his stained sweatpants cut off at the knees, the scars on his left leg are open to the air. "I ain't stupid. I know what withdrawal looks like."

"It's not—"

"You think I don't?"

I don't want to have this conversation anymore. Lady paces between me and Dad, ears pinned back, and I resist the urge to jam the heels of my hands into my eyes. I pull on the shoelace a few times instead.

"No," I say. "I know."

"And going out after dark? Alone?"

"I know."

"What did you do?"

I don't know how to answer. Dad comes over, takes the photo album out of my hands, and sets it on the table.

"Miles," he whispers. "Please."

My name. It's the first time he's said my name. My eyes burn. Don't cry, don't cry, don't cry. I wad the shoelace up in my hand and squeeze until it hurts.

I'm doing all of this to protect you. Because I don't want you to get involved. You're already dealing with so much, and so much of it is my fault.

"Please don't tell Mom," I whimper.

"You know I can't promise that, bud."

I answer anyway. "I flushed the pills. All of them."

Dad takes a second to let that sink in, then purses his lips and nods. He's studying the floor. Mom always reminds him to look at the corner of the eye like she does, but it never sticks for him. He can't manage it.

"I got scared," I say. "I remembered what happened to you, and what's going on with Cooper's dad, and I didn't—" I sniffle. "I didn't want them near me anymore."

"You had surgery," Dad says. "They had to open you up." I shake my head like that means anything. "Of course it's scary, but we wouldn't let anything happen to you."

I'm already crying. Lady whines and paws at my leg. Dad grabs me by the back of the neck and pulls me into a hug, and he presses his face to my shaved head and won't let go.

He can't promise that. I know that's what parents are for, but nobody would ever be able to actually keep me safe, not for sure.

"Okay," he says, rocking me gently back and forth. "I know it hurts. It'll stop soon."

✦

We don't talk about why I went out. He don't bring up the bandana hanging out of my pocket or why there are flakes of rust on my hands. Instead, when I finally let go, Dad gets me a glass of ice water and a wet washcloth to wipe my face and makes me sit at the wobbly dining room table while he cuts a banana into bite-sized pieces. "BRAT diet," he says. "Bananas, rice, applesauce, toast. It'll help with your stomach until this is over. Boring as hell, though."

I clutch the ice water to my cheek, because the cool plastic is nice. "Sounds like my usual."

Dad snorts and brings over a little plate. I've never been a fan of bananas, even when I'm doing okay, but he's so worried about me that I have to try. It'll be a miracle if I keep it down. I take the smallest bite, trying to get used to the texture, but opening my mouth enough to get anything in triggers my gag reflex immediately. Dad rubs my back and makes me finish the glass of water before getting me another.

We decide my best bet is mashing the banana pieces into a paste with a fork. I have to take a breather between swallows.

"Get down what you can. I know it's tough." That's an understatement. Then he nods at the photo album, maybe to distract me, give me something else to focus on. "What's that?"

Not a good choice. My stomach bottoms out. Sure, the most incriminating things are in the document case, still hidden safely at the bottom of my dresser, but I have the accident photocopies in there. I struggle to come up with anything that'll keep him from opening it up. "It's, um. A project I'm working on. Kind of personal, though." Then, because it seems like a good nail for the coffin, I add, "You know. Gender stuff."

"Gender," Dad says, "stuff."

"Yeah." I glance down at the plain cover, fidgeting with the fork. "You know. Appalachian masculinities, that sort of thing."

The words *Appalachian masculinities* seems to throw Dad off, like he's not quite sure what to make of the phrase. If I really was going to make something like that, an illustration of *Appalachian masculinities*, I wouldn't have to go far. I've grown up with ex-moonshiners wearing Realtree camo and cleaning hunting rifles on the dining room table, mechanics coming home with oil still on their hands, Papaw and Dad and Mr. O'Brien on the back porch with a round of beers discussing the best way to protect their families in the wake of some cruelty or another. When you grow up with mountain men, your idea of masculinity is that one: pickup trucks and big game and taking care of each other.

Dad says, "I guess I don't get it."

He don't have to say what he don't get. I know what he's talking about. "That's fine," I say. "You ain't gotta get it."

"Makes me feel old, actually. You wrote that whole essay for us and I'm still confused." He laughs a little. "Your mom, she, uh, didn't take it all that great. Don't think she actually managed to finish it. Got too upset. Said something about never getting to see you in a wedding dress." Ain't no reason for him to be telling me this, but I listen anyway, poking the plate of mush with the fork tines. "Dunno what she was on about with that, since I always figured you were gonna get hitched in flannel."

Okay, fine. That makes me smile. It's not a great smile, but it's there.

"I guess," he says, "my main question is, how do you know?" *How do you feel?* I don't know. I never know. "Because there's nothing inside me that tells me I'm a man. I just am."

I shrug. "Exactly."

Dad leans back in his chair. "Huh."

I finish the banana eventually and chug the water. Dad gets the washcloth wet again and stands behind me to clean behind my ears, then gets my wrists too. Pulse points, he tells me; it'll help. And when's the last time I've washed that shoelace? Give it a soak tonight.

When I get up to go back to bed, to see if I can at least try to get some sleep, Dad catches my wrist.

"If you need anything," he says, "you let me know. And be careful."

I reply, "You too."

He snorts, but the look he gives me as I gather up the photo album and catch Lady's attention makes me think that he's trying hard to figure out exactly what I mean.

CHAPTER
TWENTY-THREE

i wake up to arguing from the kitchen. I'm cradling
Squishy Pillow, curled up as if trying to protect myself
from a storm, and my vision struggles to clear no matter
how many times I rub my eyes, but I feel . . . not as bad as
I did last night. There's no bile burning in my throat, and
the food Dad gently cajoled into my stomach hasn't come
back up. Lady snores on the rug beside my bed. I stare at
my ceiling, listening to the muffled noise of Mom and Dad
snapping at each other in the kitchen. It's damp outside.
The ceiling fan whirs. The savory smell of sausage gravy
and biscuits creeps in, and I think those technically hit
that diet Dad was talking about. Beige and simple.

He said the only thing I had to do today was rest and, if
I could manage it, shower. He's taking a day off from the
garage too, so if I need him to run a bath, all I have to do
is ask.

Not sure I deserve it.

I check my phone for Cooper's response, even though the bright screen hurts my eyes. There it is. *Atta boy*. And the railroad spike sits on my bedside table, even though I didn't believe it would still be there when I woke up.

"Why didn't you *tell me*?" Mom demands across the house. I sit up with a groan. Lady is awake now, watching the door. My parents don't argue all that much, and when they do, their voices never rise. It's all harsh whispering and warbling awkwardness before they walk away to cool down. They haven't gotten to the cool-down part yet. They probably think I can't hear them, which is funny, since you can hear everything in this piece-of-shit house. "Seriously, Jeffery, *withdrawal*? This isn't some stupid painkiller, this is OxyContin—"

"I know damn well what it is," Dad counters, and Mom goes quiet. Dad follows up gently. "I just wanted to be sure. You know how our kid gets. Gang up, and we'll never get anywhere. She's—he's sensitive."

I didn't think anybody would ever describe me as sensitive.

I change clothes because seriously, this sweating thing is getting out of hand; down another glass of water, because I know Dad will tell me to; and wander into the kitchen with Lady at my side. Mom is still going, clearly not hearing the floor creak or Lady's nails on the hardwood as we get closer.

"Which is exactly why I want to get someone else involved. Someone who actually knows what they're doing, because clearly we didn't do all that well the first time."

"Someone else?" Dad says, ignoring that *the first time* was him. "This is family business. Ain't no need for that. Besides, Cooper's been helping out, hasn't he?"

"The O'Brien's boy is a child, and the last thing that child needs is to get mixed up in this."

I pause on the threshold and clear my throat to catch their attention. "Morning."

Dad gives me an apologetic frown from the stove where he's stirring the sausage gravy, next to a pan of biscuits cooling on top of the oven. God, I hope the nausea stays down, because this is the first time I've been hungry in days.

"Hey, bud," he says. "You holding up okay?"

Mom, though, snatches up a bunch of glossy brochures from the counter. She's got her outside clothes on even though it's too early to be dressed for anything.

"Now?" Dad says. "Really?"

"Now," Mom says.

She hurries across the kitchen and pushes the brochures into my hands. I fumble, turn them over in confusion, try to catch up with what's happening. I'm still fuzzy from waking up and literally everything else that's been happening over the past few days.

Dad shakes his head. "Ignore all that. You can worry about this when you're better."

"*Jeffery*." Mom glares at him, then turns to me. "Pick one," she says, "or we'll pick for you."

Dad goes, "Christ."

I look at one flyer. And another.

Appalachian Community Health Center, Twist Creek Office. Then, *Celebrate Recovery.* Another: *Virtual Mental Health Resources.* Another: *Pearson Group Sessions for Teens and Young Adults.* I can't tell if these flyers are written in a condescending tone or if my fight-or-flight response has kicked in. Mom can't be serious. There's no way. I pick out one of the middle fliers and show it to her as if she's not completely aware of what she's suggesting.

"This is a drug counseling office," I say, forcing a laugh to cover up the fear creeping in. I wonder if she can tell I'm using the corner-of-the-eye trick. "For, like, alcoholics? And it's in Tucker County? That's ninety minutes away, maybe two hours if traffic sucks."

"There's not a lot of options," Mom says defensively. "Mental health resources are abysmal here."

"I don't—" I glance to Dad for backup, but he turns away and goes back to stirring the gravy. "I don't need this."

"Your father told me what happened with your medication."

"Yeah," I say, "and I ain't dead, am I? Am I in the hospital right now? No." Mom is not impressed with my low blow. I turn over another brochure, the Appalachian Community Health Center, my nervous laughter getting away from me. The sunny faces and bright printer ink ain't right. I'm not going to therapy. Absolutely not. *How are you feeling*, they'd ask, and I would only be able to respond, *I don't know, I don't know, I never know.* "We can't afford none of this. This is gonna be, what, a fifty-dollar copay? Once a week? That's two hundred a month. Plus whatever else they spring on you, because they're always springing something."

Mom says, "Don't think about money. That's our job, not yours."

That's bullshit. I've been poking my nose in family finances since I was a freshman in high school, and I ain't got the patience to play at saying the right thing today. I push the brochures back at her, but she won't take them. "No way in hell. I ain't going."

There's a knock at the door.

"I got it," Dad says, as if eager to cut this all off. Mom backs away from me with a sigh. Lady whines.

He opens the door and Sheriff Davies is on our porch.

Cop car idling in the driveway. Sunglasses perched on top of his blond head. Smiling that rat-eating smile with all those little white teeth crammed in his mouth. Lady cringes against my leg, ears flat back against her skull.

"Good morning," Sheriff Davies says, all drawl and fake charm. His dark uniform looks like it was specifically dyed to hide bloodstains. "Sorry to drop in on you so early, but I wanted to swing by on my way through town."

Mom takes a step back, putting her body between me and him. Dad's fingers twitch. He put the gun back in the safe. Ain't got nothing but kitchen knives.

"Sheriff," Mom says carefully, "we're in the middle of a family conversation."

"Won't take but a minute." Sheriff Davies steps over the threshold—it feels like he shouldn't be able to, like he should be a vampire that needs inviting in—and tracks wet footprints onto the kitchen floor. "Smells heavenly in here. Don't mind if I do." He takes a biscuit from the tray, breaks it in half, and dips it into the pan of sausage gravy to take a big, showy bite. "Mm, that's good. Might want to take this off the heat, Linda. Seems about done to me."

Dad comes over to turn off the burner, because he was the one cooking. Besides, Mom ain't moving. I can see the muscles in her neck getting tight. Her eyes are trained on the gun at his hip.

I do a quick mental check. The lockbox with the photos is inconspicuous in the next room. My photo album and document box are hidden in the dresser. The railroad spike and bandana are in my room across the house. The camera behind Big Kelly's is broken, Cooper kept his mouth shut, we should be fine. We're fine.

"I just wanted to see how Miss Abernathy is doing." When his gaze lands solidly on me, Mom reaches out to take my hand. I'll be fine. We agreed on the reality that I don't remember. He's got no reason to think I killed Eddie. He's got no reason to think Eddie's dead at all. "It's been quite the few weeks, hasn't it?"

I nod, fiddling with the brochures in my free hand. I want my shoelace. I left it on my desk. "Something like that."

"You healing all right?"

"Yes, sir."

"Good. Careful with those prescriptions. You know, given"—he pauses, gives Dad an apologetic smile—"how things have been."

Dad sucks in air through his teeth. Sheriff Davies scoops another mouthful of sausage gravy and swallows the rest of the biscuit whole. Gotta unhinge your jaw like a snake to do that. I don't think Mom's breathed since he walked in that door.

"Well," Davies continues, "truth is, I'm also here to ask if y'all have seen hide or hair of the Ruckles' boy, Edmund." He won't take his eyes off me. "Eddie, right? You're in the same grade, ain't you?"

I nod. "Yeah, we are." Don't say *were*. Stay in the present tense. Mom and Dad snap a glance to each other over my head. "Something happen to him? He okay?"

Sheriff Davies makes a clicking noise that's probably him thinking, but it sounds like a bug. "Kid was supposed to start his first shift at Big Kelly's a few days ago, but he never showed. Found his bike out back, but not him. His folks says he has a knack for disappearing every so often, so they weren't worried at first, but it's never been for this long." He spreads his hands. "Kelly said you were there right before he was scheduled. Picking up your paycheck. He was your replacement, wasn't he?"

"Was he? Didn't see his name on the schedule."

"So, you didn't see him," Davies replies dully.

If he knows something and he's trying to trap me, I'm screwed—but Davies don't strike me as the hardcore mind-games type. If he knew something, he would've had me dragged down to the station in Pearson by now. "No, sir. Maybe he went in the front? I use the back entrance and all that."

Davies shakes his head. "Pulled camera footage out front, nothing. And that back camera's busted too. Shame."

"Shame," I repeat.

"Well." He reaches into his breast pocket and pulls out a business card before handing it to me. Mom intercepts it. "You learn anything, don't be a stranger. Be kinder than these parents of yours, you hear?"

Mom shoves the card in her pocket. "Don't want you to be late for nothing," she says, an overly polite *get out of my house*.

"Of course." Davies's eyes flick down to the brochures in my hands. He plucks one off the top, squints at it. I can smell his cologne, and it don't cover up the rot. "What's this? Therapy groups?"

"Sir," Dad cuts in, trying to pull him away from me, but I don't want Davies to so much as look at my father. I answer instead: "Stuff like that."

"Which one you planning to go to?"

I hesitate.

"You really should go," he says. "Might help, considering everything you've been through."

I grab one from the stack and give it to Mom. "This one."

Pearson Group Sessions for Teens and Young Adults.

"Right," Mom says.

When Sheriff Davies leaves, he takes another biscuit for the road and knocks his sunglasses back into place—and I didn't notice it until the door was closed but Lady has not moved, has barely even breathed, her teeth showing

through her black lips like she's spent the past five minutes
staring down a wolf on the edge of our property.

Eventually, Mom unfolds the brochure, and says, "This
one?"

Yeah. Whatever. "That one."

Saint was right. I'm never going to let Davies treat my
family like prey ever again.

✦

Cooper

You free to talk Tuesday?

Just heard Paul's parents are out of town on the fourth

Sounds like a clean shot to me

CHAPTER
TWENTY-FOUR

The withdrawal symptoms lessen. Dad wakes me up every morning with a glass of ice water—at first so the vomit don't burn as bad coming up, and then just to make sure I'm hydrated. Mom picks out my clothes and checks my eyes, counts my pulse under her breath. She holds my face in her hands a little too long every time she does. I keep down snacks, then small servings of buttered noodles, and suddenly one evening I'm polishing off a bowl of chipped beef dip and I slump over in my chair, laughing because *finally*.

"This was a real stupid thing for a smart kid to do," Mom says that night, taking the bowl from me and dunking it in the dishwater. "But I figure you know that already."

"Yeah," I say, and bump my head against her shoulder. "I know."

Then, like an ambush predator that's finally decided to show itself, the first day of therapy arrives. Now, I

don't got nothing against therapy. It's a crucial, sometimes lifesaving resource that needs to be normalized in
communities like mine. It's also expensive, inaccessible,
and horrifically flimsy in the face of a century-old blood
feud. Can't talk-therapy your way out of a gun pressed to
the back of your head. But Mom still picks me up after
her shift at the nursing home and drives across the Twist
Creek Bridge and down the winding mess of roads to
Pearson. Neither of us is happy with the situation, but
we both know that if she don't hold me to this, it'll never
happen at all.

Looking at Mom in the driver's seat, I wonder if she
feels the same way about therapy that I do and she's just
reaching in a terrified flurry for anything she thinks might
help me. I don't like thinking about my parents being
scared, but I think about it all the time.

Anyway, Pearson is flatter than McLachlan and twice
its size, though that don't add up to much. There's almost
six thousand people in the county, with a thousand of them
here. The demographic percentages are bleak. According to
the census, there'd been a Black family here at some point
in the past few years, but I think they left for Martinsburg,
and who could blame them? Everyone is crammed into one
square mile around the single stoplight, the median income
per household is barely scraping thirty grand, and almost
20 percent of the population lives below the poverty line, a
nasty number compared to the national average.

I'm full of depressing statistics. Maybe that's why I don't
have friends.

I shrink against the seat as we drive by the blocky sheriff's office. There are officers besides Davies, obviously, but they've split up the county like wolves fighting over territory. They leave Pearson and McLachlan to their boss. When I was in middle school, a deputy got killed, and while the official story is suicide, Papaw maintains it was Davies that did it. "You know how it goes," he'd said. The deputy's mamaw spits at cop cars when they go by.

As for the Pearson Methodist church, it's sandwiched between a laundromat and an old restaurant building. Even though I'm doing better, in a physical sense at least, Mom still fidgets as she drops me off in the parking lot. She takes a piece of gum out of its pack, bites it in half, and saves the rest.

"I need to grab groceries for Mamaw and Papaw," she says, "so I'll be back a little bit after you wrap up. You gonna be okay?"

"Should be," I say flatly. I've got my shoelace. Ain't no way I'm chewing on it in front of everyone here, but at least I'll have something to tie into knots. "He ain't gonna do nothing to me in front of God and everybody."

Mom is unamused. "Promise me."

"Promise."

She drives off. An awkward folding sign points out the stairs to the basement, tucked under the church's front porch. The door's been propped open. I slip inside as quiet as I can, already pulling the shoelace into a ball of butterfly knots.

Oh, I hate this.

My fourth-grade teacher, Mrs. Amsler, is setting out a bunch of plastic chairs across the checkered floor, flanked by folding tables sparsely peppered with cheap snacks. Two kids from school are already here: Kent Sanderson, who spent the last few months losing his shit after his sister died of an overdose, and Claire Snyder, whose dad is the one who got nabbed by the game warden. Neither of them make eye contact with me.

"Evening, Sadie," Mrs. Amsler says softly. I nod in acknowledgment because I can't manage much more. "Your momma told me you'd be coming down today. Here, get some water, take a seat."

I do as I'm told, then tie up the entire shoelace in one giant convoluted knot, pull it as tight as I can, and try to pick it apart. A few more kids trickle in. They chat a little bit, picking seats next to one another, grabbing snacks and whispering. I uncap my bottle of water, down the whole thing, and chew absently on the bottle cap.

I wish I could have brought Lady.

Once everyone arrives, we begin. Mrs. Amsler opens the session with an icebreaker question, the two truths and a lie thing. She asks if I want to start, and I do not. The looks I get when I say no make me want to crawl out of my skin. There could be a lot of reasons for that. The fact that I haven't healed perfectly, that my nose is off-kilter and my eyes uneven. The fact that I'm an Abernathy, and people close to the Abernathys get hurt.

But it's more deep-rooted than that. It started before the accident, before my classmates were old enough to pay attention to who my parents were. It's like everyone knows there's something off about me, and they don't like it, and they don't quite know what to do about it.

It's what I spent so, so long trying to fix. And it's hard trying to bridge the gap between me and everyone else. To do all the work, mold yourself into what you think people want, only to have it fall apart when you're too tired to keep it up anymore. People are exhausting, and frustrating, and so much work. Fake eye contact, stay still, stop chewing on things, stop being so goddamn *weird*.

Why is it so hard for me? How come everybody else seems to handle it fine?

"Sadie?" Mrs. Amsler says sweetly. "Would you like to share?"

Everyone else has been talking for a while, and now they're all watching me. I have no idea what the topic is. Are we still on the icebreakers? My leg is bouncing. I want to leave.

"Um," I say, "is there a bathroom down here?"

Mrs. Amsler's smile does not drop. "You'll have to go up to the church. The door is unlocked."

"Thanks," I say, and bolt.

As soon as I'm up the stairs, I gasp for air, pressing the heels of my hands into my eyes, even though it hurts. All my muscles scream for me to start walking—in any direction, just away. Or at least get out of view of the goddamn street, because I don't want to be caught alone if Sheriff Davies decides to stroll by. Pick a direction and go. So I start around the side of the church, down the narrow alleyway between it and the restaurant. There's some trash cans, a milk crate, cigarette butts against the brick wall.

I need a moment to breathe. That's it.

A door creaks open. My head jerks up.

A voice: "Sorry, buddy. Didn't mean to startle you."

The side door of the restaurant slaps shut as a waiter dumps an armful of collapsed boxes by the dumpster. I know they're a they—it's hard to miss the *Suck my they/them dick* pin hastily jammed onto their apron.

"You're fine," I mumble, scrubbing my face so they can't catch whatever confused, wrinkled expression I've got going on. "I'll get out of your way. Sorry."

But the waiter don't say nothing.

They're staring at me.

Eventually, they say: "Holy fuck, Abernathy, that you?"

✦

The last time I saw Dallas Foster was five years ago. They were twelve years old, and Cooper and I were visiting them in the only burn ward in West Virginia—a tiny wing of a Huntington hospital that would nearly drive the Fosters to bankruptcy. Mom had driven Cooper and I down, but we could only stay for the day because Dad and Mr. O'Brien couldn't be left alone for long. Mrs. O'Brien's funeral had been two weeks earlier.

In the burn ward, Dallas reminded me of a mummy. They were all tubes and bandages and mess, wrapped up in compression garments and skin shiny like raw meat. They'd only been awake from the medically induced coma for a few days.

"Sorry we couldn't make it," Dallas whispered about the funeral, which was a wild thing to hear from a seventh grader who had almost died.

"It's fine," Cooper said.

In the silence that followed, we heard the moment that Dallas's parents realized my mom was there and the sudden eruption of screaming in the hall. *This is your husband's fault, you bitch!* I'd turned to rush out, but Cooper grabbed me.

"Amber's got it," he'd said.

"Amber's got everything," Dallas added.

But I kept watching the door to the hall because I didn't want to look at Dallas. It wasn't right. They'd been the kind of kid who hit their growth spurt early, started shaving in middle school, probably would've been courted for varsity football if they'd had any interest, which they didn't. They hated their parents and spent all their time with their brother, and sometimes they called Amber *Mom* instead. They wanted to grow up to be just like her. They were loud, and smart, and mean in a way that was funny because they were only mean to people who deserved it. Then suddenly they were in a burn ward, an open wound in the shape of a person.

Sure, Dad didn't do it. Sheriff Davies did. But hell if you could explain that to Dallas's parents—Dallas was in the car, Dad was driving, you know how it goes. So when we left that day, Dallas's parents never let us see them again. They moved out of Twist Creek to . . . somewhere. Texts no longer went through, and then reached strangers. Facebook account deactivated. Chat logs missing. Gone.

Now they're right in front of me.

And they look *right*. Exactly how I'd imagined them when I pretended we'd run into each other again one day. The redheaded spitting image of their brother: tall, fat, and built like a bull, the same bright eyes and toothy smile and messy hair. They've even got the beard, or at least the kind of beard they can manage at, what, seventeen? Eighteen? When a good chunk of their skin ain't growing hair anymore?

Then the burns. Across the face, the neck, the hands. Half an ear gone, their mouth pulled into an asymmetrical shape half fixed by surgery. They're bald at the left temple, and their skin has mottled into different colors and textures, a patchwork quilt of scars and grafts and medical miracles.

They look . . .

Like they managed. Like they pulled through. Despite everything Davies did.

I point at the pronoun pin and say, quietly, "So we're both trans now?"

For a moment, there's silence. Dallas just stares at me. And I wonder if I've said the wrong thing, or somewhere along the way they decided to agree with their parents and blame my family for everything—

—and then they burst into loud, sudden laughter. They grab me in a hug, squeezing tight enough to hurt for a moment before pulling back, holding me by the arms, shaking me in excitement. It's clear their hands don't got the same range of motion they used to, but they're *laughing* and it's *contagious*.

Jesus, I missed them so much, and they're okay, and they don't hate me, and they're back home.

"I knew it!" Dallas crows. "I knew it, I could've fucking called it, oh my god. Of course you're trans. Of course you are." Nobody has ever been excited to hear I'm trans before. My head spins. "I'm so sorry I ain't been able to track you down, I dropped out of school last year and left Charleston and moved in with Michael and Amber a few weeks ago and the ADHD's kicking my ass, oh god, how are you? New name? New pronouns? We—"

They'd been rambling, and now they're suddenly stumbling over their words. They grab my jaw to tilt my face like we didn't spend half a decade apart. Their skin feels exactly how it looks, rough and uneven.

"What happened to your face?" they ask. "You good?"

I pull out of their grip. "One question at a time, Foster." They hold up their hands in surrender but don't let the distressed expression drop. For once I'm not exhausted by the concern. This is how it goes between friends. Friends, right? I don't know if we can call ourselves that after so long. "It's Miles now. He/him. And what do you mean, you dropped out? Of school? For good?"

Dallas shakes their head. "Your face first, man."

My instinct, for some reason, is to hesitate. To not tell them, like if they don't know what's happened then the feud won't touch them again. They've been through enough.

Physically, going on a scale of bodily harm, they've had it so much worse than me: my days in the hospital versus the slogging years of recovery, whatever it takes to heal from something like this—the rest of your life? It's not like I can tell them everything. I can't say that Eddie is dead, that Paul is next, that Cooper and I refuse to let this get worse.

But they deserve to know the Twist Creek County they came back to.

I point my eyes down the alleyway, towards the road. Right where you'd be able to see the sheriff's office. Dallas tracks my gaze.

I say, "It was going to happen eventually, right?"

Dallas says, "Shit." They grab the side door to the restaurant. "Inside, now."

CHAPTER
TWENTY-FiVE

I don't need to reiterate the political climate of Twist Creek County, do I? Last year, Big Kelly put a Democrat bumper sticker on her car and got her tires slashed. Lawn signs from the 2016 presidential campaign still stick out of yards and roadsides like thorns: MAKE AMERICA GREAT AGAIN, TRUE AMERICANS ARE REPUBLICANS, KILL ALL COMMIES. We even had a voyeuristic blue-state film crew come through last year, using interview footage as B-roll for a documentary on the rise of the rural far right. I watched when it aired a few months ago. It was all clips of abandoned trains, old men smoking in abandoned shops, *Unemployment is more than twice the national average and the North Mountain Coal Company left us to rot, but remember, Trump Digs Coal.* We seceded from Virginia so we didn't have to join the Confederacy, and now you can find a half dozen traitor flags while walking down Main Street.

So when Dallas ushers me into the restaurant and I see a black flag hanging on the inside of the door, I do a double take.

A black flag with the circle *A*. The anarcho-communist black-and-red rippling in streamers on the industrial fans. Words spray-painted on the kitchen wall next to a stencil of a hissing cat: ALL PROFITS ARE STOLEN WAGES. One cook does prep work while another throws burgers on the flattop, a dishie shoves a pan under the water to soak, a waitress sorts silverware. The dishie whistles as Dallas comes in. Dallas whistles back.

"Amber and Michael own this place?" I ask, like I can't quite believe it.

Dallas shakes their head. "Don't call them capitalists where they can hear you. It's a worker co-op; they just got it up and running."

This place is perfect, and my knee-jerk reaction is fear.

I cover my nerves with a shaky smile as Dallas guides me through the kitchen. "Amber's idea, yeah?" She's always been the most outspoken about, well, everything. I was always surprised Davies didn't go right for her—or maybe that's what he tried to do when he ran the car off the road that night.

"Don't worry," Dallas says. "She radicalized my brother before she married him, thank god."

Dad was going to reach out to her. I saw her name on one of the emails that night before the party. It wasn't much, the *To* line and nothing else, but it was enough. He was thinking about it. He was planning to try again.

And look what happened to us.

I pull hard on the shoelace. "You know Davies's gonna kill y'all for this, right?"

I didn't mean for it to come off as a joke, but it must have, because Dallas gives me a nasty smile. "Fucking with us is part of his job description, babe. Can't let it stop us."

Then they're bustling me out to the front of the house, where it's all cheap booths and old tables and blown-up printouts of mine revolts hung on the walls, a WELCOME TO THE RED HOLLER banner hung beside the door. There's the start of a stage against the back wall, not quite put together yet. String lights flicker, a jukebox plays some folksy song featuring a barely tuned guitar, and a man behind the cash register barks when Dallas and I come into view.

"Dallas!" Michael Foster snaps. Swear to god they're Dallas's uppercase, just less queer-coded. "What are you doing? You're on break! Don't fucking do shit on break."

There ain't a lot of people eating—a woman in a Dollar General uniform drinking an iced tea in the corner, two truckers demolishing a pizza—but that still gets a quick laugh.

"I ain't working," Dallas counters. "I found a stray."

Michael's eyes slide to me, and he has that moment of recognition I've been getting a lot recently. My chest aches. I forgot how much I liked Michael. He was always slipping me five-dollar bills and cool rocks Amber found. He stumbles out from behind the counter, clapping his hands together in excitement. "Sadie! That you?"

"Um," Dallas says, giving me a panicked look. I don't know why. "That's not—"

Oh. My name. Dallas is worried about my name. Is this what it's like to be around other trans people? Not just using your name, but defending it?

"Actually," I say as soon as Michael is comfortably close enough, considering I ain't planning on announcing this to the entire restaurant, "it's Miles now. It's recent, though, so don't worry or nothing, you're fine."

"Nah, don't make excuses for me," Michael says. "Miles it is. You're . . ." His voice trails off as he searches for a word, but Dallas shoots him a glare and he swerves immediately. "Bigger! You got big. I mean, look at you. Last I saw you, you were, what, eleven? I feel old."

"Dude," Dallas says, "you're thirty. You're ancient. He's had a day, don't be weird." Michael holds up his hands the same way Dallas did. "We're gonna hang out for a bit."

Michael says something else, but I don't hear him because I've caught sight of the corkboard by the front door. No *way*. It's a mess of printouts and business cards: offers of free stuff, book club notices, Planned Parenthood pamphlets, phone numbers for food banks and pro bono lawyers and thinly veiled abortion help. They've put together a setlist of indie bands for the rest of the summer, all with names like All Cats Are Beautiful and Trans Punk Rebellion. There's even a stack of Molotov cocktail stickers with a holographic flame.

As if calling this place the Red Holler wasn't enough. This ain't just a target on their backs—they've practically put a neon sign on the front door, saying, HEY SHERIFF DAVIES, WE'RE DIRTY FUCKING COMMUNISTS.

I take a half step back from the board but immediately bump into Dallas.

"Oh," they say, "careful." Their voice is low enough that it rumbles. Jesus, they really grew up. It's hard not to remember the middle schooler I left behind in the hospital. "Sorry, just told Michael to give you some air. He gets excited about stuff."

"Thanks." Figures they'd remember that I like my personal space. It's kind of my whole thing. I nod to the stickers, the Molotov cocktail that is very clearly ignited. "Didn't think you'd be cool with fire after, you know. Everything."

Dallas playfully pushes their arm into mine and grabs a sticker. The glitter finish gleams. "Yeah, well, start smoking and you'll get yourself some exposure therapy for the price of a lighter. Cheaper than a shrink, if you ask me."

They laugh a little, but I don't. That's not very funny. They've always said things that were a little out of left field, a little uncomfortable sometimes, but that's . . .

They're joking about it because it's true, and it reminds me of how Cooper started drinking a few months after the accident. He was thirteen. Davies messed all of us up real bad.

It gets quiet between us. Dallas's expression falters. "Want one?"

"I'm good."

Dallas puts the sticker back, clearly knocked out of their rhythm. I can't tell which one of us made this awkward. Maybe I should've laughed, or I shouldn't have brought up fire in the first place. "Right," they say. "How's Cooper?" Thank god, a subject change. "Haven't run into him yet."

"Oh, he's okay." Can't say we hid a body, can I? "We didn't really talk after the accident, but he's been great after"—I gesture to myself—"all this. Especially since Eddie Ruckle went missing a few days ago. Davies ain't happy, and he's making it our problem."

"Eddie Ruckle's missing?" Dallas tilts their head. "Should I feel bad, or is he still a freak?"

"No, still a freak. I dunno. I ain't real upset about it." I unwind the shoelace from my wrist, and I stick it right in my mouth. Dallas never cared about me chewing on my hair or shirt collars when we were little, either. "Has, uh, Davies given y'all any trouble?"

Dallas makes a rasping noise in annoyance. "He dropped by last week while we were doing morning prep. Didn't let him in, and he didn't take it great. Lost his mind, threatened Amber, you know how it goes." They sniff. "I mean, Amber didn't know she was being threatened, the autism will do that, but Michael went ballistic."

The first thing that comes to mind: wait, Amber's autistic? I didn't think people were allowed to—I dunno, volunteer information like that. It makes sense, I think. I guess? Maybe I was young enough when we met that I never noticed anything different about her.

And second: Davies knows about this place, and he don't like it. Of course he don't.

"What was he pissed about?" I ask.

"God knows. Everything? But can't imagine he's thrilled we posted all this." They pluck a piece of paper off the corkboard. "We're hosting an unofficial town hall since the county commission wouldn't let us have one at the courthouse. But first we have a voter registration thing coming up and a Fuck the Fourth party pretty soon."

Christ. This is dangerous, this is so damn dangerous, they have to know that.

"I," I manage, "should go. My therapy group's probably wondering where I am."

Dallas snorts. "We have therapy around here?"

"I mean, I don't like it, but."

"So skip," Dallas says. I balk. "The hell are they gonna do if you don't show back up, cut off one of your fingers or something?"

I rub my left pinkie, where the fingernail has, in fact, gone missing. The less trouble I stir up, the safer we'll be when Paul disappears too. "Maybe I'll skip next time."

"Hold you to that. Wait—can I get your number?"

I hesitate, but they offer their phone, and I put in both my number and Cooper's. We're friends catching up, that's it, that's all. "Figure Cooper might miss you too," I say. "He's usually at the Sunoco outside of McLachlan."

Dallas beams. "Hell yeah. Thanks, man."

And as I open the door to leave, they add, "Hey." I pause, glance back to them. "I'm sorry it's getting messy

again. If it means anything, being a guy looks really good
on you."

I know that. I also know that being friends with an open
leftist, as long as Sheriff Davies has a stranglehold on Twist
Creek County, does not look good at all.

✦

Dallas
Fuck, dude
Good for you!!!!
Figuring it out and everything 🫡
Did coming out go okay? You good?

It's late, and I'm tired. I almost don't respond.
But . . .

Miles
it went? idk, don't mean to be a bummer
cooper's fine with it, dad's getting over it, it's a whole thing
with mom. nobody else knows lol
don't really have anyone to talk about it with?
b/c cooper's cis and everything

Dallas
I shall be a receptacle for gender feelings 👀
The shaved head is an aesthetic tho

I hadn't realized how badly I needed to talk to another trans person until today.

We spend all night catching up. Dallas dropped out of school for a bunch of reasons—the inevitable collapse of grades thanks to an ungodly time in the hospital, the ADHD barely managed with energy drinks and nicotine. Being nonbinary *and* disfigured *and* fat *and* disabled in West Virginia public schools? Forget it. Might as well get a GED on their own time. They're thinking about going to court to get officially emancipated from their parents, but they're about to turn eighteen soon, so it might not be worth the trouble. The burns don't hurt no more, mainly itch these days, but they're paranoid about contractures.

Dallas

You know they have to surgically release that shit?? They stitch corpse skin to you (!!!!) so the joint can bend again and it's the WORST 😭😭

If I'm gonna be 100% honest though, more than anything I just want people to stop being weird about it. Someone saying "what the fuck happened to you bud" is def preferable to pretending I'm not there

Miles

can i say smth weird

hope this is okay but they kinda suit you

Dallas

😭😭😭

Miles

sorry lmao

you get what i mean, right? like, you survived, you made it,
there's proof

Dallas

I'm messing with you!!! Lmao no I get it

They've grown on me actually. Like I'm not ME without them???

And maybe I'm a freak but did you know how many people are
into the Freddy Krueger look

Miles

FREDDY KRUEGER

BITCH

i was gonna say prince zuko

I update Dallas on everything I can think of. How Dad's
doing these days. How the O'Briens have been holding on the
best they can, in their own way. (Dallas texted Cooper but
didn't get a response; I said he's probably tired.) Pictures of
Lady and the books I've been reading. How I've been healing
after the attack—flushing the OxyContin and the resulting
withdrawal—and how much I really don't think therapy is
going to help, not when I'm the kind of person I am.

Miles

i only really ever felt comfortable around you and
cooper is the thing

and then you moved and cooper kind of collapsed

i never made any friends after that and idk i'm kind of okay with that? i don't like people lmao but i can't even explain why i don't. because i know it don't seem like i struggle but I DO

and sometimes i even forget it's hard

being exhausted is my baseline

Dallas

I swear I'm not making this about me but it was like that with the ADHD for me too. Nobody believed I was having a hard time b/c I was covering it up so well??? I had to have a full-on breakdown and start screaming before anyone gave a shit :0

Miles

SEE! YOU GET IT

It's three in the morning by the time I realize I need to go to bed. The screen hurts my eyes and Lady is asleep on my feet, gently snoring. I scroll back through the messages. Linger on them. Resist the urge to screenshot, just to have them.

I take their name out of my contacts.

Miles

i missed you

i'm glad you're back

304-555-6392

I missed you too :')

Conversation deleted.

CHAPTER
TWENTY-SiX

I meet Cooper at the Sunoco station that Tuesday. It's at the top of a hill a few minutes outside of town; he's here most of the time, unless he has to go to the one in Pearson to cover a shift. I prefer this one because it shares its parking lot with a dinky trailer serving the best ice cream for fifty miles.

But—

"Really?" I say, leaning against the counter. It's scattered with pen cups, change trays, and notes taped down to the wood: NO $100 BILLS and SMILE, YOU'RE ON CAMERA, plus those birthdate reminders for cigarettes. Lady sniffs the bags of candy by the checkout and decides that Skittles ain't for her. "We're talking about this here?"

Hell of a place to plan a murder if you ask me.

Behind the counter, Cooper shrugs. "Sent Jay home, and the cameras ain't got audio. We'll be fine." I roll my eyes at him but he pops open the register to grab a twenty dollar bill. "Ice cream?"

Hard to say no to that. I need something to settle my stomach.

Cooper puts a BE BACK IN FIVE MINUTES sign on the door and walks out with Lady and me to Mack's Ice Cream Shack. Working here is a rite of passage for hot girls at Twist Creek High—the uniform might as well be jean shorts and French braids, with a boyfriend or two usually hanging out at the picnic tables to make sure nobody tries nothing. It's nicer here when it's night and the string lights get lit up. Otherwise, you can see all the ugly generators and iceboxes, and it loses a bit of its charm.

We don't talk about the kiss. I'm not sure there's anything to say.

"Your usual?" Cooper says. "Or have you changed your order sometime in the past five years?"

Of course I ain't changed it. "The usual."

So Cooper gets a brownie sundae and I get a small vanilla cup with M&M's. The girl working the register, Andie Booth, is in my grade. She don't look in my direction. That's fine. At least it ain't because of how fucked up I am, because I'm halfway decent these days. No more headache, only vague rib pain, and the bruises have finally turned faint. Some of the scabs—not all of them, but enough—are gone. No more nose splints, no more finger splints.

All that's left is what's permanent. The chipped tooth, the metal in my rib, my cockeyed orbital sockets. The crooked asymmetry of my nose. And the scars. There's a lot of scars.

"Oh," Cooper says, "and whipped cream for the dog."

So Lady gets something too. I grab the whipped cream cup and immediately reach down so she can lick it clean.

The sun's too bright for me to be out without squinting my face up, so once we get our ice cream, we head back into the gas station. Cooper takes down the sign and sits on a wobbly crate he's hidden under the register. I hop up on the counter. Lady's nose gets the better of her as she wanders off towards the coolers in the back of the store, towards the beer case.

"Hey now," I warn her, and she makes a quiet noise and keeps walking.

Cooper's head maybe comes up to my knee, which is bouncing as I eat. He grabs my ankle to make me stop.

"Nervous?" he says.

"Ain't you?"

He shrugs, way too nonchalant for the situation. "Too tired to be nervous. Mainly just *ready*."

That's one way to put it. "You been thinking about it this long?"

"Every day." He stabs his spoon into his brownie and cuts it up with a bizarre, simmering aggression. "When Davies showed up at Mom's funeral, I almost lost it. But I didn't want him to mess with Dad any worse, so I just sat there." He jams a bite into his mouth. "Need to prove we ain't kids. We ain't our parents, neither. If they won't do shit, we will."

I bristle. "They were doing shit."

"Like what, running for office?" Cooper snorts. "Even if they won, what would that change? Nothing."

I don't completely agree with him. If having a sympathetic figure in a local office wasn't a danger to Davies's power, why would he be so against it? *The whole reason your mom died was because they were* doing shit, *O'Brien.* But that's cruel. "That's how I feel about those photos, if I'm gonna be honest."

Cooper reaches into his pocket and pulls out the folded sheet. Of course he has it with him.

"They're not useless," Cooper says. "They're a reminder."

"I guess." Lady stalks back to the counter like she's checking I'm okay before settling herself by the front door to alert us to any approaching customers. "Anyway, what the hell are we doing."

Cooper hums. "The Millers are heading up to Ohio the Saturday before the Fourth for a family reunion, and Paul ain't going with them. Fight with his parents, I think. Noah and Davies will be setting up and he'll be alone. If it's good enough for you, it's good enough for me."

I can't believe it's almost July already. And this is honestly perfect timing—the Davieses are always preoccupied with the Twist Creek County Fourth of July Festival, so it's the one time my parents' paranoia relaxes. Our family gets a respite for a few days.

Still. "Eddie was an accident," I say uselessly.

Cooper says, "We can't rely on an accident again."

"I know."

"The premeditation, it—"

"Changes things," I finish for him. "Yeah."

"So." Cooper gestures at me with his spoon. "I was thinking about that. Fire would be thematically appropriate but hard to pull off."

"No metaphors," I say. "And nothing fancy."

He laughs. "Right. Exactly. Figured it'd be easy to just shoot him, but Dad ain't got any guns, and I can't buy one for another few months yet."

It takes me a second to decide whether or not to say anything. Then I mumble, "My dad has one."

Cooper glances up at me. His eyes gleam. "He does?"

"It's a home defense handgun." Like I'm already trying to walk it back. "It ain't much."

"Can you get it?"

Too late now. I nod. "I know the code to the safe."

"Good," he says. "That'll make it easy. And fast. Before he even knows we're there."

I'm about to respond when my phone chirps. Ugh. I dig it out of my pocket, both grateful for the distraction and worried that it's Mom or Dad asking why I ain't answering the house phone. I didn't say I was headed out.

"Everything okay?" Cooper asks.

But it's not Mom or Dad. It's Dallas. Even after I deleted their contact info and all of last night's messages, I still recognize the number. The text is accompanied by a photo of a hand holding two cheap paper tickets in front of the Red Holler register.

304-555-6392

Btw if you and Cooper want to come to Fuck the Fourth, I've set aside two tickets for you 😊 Got a cool gig lined up, gonna be loud!!

"It's, uh," I say, "Dallas."

I should not be going *anywhere* near something called Fuck the Fourth.

Miles

oh shit

shows aren't really my thing but thank you

it sounds really cool

"Dallas?" Cooper says. "Dallas Foster? He texted me yesterday. How'd he get our numbers?"

"They," I say.

"They?"

"They're—" I gesture vaguely. "They're nonbinary. They/them."

"Right, whatever, how did *they* get our numbers?"

I shrug, even though I'm suddenly convinced I've messed up in some undefined way. "I gave it to them? We ran into each other yesterday, at that restaurant Amber and Michael opened up. By the church in Pearson? They're doing good. Really good, actually. Considering everything that happened."

The muscles in Cooper's throat stand out. I don't like that.

"I told them you were tired," I continue to fill the silence. "That's probably why you didn't respond. But I thought you might—I don't know. Thought you might want to hear from them."

Even if it's dangerous. Because I missed them. I thought Cooper missed them too.

304-555-6392

I figured!!! You never really liked doing things lol

Just thought I'd check 🏴

I close out of the texts and put my phone back in my pocket so I don't have to see the messages.

I definitely did something wrong.

"Did," I say carefully, "did you and Dallas not get along?" I'm racking my brain trying to find evidence for the claim but come up with nothing. Sure, Dallas could be loud, and sometimes they said stuff that was a little out of line, but any disagreements were us being kids. Nothing that ever really stuck deep. "Did something happen?"

For half a second, Cooper looks at me like I've insulted his dead mother. Then he takes one more bite of his ice cream, sets it aside, and stands. Leans against the counter, right next to my knees.

His face is so close to mine.

"The more people you bring in," Cooper whispers, "the worse this is going to get."

I recoil. "The fuck are you talking about? You think I told them?"

"You ain't got to say nothing." He pushes forward. I bare my teeth on instinct, like a dog. "All you got to do is stand beside him and you're giving Davies another reason to kill you."

I snap, "*Them*."

Cooper coughs in furious exasperation and Lady is suddenly standing, breathing hard. Her ears are back.

"Them," Cooper repeats coldly. "Fine."

"Do you want the gun or not?" My voice has become the same kind of thing it was when I spoke to Eddie, rough and not quite mine. "Because if I back out, you're on your own and you know it."

That—a threat—seems to get to him. The anger on his face tightens, suddenly sharper, before it collapses. It's weird, manually tracking his emotions across the muscles and skin, naming them one by one instead of unconsciously translating them the way everyone else seems to. So I can tell Cooper O'Brien is tired. He's a seventeen-year-old a few weeks out of high school, managing a gas station all by himself because there's nothing else he can do, and he's scared and cornered and ain't slept well since he was twelve, because his daddy is sick and hurting and, Christ, they're all sick and hurting, ain't we all?

His forehead falls against my shoulder.

I don't breathe. I don't want to startle him. His head lolls slowly to the side, hair pressing against my neck, and I can see his dark eyes staring off past me.

"Just be careful," he says.

His mouth is so close to my skin, and I think about the kiss. Both of us kneeling on the floor of his bathroom. My shaved head. The overflowing trash can and old towels and soap-stained shower curtain. And I think about the adrenaline high, the ache of my injuries, Eddie's blood on my shirt and his corpse wrapped up in the blue tarp and his broken nose a hell of a lot like mine.

Violence for violence, right? Be a man, be an Abernathy, right?

I reach up and tuck a stray piece of hair behind Cooper's ear because I remember seeing Mrs. O'Brien doing that once. "I will."

His breath hiccups a bit in his chest. "Okay."

There's a silence now. Him breathing. The distant hum of the drink coolers and HVAC. My heartbeat.

"If you don't want me to kiss you again," he says, "tell me."

And I have no idea. I don't know if I want him to. I don't know what it would mean if I did want him to, or what it would mean if I didn't. The word *boyfriend* flits through my head and it makes me—I don't *know*, I can't tell, I can never tell—uncomfortable? Unsteady? What?

I think, if I had time to give some sort of response, I'd tell him sure, yeah, he can do what he wants, I think I'd like it. Just don't give it a name. Please don't.

I'm saved from answering by the bell ringing above the door. Cooper jerks away from me, nearly stepping in the bowl of ice cream he left on the ground. His eyes are glassy, like he's trying not to cry, like he wanted to kiss me to distract himself from whatever the hell's going on his head.

For some reason, that's easier to stomach than the idea that he might *like* me.

Lady starts to growl, and Noah Davies says, "Hey now. No need for that."

Goddamnit.

"Noah," Cooper acknowledges. "Paul."

It's weird to see Noah and Paul without Eddie. It's always been the three of them skulking around Twist Creek County, and they're incomplete without that rat-faced creep peering at roadkill and too-young girls. He was always itching for a car crash or hunting accident he could upload to LiveLeak. I don't know if he ever *actually* jacked off to any of that stuff, but I don't know why else he'd be so obsessed with it. If it were a fetish, at least then I'd be able to wrap my head around it. Otherwise, what else is there?

Without Eddie, though, the set of them is amputated, and they're pissed they've lost a limb. Paul wanders towards the drink case, pulls out a Sprite, cracks it open. And Noah is looking at us, smiling like he's gone into rigor mortis.

Lady shows her teeth. The fur on her back stands up. Stupid dog. I slide off the counter, push Cooper out of my way, and grab her by the collar. She can hold her own against a bear, I know she can, but Noah and Paul are more dangerous than bears. Bears are just trying to protect their babies. Noah and Paul—

Well. We've all seen the video.

"Careful now," Noah says. He's taller than me. Not as tall as Cooper but close. And he's so much like his daddy, that kind of too-handsome that wraps right back around to not being handsome at all. "Don't want nothing to happen to that mutt of yours."

This motherfucker. I sense the start of a bark in Lady's throat, and I tighten my grip on her collar, pull a little bit, *Don't you dare*. I've thought about Noah hurting her every damn day since that video started making its rounds.

"What do you want?" Cooper says.

Noah's attention on Lady dissolves as he snaps his fingers. "Right. The usual."

Cooper reaches into the case by the register and pulls out a can of Skoal. It's got that big *WARNING: This Product Can Cause Mouth Cancer* warning right at the bottom. "Six bucks."

"No, it ain't."

Cooper grits his teeth but slides the can across the counter. Noah takes it with a nod, immediately peeling off the plastic. "Appreciate the cooperation. Miller, you want some?"

Somewhere across the store, Paul snorts dismissively.

"Fag." Noah tosses the plastic on the floor, packs the can with a few quick snaps, and settles a wad of chewing tobacco between his lip and gum. "Just wanted to say, Coop, it's real admirable what you're doing for Miss Abernathy here. Taking care of her after such an awful thing."

Cooper snorts. "It's the right thing to do, after everything. Ain't that right, Sadie?"

"Yeah," I say, because it's expected that I reply, and if I say anything else, I think I might scream.

Paul wanders back out from the drink coolers, nursing the Sprite, more haggard than he'd been that night at the party. He's hanging back, eyes averted. He reminds me of the pictures Eddie used to drop in unsuspecting group chats or hide in the shared files on the school computer—torture victims subjected to sleep deprivation, zombified by exhaustion.

You're dead, Paul.

As if he hears me, Paul's eyes slide sluggishly towards mine. His cracked lips are parted. He could be a cis version of me if I squint. Close-cropped hair, worn clothes, never quite comfortable.

He was the one that held the dog down. Did he hold me down too? Was Noah gonna cut me open before Cooper found me?

"You two a thing now?" Noah says.

My heart skips a beat. "None of your business."

Noah shrugs. "Just asking. It'd be cute if you were, you know. But be careful." He grabs a pack of condoms from the display at the end of the nearest aisle and chucks it Cooper's way. Cooper catches it before it hits his face. "We ain't had a shotgun wedding this year. Think we're a bit overdue."

"*I* think you should leave," Cooper says.

But for some reason, I say, "Y'all heard anything about Eddie yet?"

Noah's attention lands sharp on me. Lady presses closer to my side. Paul has the lip of the bottle between his teeth, about to chip a piece of enamel on the hard plastic.

"Not a peep," Noah says slowly. "Damn shame." His mouth works the chewing tobacco for a moment. "Why? You know something?"

Even I catch the implication: *Was it you?* We agreed I don't remember a thing. Don't matter if it's true, as long as that's the version of the truth we decided on, Davies and me. But the way Noah's watching me, he's trying to figure it out. Did I break my promise? Did I remember? Did I retaliate?

"No," I say. "Just wanted to ask."

Noah reaches behind him for Paul's Sprite. "Can I get some of that?" Paul hands it over, and Noah spits into the bottle. The dark snuff-saliva infects the soda immediately, spreading like blood in water as Noah gives the bottle back. Paul stares at it dully. "It's scary, ain't it? First you, then him? Got some kind of monster on the loose."

"Seems like it," I say.

I thought it'd be gratifying for a Davies to call me a monster, even in a roundabout way. But it's not. Monsters don't get to be innocent. Monsters don't get to beg for mercy. They don't deserve it.

◆

My question is, though—was it like this before?

Back when my parents were young, or Papaw and Bobby, or Lucille. Was this what it was like? The Davieses and us circling each other like rabid animals, existing in the same room with bared teeth. The existence of tenuous quiet between bouts of violence.

For some reason, my first instinct is to claim that it was wilder back then. Louder, bloodier, bearing down on us like a war zone, only letting up around the time of cell phones, of instant photographs and 911. But it wasn't. Even the Hatfields and McCoys took—what, thirteen years?— to go from their first murder to the next.

Life has always been days and months and years of dread interspersed with seconds of sheer terror.

Honestly, I can't think of any other way for us to exist.

✦

By the time Noah and Paul have left and we've collected ourselves enough to move, our ice cream's melted. Cooper grabs both the Styrofoam bowls and takes them over to the trash. I've been chewing on the shoelace, and now there's a fiber stuck between my teeth and a wet spot against my wrist.

CHAPTER
TWENTY-SEVEN

I won't take the gun until the night of. We have a few days—give or take.

Eddie's parents don't seem to care much that he's gone. Neither does anyone else. I bump into his stepsister on Main Street while taking Lady for a walk, and she stops to pet her, and it's the first time I've seen this girl smile. She's also one of the first people who, when she sees my face, does not flinch.

◆

Cooper comes over when Mom and Dad are at work. To keep an eye on me, he claims. I don't quite believe him but that's fine. It's nice to do anything besides think about the past few weeks. He brings boxed-up food from Big Kelly's and we eat on the back porch while Lady begs for fries. "Don't," I warn Cooper around a mouthful of chicken tenders. "She's already spoiled."

After a bit, Cooper says, "You didn't answer me yesterday."

I swallow my food. "Huh?"

"About the—"

But what else would he be talking about? "*Oh.*" Right. *If you don't want me to kiss you, tell me.* I finish my lunch and stand up to throw the take-out box in the burn barrel by the back stairs. "Man, I don't know. I've never done this before." I watch the trees instead of him. "Are you queer?"

"What?" Cooper says.

It strikes me that he's probably never heard the word used as an identifier instead of a slur. When I spoke, he probably heard *Are you a queer,* which tastes entirely different in the mouth. I move my hands aimlessly. I left my shoelace on the kitchen table, and without it, my fingers never have any idea what to do.

"Are you—" I don't know another word for it. "Bi or something?" He's still staring at me like I'm the weird one for asking. "You ain't said so, which is—which is whatever, I guess it's not my business. But if you're asking questions like that, I just want to make sure you actually like guys." My face is warm. "Because, you know."

Lady watches us curiously.

"I'm not a tomboy to you," I say, "am I?"

Cooper says, "No? Of course not."

I don't got a response to that. We both go quiet.

◆

I keep talking to Saint. Sometimes he's there, sometimes he's not, but it don't matter. It's a coping mechanism, I think, which tracks for me; a combination of *painfully self-aware of my issues* and *unable to do anything about it*.

"I think you'd get a kick out of this book," I say to the open window, thumbing through the pages. The railroad spike sits on the windowsill like a talisman. "It looks boring, but it's actually really good—about the profit system that's cropped up around evictions, the need for universal housing vouchers, that sort of thing. I mean, housing should *definitely* be free, but vouchers would work in the meantime, while we figure that out." I turn the page. "One of these days I'll get my parents on board. Mom's gonna be the tough one."

Do I think he's real?

Does it matter?

CHAPTER
TWENTY-EiGHT

I go to the garage with Dad the next day. Everyone I know has to work, and I ain't thrilled about the concept of being alone after Noah showed up at the Sunoco. I keep thinking about the video, the dog screaming, the blood in the grass.

Maybe I'm more worried about Lady than me. That's why she comes with.

Dad walks—limps—the gravel road to Main Street and then half a mile down the road between McLachlan and Pearson, where Uncle Rodney's auto garage sits in the midst of a few trees. He's got a pile of tires languishing behind a chain-link fence, some ripped-up cars around back. There are a few packages on the front step too, and Uncle Rodney is there sifting through them all, checking them against a list on his phone. We didn't always order parts online. Used to be that we'd go to the salvage yard a county over, where you can rip pieces out of scrap cars and pay by the part. It was cheaper that way, and more fun, but Uncle Rodney can't be bothered, and Dad tries not to walk too much, so.

I guess we should be grateful anyone comes here. Uncle Rodney don't own the shop, just runs it, but the Abernathy name is still bad for business if we ain't careful.

"The hell you bring that dog for?" Uncle Rodney barks when he sees us.

Lady barks back.

"She ain't gonna cause too much trouble," Dad replies. Uncle Rodney grunts and pushes his way into the office, arms laden with cardboard boxes.

I pick up a package he left behind. Taillight replacement.

Uncle Rodney is a large, bearded guy who only wears Big Dogs shirts and old ripstop pants, ratty baseball caps and shoes held together with duct tape. He rolls his eyes when Lady trots in but gives her a scratch behind the ears anyway. He's haloed by a $25.00 BITCHING FEE sign.

"How are you and Cooper getting on?" Dad asks, grabbing a clipboard so he can see what's going on today. "Everything okay?"

"Yeah. We're good." Nothing else to say about it.

We head out to the garage, where there's an old truck that's beat to hell. He runs me through the issues: hood won't open, sideview mirror barely hanging on, AC needs replacing, belt's about worn out. Big ol' "failed inspection" sticker on the windshield. Poor bastard. Most people around here have a mechanic they're friendly with that'll sign off on the inspection without checking a thing.

Dad hands me a filter and an oil drain bin. "And this. All you."

"Child labor," I say, even though I'm grateful for the chance to do some work with my hands.

Dad says, "You little shit."

But I'm good at this, and small enough to get under the truck without putting it up on jacks, so I grab some tools and scoot down to reach the oil filter. Lady paces through the garage before sitting her ass down in front of the fan in the office.

"Gotta admit," Dad says above me, "it's not as cool to say I taught my *son* how to work on a car." He's moving around the garage, grabbing supplies, while I try a few different socket sizes to get the plug off the oil pan. At least he ain't talking loud enough for Uncle Rodney to hear. "Used to say, oh, I'm making sure my daughter can do everything herself, and be all progressive." He taps my shoe with his foot to show he's kidding. "Good going."

The socket fits snug, and I throw all my strength against it to get it to budge. "Not sure we're at the *making jokes about it* stage."

"Damn," Dad says. "We'll get there."

The bolt gives just enough for me to pull it free and a cascade of black oil erupts into the bin. Then it's just putting the bolt back in, yanking off the old filter, and popping the new one on. Between the garage and the auto shop classes at school, I've probably got decent footing for a career. It's not even a gender thing; it's getting my hands dirty, and working with my family, and doing something I'm *good* at. I think I'd like it. But Dad's already one mechanic that ain't licensed to do inspections, and Uncle Rodney certainly don't need a second, and who the hell else would hire me? So. You know.

Someone comes through for an inspection, and Uncle Rodney decides he's actually going to put them through the wringer. As he starts down the inspection checklist, I pull myself out from under the truck and wipe the oil off my hands. Dad leans into the cab to replace the cable that opens the hood.

"Oh, Dad," I say, propping myself up on the fender. "I ran into Dallas a few days ago."

Dad don't look away from his work. "Really? How's he doing?"

I fumble over whether to correct Dad's use of *he*, torn between Dallas's brazen queerness and how Cooper reacted to my correction at the gas station. I decide not to make a fuss. "They're good. Have you been to the restaurant? It's cool."

Dad shakes his head, then fumbles like he's trying to come up with an excuse. My parents can't hide nothing from me—we're practically the same people. "Ain't had time," he decides on. "Can't make it down with your mom at work so much."

The real reason is obvious: he's afraid to see them again. I get it. Maybe he's afraid of the same things I was. That the Fosters blame him for everything, or that Davies will get worse if he catches us together.

"It's . . ." I try to find a word to describe the place that ain't *anarchist* or *socialist*, because we all know how most grown-ups react to those words. "Community-focused. They're doing, like, voter registration workshops and stuff."

Uncle Rodney drops the hood of the car he's working on. *Bang.* I flinch. "They're fucking themselves over."

Dad winces, less at the bang and more at Uncle Rodney himself. "C'mon, man."

"Practically begging for Davies to bring his foot down, if you ask me." Uncle Rodney grabs the inspection clipboard to make a few checks. "What'd they even come back here for? Sure they were doing fine wherever they were. When one of them gets hurt again, I ain't gonna feel bad— it's on them."

Dad and I glance at each other through the driver's side window.

Uncle Rodney was a toddler when Bobby Abernathy was killed. Sheriff Davies's daddy left Bobby slumped over the steering wheel of his truck, two jugs of moonshine still under a tarp in the back seat. Papaw got drunk and told me about it when I was in middle school, talking over a late-night rerun of *Top Gun*—how he found Bobby's body, how he had to bury his brother his damn self because Lucille was in prison and no funeral home would take an Abernathy. I wonder, if I'd died that night at the party, or if Dad had never made it out of the burning car, if the same thing would've happened to us.

"*Bobby was soft,*" Papaw had said. He don't talk much unless he's drinking, and I was twelve years old and trying so hard to listen. "*He must've been so scared.*"

He didn't talk about how he'd gone and killed a Davies in retaliation and the bloody, terrible silence that followed. He didn't have to. I think I already knew.

"The Fosters do good work," Dad counters. "I'm glad they're back. Amber especially—that girl's smart as a whip. She knows what she's doing."

Uncle Rodney grimaces. "She can be as smart as she wants, but if she ain't got common sense, it's a waste." He shakes his head. "Thought it'd be enough that she got her husband's brother burnt up like that. God knows what she thinks she's doing now."

It's just like so much of my life; adults talking grown-up business while I stand to the side, wanting to speak up but not wanting to get in the way.

One day I'll be in their place.

Then I think about Paul, and the code to the gun safe, and I wonder if I already am and they don't know it yet.

✦

Dad and I eat lunch outside in the grass, under the shade of an old tree—tuna salad and crackers for him, a bologna sandwich with chips for me. We pass a thermos of Kool-Aid back and forth. I give in to Lady's begging and toss her the sandwich crusts I peel off as I go.

We're comfortable in silence. We always have been. So of course I have to break it.

"Hey, Dad?"

"Yeah, bud?" He ain't looking up from his phone. I wonder what he's reading. Probably some news article, bypassing digital paywalls on the *New York Times*. Or researching how to put solar panels on the house. Mom would freak about the upfront cost, but it'd help with the electricity bills if we could get the landlord to agree.

I bite a chip in half to stall. "I, uh. The night that I . . ." That gets his attention.

"Got hurt," I finish. "You fell asleep at your computer. I saw what you were working on. The emails, the maps, that stuff. Figured Mom would be upset if she saw, it so I, you know, hid it. Covered it up. Whatever." I pick at another piece of crust before tossing it Lady's way. "Were you actually going to try? Running for office again?"

Dad reaches out for the Kool-Aid. I hand over the thermos, but he just fidgets with the handle.

"I was thinking about it," he says. "You know, I love this country. I've always had a lot of faith in it, even when it does the wrong thing. And there's been a lot of wrong, ain't there? Internment camps, Vietnam, Iraq; we could sit here all day. But despite everything, I still believe, here"—he points at his chest—"that it's the best country in the world."

I don't believe that at all, but I let him keep talking.

"It's got the building blocks," he says, "the *potential*. It could live up to its promises and make up for its mistakes, if it really tried. And for a minute, I really thought we were headed there.

"So last year's election rattled me. I thought, look at this cruel, greedy liar running for president—ain't no way he'll win. As a people, as a country, I figured we were better than that. We weren't gonna fall for some egotistical asshole making fun of disabled journalists and treating women like shit, right?" He shrugs. "But here we are. And that night, I remembered how I felt all those years ago, before we all got hurt. Like everything was so *wrong* and I had to *try*. Because, hell." He offers a tight smile that makes him look a lot older than he is. Same as Saint, with the coal dust permanently etched into the lines of his face. "That's not the world I wanted you to grow up in. I wanted to do better for you."

The smile falls.

He says, "It's just—"

"We could try again," I say. "Next election cycle. You have a few years, but you've got your work cut out for you. Might as well start now."

Dad shakes his head before I can get any further. "I ain't letting you get hurt again."

What? "I told you, this wasn't Davies."

"I don't care. I'm not risking it." His voice is final. "If we step out of line, they *hurt you*, Miles. Do you know how thin this line we gotta walk is? Between defending ourselves and not making things harder than they already are? No way in hell I'm putting you in more danger. Not now."

What? No. Is he backing down for good? Because of what happened to me? He can't do that. I fumble for something to say, my hands tapping together nervously. "You really should email Amber." It sounds pathetic, and I know it. Dad sighs. "I saw her name in your drafts. I know you were thinking about it. Or I can ask Dallas for her number."

"*Miles*," Dad says.

I fall silent and shove my fingers into the grass so they stop moving.

He says, softer this time, "It ain't worth it. Amber's smart as hell, and she's doing good, and sure, maybe I'll go say hi. But I care about you too much to get mixed up in that again."

I grit my teeth and look past him, towards the tree line. Saint is there—head tilted, listening to his great-grandson give up.

If Dad won't do anything, I know someone who will.

And maybe those photos will finally be good for something.

CHAPTER
TWENTY-NiNE

Cooper

I know I didn't say the right thing yesterday

This whole thing is sensitive and I'm new to this. I'm trying to figure it out too

Can I make it up to you?

I glare at my phone, halfway through the bowl of cereal I'm eating for dinner. *Didn't say the right thing?* He didn't say shit.

Sure, I ain't been able to stop thinking about the kiss either. Trying to figure out what it means, what I want it to mean, all that. But when I first get the text, I'm pissed about it, because why the hell is he so fixated on it? We got bigger things to deal with.

But if it's a distraction—something to forget what we've done, what we're about to do—I can work with that. Probably.

Miles

i'll think about it

give me a bit

Besides, I'm busy tonight. I'm gonna brave the Red Holler and talk to Amber Foster for the first time in five years.

✦

When Mom drops me off at the Pearson Methodist church, I wait for her to drive off, nervously fiddling with the spare set of photocopies in my pocket before I step right into the Red Holler instead. They've done some work since the last time I was here. The string lights are shining and the stage is in better shape. Dallas lounges behind the counter, scrolling on their phone to eavesdrop on Michael talking with some rough contractors. I think it's about our new governor. Still can't believe West Virginia decided to hand the office to some billionaire coal operator. Didn't we make a state identity out of hating those bastards once?

"I'm just saying," Michael says, "he's fucking over his miners. You seen them safety reports? Every one of his worksites is a meat grinder."

"You're a Democrat," one of the contractors counters. My hackles raise instinctively, and by the looks of it, so do Dallas's—they pick their head up, stare across the counter. "You don't get to complain. He's one of yours."

Michael scoffs. "Don't call me a *liberal*." Then: "Oh, hey, kid!" He reaches over to elbow Dallas. "Your stray's here."

Dallas perks up, and I offer an awkward smile, maybe a wave. They're wearing different buttons this time. *Ronald Reagan Is Burning in Hell* and *Fags Do It Better*.

What is it like to be so out? I'm too chickenshit to tell my own grandparents I'm not a girl.

"And suddenly," Dallas says, "I'm on break." They pop out from behind the counter, cracking into an asymmetrical smile. Part of their face don't quite move the way it used to. "You bailed! Want a menu? Can't sneak you any drinks—ain't losing our liquor license—but anything else is fair game. On the house."

"I had dinner," I protest as Dallas steers me towards a booth, not saying all the other things that are on the tip of my tongue: I'm sorry I ain't texted them all that much, I've been scared for them every day since I learned they were here, I've forgotten how to be friends with people and I promise I've missed them even if I don't show it.

Completely ignorant to all that, Dallas gives me a sideways look. "Was your dinner some gross breaded chicken and canned green beans?"

I mumble, "No, it was cereal," even though that is, in fact, what I had for dinner every day when I was little. "Cheerios." Then I add, as if this makes it better, "The multigrain ones. The plain stuff is like eating cardboard."

"Oh my god, you poor thing." Dallas pushes me down in the booth and drags a chair over so they can sit straddling the backrest. I convince myself to leave the photocopies alone by untying the shoelace from around my wrist and wrapping it in a pattern around my knuckles. "Pick something or I'll pick for you."

I grab the menu from them with a huff, because they're right, it barely counts. It's not that I particularly like Cheerios, or whatever meal substitute I throw together. I don't have to like it, as long as it's something I can actually stomach. "If you insist. Is Amber in today?"

"She's out back taking a breather," Dallas says. "Too many people talked to her today, so now she's"—they gesture like they're scrambling up their head—"frazzled. Give her a minute."

That makes sense. I get the same way. "Minute's fine. Are the fried chicken biscuits too much?"

"We can split." They flag down another waiter and pass the order along before grabbing their phone. "Let me text her real quick, let her know you're here. Why, what's up?"

"It's been a while is all," I lie, even though I'm not sure why I ain't telling the truth. Would Dallas be upset if they see the pictures? Would it be a trigger or something? I get why Dad has kept them under lock and key for so long, but I would totally understand if a Foster felt betrayed by him sitting on evidence for so long. I swerve to another topic for good measure. "Sorry Cooper's being a dick, by the way. If he still hasn't responded to you."

Dallas shrugs. "What he does ain't on you. Hell you apologizing for?" Then: "Wait." They lean in. "Are you two—"

"No." I recoil. Whatever they're about to say—*boyfriends*, or *together*—absolutely not. "Jesus."

But . . .

"Maybe?" I say after another second. My knee-jerk reaction fades to something more bizarre. "It's complicated."

Dallas says, completely missing the point, "Holy shit, we all turned out queer."

"Maybe," I say again.

There's a bit of quiet. One of the contractors puts a Nickleback song on the jukebox, and Michael goes, "*Why do we even have that option?*" Someone else laughs.

"Maybe?" Dallas repeats, cottoning on.

I shrug. The waiter brings out two glasses of water, and I grab mine to postpone responding. Dallas seems more than happy to wait me out, though. The bastard.

Don't take long for me to break. Apparently, I've been waiting for an excuse to spill.

"So I told him I was trans after I got out of the hospital," I say, "and he's been cool about it. Better than cool, right? For a bit he was the only person who actually used my real name."

"Oh," Dallas says, "that's nice of him."

"But then he kissed me, which, sure, okay, I—I think I had a crush on him, so I wasn't exactly complaining about it, but also maybe I didn't? And it's weird, because as far as I know, he's straight. Maybe he ain't and he's trying to figure it out—I get that's a lot to work through—but the least he can do is say that him liking me makes him queer, right?" I pick at my straw. Dallas watches me unblinking. "Because, yeah, it's his business, and he ain't got to come out to nobody if he don't want to, but if he thinks he's straight, then the only logical conclusion is that he sees me as a girl. Does that makes sense?"

Another silence. I slump in my seat.

"Plus," I add slowly, "I don't think I've figured out the difference between liking someone and *liking* them yet. So there's that too."

I grab my water again and jam the straw into my mouth. I finish off with, "Sorry."

"That everything?" Dallas says.

"I think so."

"You're very . . ." Dallas props their chin up with their hand. "I mean, you've always been this way, but you're real honest."

"I ain't honest," I retort; not honest enough for it to be something to point out, at least. Pretty sure I'm the normal amount of honest. "Everyone else lies all the time."

Everyone except for Mom and Dad, I should say. I'm *fine* at home. It's everybody else that's the problem. Never saying what they mean, never being upfront about a damn thing. Sure, I can play the game, but it's a *game* and I'd really rather not.

Like Davies. *It'd be a miracle if you remember who did it.*

For some reason, me pointing out the obvious makes Dallas laugh. "I didn't say it was bad. Like, you're—I don't know. You say what you mean. No dancing around it or whatever."

"The auto shop teacher called me *no-nonsense*."

"That too." Dallas sucks on their teeth for a second. "I dunno, I'm no therapist, but it sounds like you're both figuring shit out."

"I've figured my shit out."

"Uh-huh," Dallas says. "You're sixteen."

I chew angrily on the straw. "Fuck you," is the response I decide on. "You're seventeen."

Dallas flashes a grin. "Almost eighteen." I flick the straw wrapper at them.

That's when a woman bustles up to the table with a plate of fried chicken sliders, nudging Dallas out of the way so she can set it on the table between us. Her curly hair is pinned back, and beaded chains dangle from her glasses, every inch covered in chunky jewelry and cat-themed paraphernalia. Her nails are painted rainbow, and she clatters when she moves.

"Amber?" I manage.

She does not smile, and her face is entirely unenthusiastic, but all the tension goes out of my shoulders when I see her.

I loved Amber Foster when I was little. I refused all but a handful of foods for *years*, so she memorized the list and made sure I'd have something at every cookout and potluck. She gave me silicone bracelets to play with when I got in trouble for chewing on my hair and told me it was perfectly fine to wear my socks inside out if I couldn't handle the seam against my toes. My parents tried their hardest to make sure I turned out "normal," but Amber made sure I was comfortable just how I was.

"Well, well, well," Amber says, "look who the cat dragged in." Her voice is completely flat. She explained once that she wears bright clothes to counteract her personality; when she and Michael first met, he thought she hated him.

Now that Dallas's brought up that she's autistic, okay, maybe I can see it.

She says, "I hear you're going by Miles these days?"

I nod. "Yes, ma'am."

"Don't call me ma'am. Makes me feel old." She slips into the booth across from me, ruffling Dallas's hair as she goes. They grin and lean into her touch. I take two sliders, put them onto my plate to cool, and try to catch the song that the jukebox moves to next—another Nickelback song, unfortunately. "Dallas says you wanted to catch up, which works out because I was about to ask after your daddy. Maybe you can pass something along for me."

I sit up immediately, but Dallas wrinkles their nose at her and says, "No pleasantries?"

Amber *tsk*s. "What pleasantries? Sorry you almost died, I'm sure you ain't too upset about the whole Ruckle thing, hope you're having a fun summer break." Dallas cackles. "I've been updated on everything, so figure there's no point in making you repeat it."

"Not my idea of a good time," I admit. I am *definitely* a fan of the way Amber does things. Though I'm not gonna lie, I ain't sure Dad will be up to talking, especially not after the conversation we had at the garage. If it's got anything to do with the Red Holler's politics, he'll bolt faster than a squirrel from a BB gun. "What do you want to ask him? I can give you his number if you want."

"I don't like phones," Amber says simply. Dallas shoots me an amused half smile, as if to say I walked right into that one. "I wanted to ask if he has anything on Davies he wants to, say, *share* with the county. If that's what we want to call it."

My stomach immediately erupts into butterflies.

The photos.

Of course she'd be the one who could help us. Of course it was always going to be Amber. The disabled anarchist that got a worker co-op off the ground, of *course*. If anybody knows what to do with the photos, it'll be her.

"Oh," I say, trying not to sound too excited about this. "What for?"

"Michael and I are working on a project," Amber explains to the empty space between Dallas's and my heads. "Figured we could use Fuck the Fourth as a platform to talk about everything Sheriff Davies has done. Reach out to people who've been too scared to speak up, provide a safe space, etcetera. So we're putting some material together to hand out at the festival. Let everyone know what we're doing." She has a spark in her eye even if her expression ain't changed. "We've got some ideas, but there's only so much we can do without an Abernathy on board. Couldn't hurt to ask."

It's a brilliant idea. What better way to make a statement than to mess with the Fourth of July? Kick up a fuss, really piss Davies off?

But in the second before I give Amber Foster the photocopies, I hesitate.

The last time I gave these pictures to someone, I almost died. Sheriff Davies swept into my hospital room and made me promise to lose them. Dad don't even know I got my hands on these. Handing them over would be dangerous, and shortsighted, and one hell of a bad idea. Not to mention this is the fire that Dallas *burned* in. There's a small bald patch above their left ear where the skin didn't grow back right. I know it's awful to think, but sometimes they remind me of a wax statue that's melted a little too much in the sun. They're still funny and kind and, you know what, sure, they're handsome if I think about it for more than a single second, but they were undeniably disabled and disfigured by the accident that I am holding in my hands. There's got to be so much pain tied up in something as simple as a photograph.

If I give Amber these photos, every single person in Twist Creek County will see them.

But it's the right thing to do. It'd be another nail in Sheriff Davies's coffin, exactly what we need to make his cruelty clear. Surrounded by whatever other evidence the Fosters got, we'd be at less of a risk specifically, right? And it'd knock Davies off-kilter. There's no way it'd keep him from finding Paul's body—we'd never be so lucky—but with this? We'll have more of a chance to cover our tracks, distance ourselves, clean up the mess while he's distracted.

That's what wins out. After all, you can't do the right thing around here without putting yourself in danger. I grab the photocopies from my pocket and pass them across the table, folded. Amber blinks; her equivalent of bowling over with surprise.

"Funny," I say. "Whole reason I came down was to give these to you."

Amber takes the photocopies slowly, opening them with a deep frown. My heart beats in my throat.

She closes the paper. "These are—"

"Yeah."

"What is it?" Dallas says. They lean over Amber's arm to try and get a peek, but Amber immediately turns it away from them, pulling it out of their reach as if she knows they're going to snatch it. "Hey!"

Amber says, "How come y'all never did anything with these before?"

I shrug. "I tried, and look where that got me."

I don't need to elaborate. The hospital, the scars and permanently broken facial features, the nail that's been ripped off my hand and the metal holding my rib cage together. Dallas must know too, because their face scrunches up in worry. They glance between us like maybe they've been caught in something they ain't quite sure of.

"Seriously," they say. "Amber, what is it? Is it bad?"

I answer instead. "It's photos from the accident."

Dallas says, "What the fuck?"

"It's just an idea," I say. "We ain't gotta use them if you don't want. None of them have *you* in it, either." Of course, I don't bring up that there were at least two photos in the lockbox that *did*, in fact, have Dallas visible in them. I know too much about what a charred body looks like while it's still alive, lit up by the flash of a cheap camera. "It's your call."

Dallas puts a thumbnail in their mouth before reaching for the photocopies. Amber hands them over and refuses to take her eyes off Dallas as they carefully peel the folded sides of the paper apart.

Their nostrils flare as they study the pictures.

"You okay?" Amber asks.

Dallas nods jerkily, then remembers to answer out loud. "Yeah. Yeah, I'm—" Their laugh comes out a little uneven. "It's weird, seeing it from this angle."

"Sorry," I say on instinct. "I shouldn't have—"

"It's fine." They fold up the page and give it to Amber as if trying to get it away from them. "It'll get people's attention, right? Kind of hard to ignore what a monster the sheriff is when you're looking at . . . you know."

The silhouette of Mrs. O'Brien's dead body against the flames. Yeah. Exactly.

"Be honest," Amber says to them. "If it's too much, we won't use them. Is it too much?"

Dallas closes their eyes, breathes slow.

"Jesus," they say. "No. Use them."

Amber pulls Dallas into a one-armed hug and kisses the bald spot on their temple, squeezing their cheek for a second before letting go. I'm bad at shows of affection, so I scoot closer to the edge of the booth so I can press the side of my arm to theirs.

This was either the best idea I've ever had, or I've signed a death warrant.

✦

When Mom comes to pick me up, I'm standing outside the Red Holler with Dallas. They come out with me to get a hit off their vape, calm their nerves. (They had to explain what a vape was, since I'd never seen one before.) They admit they started smoking at fourteen, the stress of school and the hospital and everything, and Michael's only condition for living with him was that they needed to at least try to quit. This is their third attempt to wean themself off Virginia Slims.

Mom seems vaguely confused as she stops beside us and rolls down the window. "Hi, Dallas. Good to see you."

They raise a hand. "Hi, Mrs. Abernathy."

I get in the car and Mom pulls back onto the road. She takes off her sunglasses since we're facing away from the setting sun now, glancing at Dallas in the rearview mirror.

"He really grew up," she says. "Wow. Swear he could be in his, what, twenties?" I get the sense that she's trying real hard not to say anything about the burns. "The beard puts some years on him."

"They."

Mom glances at me. "They?"

"They use they/them pronouns."

A muscle in Mom's jaw tightens, like she's physically chewing over the information. I keep an eye on her to gauge her reaction. This ain't the conversation I want to have after everything at the Red Holler, but ain't like I can say so.

"Oh," she says slowly. "They, uh, don't look like a *they*."

I can't figure out what a "they" is supposed to look like, but that would be rude to say, so I flounder for something else. I come up with nothing. Mom sighs hard.

"I don't know," she says. "I don't know these things. I'm trying."

"I know you are." Which is true. She is. I think.

"Those pronouns don't make sense to me is all. Because, you know, it's plural." The usual comeback to that is pointing out Chaucer's use of the singular *they* in the thirteenth century, but Mom's already moved on. "I feel like there should be a new word for that or something."

"I mean, neopronouns exist," I say carefully. Mom worries her bottom lip, staring intently out the windshield as we turn out of Pearson and onto the long, winding road back up to McLachlan. "Like, ze/hir, e/em, that sort of thing. But it's a rock-and-a-hard-place situation. Use they/them and get told it's grammatically incorrect, or use neopronouns and be told you're making it up for attention."

"I guess." She takes a second to collect herself. "Mamaw asked about you when I was dropping off her groceries today. Your new haircut and all."

She seems hesitant to call it a haircut. We both know it was a little more dramatic than that. "She hates it, huh?"

"She asked if you were a lesbian."

"What? I don't even like girls that way. I'm—"

I cut myself off, because I don't have a good answer. Ugh, I don't know, I don't *know* what I am. I've figured out I'm a boy but that's as far as I've gotten. Maybe Dallas was right.

I say, "Did you tell her I'm trans?"

Mom shakes her head. "I told her it's not my business, and if she wanted to know, she had to ask you." I jam the shoelace in my mouth, and for once I don't care if she's going to tell me it's gross and to spit it out. "The same goes for everyone else that's coming by on the Fourth. If you want them to know, you gotta tell them yourself."

That's not fair. "Okay," I whisper.

"Okay," Mom repeats. She takes a deep breath. "I've been reading some things. About, you know, trans people."

I don't want to get my hopes up again.

"I'm just scared for you," she says. I lean my head against the window and try to pretend she don't sound like a lost little girl. "It's bad enough right now, worrying about what happened to you. And then sitting here knowing that the world is going to be so much harder for you because of who you are, and having to change how I think about you, and how much different things will be—"

She sniffles.

"It's like someone else woke up in that hospital bed, and I'm not sure who it is," she says. "I want to skip the next five years so we can get to a place where this will all be over and I feel like I know you again."

She seems to know she said the wrong thing as soon as it comes out of her mouth. When I ask to spend the night at Cooper's, she agrees as if offering an olive branch. "Just text us back when we check on you," she says weakly, "and pick up the phone too."

Miles

hey

i'm outside if you want to make it up to me

whatever the hell that means

CHAPTER
THiRTY

Mr. O'Brien ain't home—it's late, eight-thirty or so, and he's out checking on the Sunocos because he's up and about for the first time in days—so it's only Cooper and me.

It's been a while since I was in Cooper's room. Used to be that he had a lofted bed, a tank for a bearded dragon named Steve, clothes and LEGOs strewn all over the floor that you had to step over. It ain't like that no more. Now there's a blanket over the window instead of curtains, a cardboard box of old pillows, a desk covered in expense reports for the gas stations. Not much in the way of decoration neither, just a deer skull Papaw gave him when we were kids and a Gadsden flag. It's the way a room looks right when someone's fixing to move out.

I pause at the flag. The bright yellow, the curled rattlesnake baring its fangs, DONT TREAD ON ME.

"That new?" I say.

"Is what new?" Cooper asks from where he's trying to make the bed, or at least smooth out his blue plaid sheets a little bit.

"The don't-tread-on-me flag."

"Oh. Yeah, kinda." He does one last pat-down of the blankets and comes over to stand beside me. "Felt fitting, considering everything."

I don't know about that. Yeah, sure, it was designed for the American Revolution, and some leftists have used it over the years—the #ShootBack movement after the Orlando nightclub massacre, that sort of thing—but mainly it's weird conservatives these days, the kind of conservatives that go "Actually, I'm a libertarian" as if that ain't conservative with a shiny coat of paint. Small government, unchecked capitalism, individualism to the point of *Fuck you, I got mine.* The fun stuff.

On its face, I get it. Don't touch me, don't mess with us; it's very anarchist if you don't look any deeper. But it's hard not to think the wrong thing when I see it.

"Anyway," Cooper says, "I'll be right back. Make yourself comfortable."

He ducks out, so I kick off my shoes and hop up on his bed. Then I scroll through the memes I have saved on my phone and grab one making fun of the Gadsden flag: a badly drawn serpent over NO STEP ON SNEK.

I send it to Dallas.

304-555-6392

LMAOOO

They send one back: a snake with a ball gag looking seductively at a boot labeled with a bunch of giant companies. STEP ON ME DADDY.

Cooper comes back with a makeshift cooler made out of a lunch box, shuts the door, and sets it on the corner of his bed.

"When I first started drinking," Cooper says, which ain't a great opener because he started at thirteen, "it tasted awful. But one of my cousins taught me a trick." He reaches into the cooler and pulls out a few packs of cheap chocolate pudding. "Take a bite right before you drink. Kills the bitter. Plus, I got you some stuff from the store that should be more fine than not."

I inspect the cans in the cooler and pull one out. This stuff, whatever it is, apparently tastes like lemonade. "I don't—"

"I'll take care of you," Cooper says, and the tone of his voice is so soft that it takes me off guard. "Don't worry."

The main reason I've never tried alcohol ain't because it was unavailable to me, because it's always been available. I just don't like new things, let alone new things that are, supposedly, deeply unpleasant. But I'm exhausted and stressed out and honestly, after everything . . .

Mom always said that if I was gonna drink, she'd rather me do it at home with someone to keep an eye on me. This counts, right?

Cooper hands me a plastic spoon.

I take a deep breath, take a bite of the pudding to hold it carefully in my mouth, and crack open the can.

✦

"I don't know," I'm saying, chewing on the pull tab of the can because I've totally forgotten that the shoelace is around my wrist. Cooper's turned on the radio and it's playing Florida Georgia Line, who are fine except for the fact that all of their attempts at rhyming are weird as hell, and I'm rocking back and forth but I'm not as ashamed of it as I usually am. Cooper's flopped back against his pillows. "I could walk into a room full of total strangers—ain't none of them know each other, *all* strangers—and I could swear to god all of 'em met already. Like I missed out on an introduction or something. You ever feel like that?"

"I mean, no," Cooper says after a second. "They're just people. You think it's, what, a conspiracy?"

"When did I say *conspiracy*?"

"They all met before?"

"No, it just *feels* like it." I take another bite of the pudding and forget to take a sip. "Let me put it another way. It's like, it's like everyone else got to take a class in elementary school that was 'How to Interact With and Talk to Other People' and nobody ever told me about it."

"I think you're awkward," Cooper says. "And you don't like people." He considers this. "And also people are weird about y'all."

I groan. That's true. I don't really know what normal human interaction is because the Abernathy name kinda taints everything. "I guess."

"Remember when you used to cry about vacuum cleaners?" Cooper says.

Oh my god, I used to run out of the room and bury my head under pillows every time Mom turned it on. "I cried about *everything*."

"Your corn touched your mashed potatoes."

"The seams of my socks hurt. And jeans too. Christ, I hated jeans."

"Didn't you throw a fit until you could cut a tag out of your shirt?"

"I cut all of them out." I think for a second. "Sometimes it's worse if you do, though. Leaves the rough edge." I stare up the ceiling, remembering all the weird shit I did as a kid. Chewed on my hair, burst into tears when the school schedule changed, refused to talk about anything but the Vietnam War for a month straight, good lord. "Was I still doing that all in middle school? No wonder I didn't have any friends."

"I mean," Cooper says, "eventually you just turned into a bitch." He considers this too. "Is *bitch* gender-neutral? You turned into an asshole."

"I'd rather be an asshole than a crybaby."

"You're moving funny," Cooper points out.

I stop rocking and take the pull tab out of my mouth. "Yeah, I know."

✦

Cooper says, "If one more person tells me I'm a saint for taking care of my dad, I'm gonna lose it." I don't know how many cans he's gone through, it but sounds like he's about to cry. He's sitting up now, because he can't drink lying down, and apparently he's overheating. He changed out of his jeans into sweat shorts. "I was twelve and my mom was dead and my dad wasn't taking care of me, and then your family stopped coming around, and—"

My memory of the year after the crash is fuzzy. There's not much left to remember, not much that was worth keeping around. The funeral, losing Dallas, little else.

"We stopped?" I ask.

"Tapered off," Cooper says. "Got tired of taking care of me, which, it's whatever. I ain't y'all's kid." He sniffs. "And I wasn't great back then. So."

"You were a kid."

"I hit your dad."

We're quiet for a while. I can't remember that, but I can picture it fine. A pissed-off teenager getting into a fight, not meaning to, taking a swing and regretting it as soon as he realized what he'd done. Dad never told me.

"You were a kid," I repeat, because I can't think of what else to say.

Cooper scrubs his face, pressing the heel of his hand into one of his eyes. He's breathing even. Too even, the way someone would breathe if they were timing their inhales and exhales.

"I love my dad," he says. "Of course I love him. I think you gotta love your dad, no matter what he is. Or isn't. And don't get me wrong, I'm gonna keep calling 911. I'm gonna keep driving him to the hospital. I'm gonna keep working the Sunoco. I'm gonna keep doing everything, because it's my job."

He sighs.

"But sometimes I wonder if it's the—the same reason grenades, or mines—" He gestures with his hands, like he's trying to find the words. "You know how some land mines don't kill people? Just blow off their legs? So the enemy's got to burn all those men and supplies on their wounded, and it'd honestly be easier if the soldier died, so you didn't have to take care of them?"

Cooper says, "*Easier* ain't the right word. You know what I mean."

Cooper says, "Wonder if that's what Davies was going for."

I don't know what to say to that. Not sure there is anything. *I'm sorry* is too hollow. *Y'all didn't deserve to get caught up in this* is too little, too late.

"We don't gotta do this," I tell him. "If it's too much."

"No." Cooper straightens up, tries to steel himself. "We're doing it. We have to." He laughs into his drink, and it's so cold and emotionless, eyes so distant, that I don't know if I'm scared or impressed. "They're going to burn in hell."

I remind myself that this is what Saint did. When the North Mountain Coal Company didn't listen to the miners, what else did he do but grab Joseph Davenport—the son of a bitch eldest child of the North Mountain Coal Company president—and drag him into the depths of the mine with a knife between his teeth. He sent up a finger for every day the company refused to talk. *One day he will run out of fingers*, he'd written, *and on that day, I will send up his head.*

I reach out for Cooper and tuck that piece of hair behind his ear the way his mother used to.

Cooper says, "Maybe I'm something. Maybe. I don't know."

I say, "What?" because I can't follow.

When he kisses me, I let him. He forgot to shave today, and the stubble scrapes against my cheek. He smells warm. We both need to take our minds off this, and it works out, then, don't it? When he puts a hand up my shirt, I grab his wrist and push it up higher.

CHAPTER
THiRTY-ONE

We don't do anything that night. We're too tipsy, decide it wouldn't be smart, and fall asleep in the same bed. When I wake up and stumble, hungover, to the bathroom—which I can handle, because it's a hell of a lot better than withdrawal—I find he's bitten me, right on the shoulder.

I pause in front of the dirty mirror, hand over the mark in my skin. I like it. I like *this*. The sense of safety that comes with knowing another person, getting to be close like Cooper and I were last night. And sex, eventually. I know I want that. But . . . I don't want the rest. Not what it's contractually obligated to become, according to all the romance novels I read as a kid, according to *how things work*. And the worst part is, I can't even put my finger on it. What don't I want? I'm not turning up my nose at touch, or at intimacy or companionship. I like all those things fine. I want them.

Just not the way I'm supposed to want them, I guess.

I come out of the bathroom and Mr. O'Brien is there, waiting patiently for his turn. He's got a cup of coffee, plaid pajama pants, and overgrown hair tied back with a rubber band.

It's been a long time since I've actually seen him. He's aged twice as much as he should have, like what Davies did destroyed him down to the cellular level, hit fast-forward on the wrinkles and exhaustion. The same thing happened to my parents. The mines did the same to Saint.

"Oh," he says, trying to manage a smile. "Morning, Sadie. Didn't know you were over."

"Sorry," I say. I don't know how to talk to Mr. O'Brien no more.

"Don't be. My boy missed you."

Mr. O'Brien is a gentle man. It's strange to me that he ran for sheriff, because I can't see him doing anything like that. Or maybe the accident took something out of him I can't remember. I go back to bed, and he gives me a friendly, if not exhausted, wave.

When Cooper wakes up, he asks if something's wrong. I say I'm hungover and he laughs and kisses where he bit me, which I wouldn't mind if I didn't catch the way he looks at me. Soft. As if I agreed to something I didn't.

Maybe I should've told him what I did with the photos. If he knew, his eyes wouldn't be so warm.

◆

The code to the gun safe is my birthday. The night before the Twist Creek County Fourth of July Festival—the night

Sheriff Davies and Noah are helping set up the stage and all the lights, the night Paul Miller is alone in his house in the middle of nowhere, the night I kiss Lady on the head again and tell her to keep an eye on Mom and Dad—I slip into my parents' room while they're in the living room watching TV. I kneel by the nightstand, brush away dog hair, and put in the code.

It opens with a quiet click. I wince.

The gun is heavy in my because it is loaded. Guns shouldn't be stored loaded. It's simple and utilitarian too, sleek black and almost ugly in design. Just like what we're planning: Get in, kill him, get out. No metaphors, no talking, a mousetrap slamming shut—*snap*.

I put the gun in my bag and ease the safe shut.

Click.

CHAPTER
THIRTY-TWO

C ooper said he'd be waiting for me at the end of the road, where the gravel spills onto Main Street. He said we'll be back before my parents wake up. Still, I pile a bunch of pillows under my sheets and prod the mess until I can stand in the doorway of my room and mistake it for myself, because Dad said he checks up on me.

Lady watches silently from my rug. I thought about bringing her, but every time I look her way, all I can see is the video. The dog's belly split open and the bloody froth collecting in the corner of its lips. So I don't.

I kneel in front of her, pull her into a big hug, and then I'm gone, easing the back door closed just as Dad turns off the TV.

But the first person I see is Saint Abernathy. In the yard, expecting me. When I raise a hand to him, the old bandana tied tight around my wrist—*We're doing it*—I can't figure out the look he gives me. His face is too rotten to make out the expression, the railroad spike distending his jaw into a permanent grimace.

✦

Cooper is halfway through a Sprite when I climb into the shotgun seat. God knows how he's able to stomach anything. I had to skip dinner, and even the shoelace dangling from my mouth makes my stomach turn. Don't think he slept last night though, not with how much worse the bags under his eyes are. His thumb taps restlessly against the steering wheel. The yellow light of the single streetlamp should turn him golden, but it only reminds me of jaundice.

I put the bag in his lap, because neither of us actually said it but we both know it's only fair he's the one to do it this time. His hands fumble as he opens up the bag and pulls out the gun. He holds it like he's halfway sure of what he's doing. He knows how to place his hand—finger outside the trigger guard, low enough grip that the slide won't pinch—but the weight of it seems to startle him.

"You done this before?" I ask.

"A few times," Cooper says.

He adds, "Just targets, though. Never anything that could look at me."

✦

Paul Miller lives deep in the back roads of Twist Creek County, past the bridge, past Pearson, in a one-story house flanked by a garage-turned–processing plant. During hunting season, this place is swarming with men in camo dropping off field-dressed deer or packing venison steaks to take home. Mrs. Miller counts out the cash, Mr. Miller interrogates the hunters about Chronic Wasting Disease symptoms, and the boys break down the game. Or so I've heard. We don't frequent the place. Papaw does all his processing himself on the back porch.

Now, it's the off season. Anywhere else, the family business would be in a lull until autumn—the only legal game in summer are pest animals, like coyote or skunk, and most folks let pests decompose where they drop. But it works different here, because if you pay Sheriff Davies enough under the table, the game warden won't so much as touch you. (Claire Snyder's dad must not have coughed up the fee.) It's symbiosis: Davies gets some spending money and the Millers never have to weather an offseason.

Pretty good gig if you ask me. If you're willing to sell your soul to the devil.

Cooper parks at the end of the long driveway, getting out of the truck to throw the tarp over the back. He's gonna make sure it covers the license plate. On the drive down, I told him it wouldn't matter, since everybody knows everybody's damn car, but he said it'd make him feel better so I didn't push. I'm standing by the truck bed, staring at the Millers' house and trying to breathe through nausea. The shoelace is wadded up and jammed in my pocket. A few lights are on, shining through the cracks in the processing-plant door. It's one of those massive rolling doors on tracks, and its large chain lock hangs unfastened. I ain't surprised to see that Paul's up. He does his best work at night.

Saint's here too. Not so close I could touch him, but close enough. When he turns to the house, I can make out the wound where the railroad spike came out at the back of his brain stem, the blood matted into his sandy hair. Now that I know he's trans, I'm trying to find it in his features; in the size of his hands, in the way his face is built. He was never gonna get testosterone, so he had to work with what he had, and I think he did well with it. Or maybe that's the weight of a century changing the body, the bones and the meat. I don't know how this works.

First him, then Lucille, then Bobby and Mrs. O'Brien and all of us and me.

Cooper gets down from the truck bed with a huff. He's got the gun tucked in his waistband, under his shirt, and he's wearing his John Deere cap backwards. It's horrifyingly casual.

"C'mon," he says.

"I don't know."

Cooper takes my arm, but I don't move. "Come on."

When we were tipsy a few nights ago, I ended up half-asleep on Cooper's chest because he didn't want to be alone and me being on the other side of the bed was too far away. The radio murmured and the ceiling fan was set to low. "What do you need me for?" I'd asked. His eyes fluttered open. "Probably be better if I was, I dunno, doing alibi stuff."

He'd said, his lips on the scar across my scalp, "Ain't this for you as much as it's for me?"

And he wasn't wrong. Even if it is easier to deal with a dead body with two sets of hands, remember: Remember Mrs. O'Brien's closed-casket funeral. Remember Dallas in the burn ward. Remember Nancy Adams screaming over her dog, remember waking up in the hospital, remember how it's always gonna be this way. Remember that I've already done this once, and in the face of everything, what's one more, really? Think about it: What are Paul and Noah gonna do once they're grown and running Twist Creek like Davies? It's gonna be just like this.

The cycle is gonna repeat if we don't get up there and stop it.

Finally, I follow, and when I look to Saint, he's gone.

We walk in the grass so we don't crunch the gravel. The forest is dark and loud. Leaves scraping against bark, crickets, the hiss of wind and the distant yapping of some animal. Cooper checks the gun one last time, and I don't know enough about guns to understand what he's checking for. I'm running through what we'll have to do afterwards. Wrap Paul up, take him to the mine, drop him beside Eddie. When I sneak the gun back into the safe, will Dad be able to tell that it's been fired? Are bullets heavy enough that you can judge the difference by feel?

Ain't no floodlight that snaps on when we come too close, nothing that gives us away. We can hear the distant jingle of metal now, the scuff of boots as Paul works inside. The HVAC system roars, cooling the workroom to preserve the meat.

Cooper readjusts his grip one last time, puts a careful hand on the garage door, and turns to me.

Jesus, I hate that this is on my go-ahead. So I nod. For some reason, in my head, that gives me plausible deniability. Like I didn't really do it if I didn't speak. I nod, and Cooper wrenches the door open and it roars across its tracks and Cooper raises the pistol and—

It should've been done just like that. Hit Paul once, maybe a second time to keep him down, and it'd be over. Because that's how death works. It's fast and out of nowhere.

But before he can pull the trigger, Paul laughs. It's small and tired. A sharp exhale more than anything, but it's still a laugh.

Paul says, "Told Noah it was you two. Son of a bitch didn't believe me."

Silence. Cooper won't move. Won't fire. Just makes this pathetic rasping sound.

Never anything that could look at me, he'd said in the truck.

He's choking up.

He can't do it.

✦

In the quiet that follows—in the time it takes to sink in that Cooper didn't shoot, that Paul is still alive, that it was supposed to be as quick as Eddie's head hitting the wheel stop and now it's *not*—I take in the processing plant.

It's nothing fancy. Wood walls hung with deer heads and metal racks, concrete floors and tables like cheap surgery beds. A line of sharp tools. And Paul: work boots, work knife, apron cinched tight. He's skinny around the middle, which makes me think the bags under his eyes ain't exhaustion but malnutrition. A bruise pools at the edge of his jaw.

He's got a doe hung up. She dangles from the hooks shoved through the back legs, head and neck resting against the floor, half her pelt hanging down over her shoulders like loose fabric. The skinned rump is naked, all white and pink bare muscle.

Cooper manages, as if only now registering that Paul had spoken to him, "What?"

Paul nods to the gun. "Had a hunch. Got proof now. It was y'all, wasn't it?"

"Shut the fuck up."

"You telling me to shut the fuck up?" Paul ain't moving, ain't running from us, just watching with a nasty spark to his eyes. He leans forward to give us better access to his skull. "Shut me up, then. Fucking shoot me. You gonna do it, do it."

But Cooper can't. Instead, the gun falls to his side to point right at the floor.

I look to Cooper as if he's going to be able to explain, as if he accounted for this, or maybe it's a ploy, but I'm getting nothing from his face. I never get anything from anyone.

Paul trades his knife for his beer, gestures it vaguely in my direction. "Figures," he says. "Close the damn door, Abernathy. You're letting bugs in."

In my state of shock—it has to be shock—I reach behind me and slide the door shut.

I've never held a conversation with Paul. I mean, I don't talk to much of anyone, but especially not him. There's something beat-down and feral about him. He always sits with his back to the wall so he can't be flanked. Dad does that too.

The first words I manage to find are, "You knew?"

"*I* knew," he says, which means Noah don't. "Figured it'd happen eventually. He'd mess with the wrong guy, get the tar beat out of him, and never get back up again." He takes a sip of his beer and grimaces like it's gone off, though he's still resting his teeth on the glass. "And I always knew I wasn't gonna do nothing, because it'd be nobody's fault but his."

If Paul's going to talk, I'm going to keep him talking. As soon as he decides we're done here, it'll get messy, and Cooper needs to be the one to get it together first. "Noah's probably pissed about it, though."

"Course he's pissed. Eddie was *his*. He don't like nobody touching what's his." Paul takes a second. Thinks. Takes one more sip, then puts his beer down, picks up the knife to flip it in his hand. He's studying the deer to find the best place to start working again. "When Eddie went missing, Noah thought it was Eddie's stepdad. Thought he found that video of his little girl and went apeshit."

Imagine being a father and realizing your stepson hadn't just filmed your underage daughter in the shower but also posted it online for kicks. You'd black out with rage, wouldn't you? You'd tear him to pieces. She was thirteen, and in that video, she'd be thirteen for the rest of her life.

I say, "Any good dad would kill him for that."

"And that's what Noah thought." He takes the pelt and starts to pull. It makes a noise like ripping fabric, sharp and loud, and when it snags, he cuts through the strings gripping hard to the meat. "But I knew it was y'all. The moment Eddie stopped sending 4chan memes to the group chat, I called it. The Abernathy girl's smart enough to lie, ain't she? It's probably her. Or her boyfriend. But Noah said y'all knew better. You two wouldn't do something so *stupid*."

Right. Of course we wouldn't. Not on purpose.

Cooper cuts in, his voice wavering. "You ain't running?"

Paul shrugs and yanks the chain hanging at the end of the pully. The deer jerks upwards. The head hangs a little off the floor now, snout pressed against the concrete like it's trying to figure out the blood-and-soap smell lingering in the cement. Then Paul takes one of the front legs and starts to cut at the knee, working through the meat before twisting it around like he's trying to snap a still-green twig. It cracks off and he tosses it to the floor.

"You know what Davies did?" Paul asks. His voice is still flat, but I can see his knife hand begin to shake. "To my parents? To this place?" He don't wait for us to answer. "Mom and Pop couldn't pay the mortgage, so Davies bought the house. And the business. And the land. Then he gave it right back to us and said we could rent it cheap, so long as we agreed to work for him. *Split the profits*, he'd said."

He takes off the other leg, slits the skin all the way up, and pulls. Pulls. Until the skin is hanging from the doe's naked neck, a bizarre collar dangling down to the floor.

"But here he is, coming back around every year, asking

for a little bit more. Reminds us we're living and working on his land and he can do whatever he wants. So now he takes half of what we make and rent on top of that, and when my dumb ass told Noah I wanted to leave?"

He drops the knife and picks up a bone saw to hack through the neck.

Paul says, "He put the barrel of his daddy's gun in my mouth and told me if I said that again, he'd blow my jaw off. Cause I got to be the one to run this place for him when he grows up."

The saw cuts through the spine, and the deer head hits the ground in a heap. Like Eddie did. *Thump.*

Paul starts to laugh. He grabs the head by the snout and throws it onto the table, skin dripping down the side.

"I should've let him," he says, and I can't tell if he's about to laugh or cry.

The Davieses have a way of doing things. Wrenching your jaw open and shoving something between your teeth, one wrong move away from obliterating you. They'll pull the trigger or bring down the hammer. End you just like that.

A traitorous pang of guilt hits me in the stomach. Paul reminds me of Dad, of me, maybe. More shattered versions of us in a worse world. The way he shakes when he works, the way he was forced into this here spot by people so much more powerful than him.

We don't got to do this the hard way, do we?

I say, "If you want to run, we'll cover for you."

Paul's attention snaps to me.

Cooper says, "What are you talking about?"

I turn to Cooper with a growl. "Shut *up*." Back to Paul with a deep breath. A hand outstretched. Paul stares at it like I'm the one with the weapon. "Look, man. You were right. I killed Eddie. But it was an accident."

"*Christ,*" Paul whispers. He could have predicted this all he wanted, but maybe it wasn't really *real* until I said it.

"I didn't want to. And I don't want to do this either. So if you want to leave, leave. Get out. Go to Maryland or Virginia or Georgia and let Noah figure I killed you too."

Paul scrapes a hand over his shaved scalp, tapping the flat of the bone saw nervously against his leg. For the first time, he looks like a child. Someone who just graduated high school, Cooper's age, skinny and exhausted and cornered. Cruel but only because he was made that way, a pit bull raised in a junkyard.

"It'd work for both of us," I say. *You shouldn't be here, I don't want to kill you, I don't want to be anywhere near you ever again.* "You get out, and I don't got to deal with you for the rest of my life."

Paul is wound tight as a spring, and I realize, probably later than I should, that he's the kind of person whose fear bubbles to the surface as anger. His teeth are bared. He won't stop moving.

He says, "If you're fucking with me—"

"You think we like doing this?" I counter. "I just want you *gone.*"

Paul groans. His eyes squeeze shut.

But Cooper grabs me by the shoulder and pulls me back. "No," he says. I flinch and try to jerk away from him.

"No, what are you doing? What are you—you're gonna let him *leave*?"

Oh, he don't get to act like this. We're only in this situation because he's the one that messed up. "You didn't shoot him, and I ain't about to, so. We gotta do this one way or another."

"I can hear you," Paul rasps.

Cooper glares at me. His finger twitches too close to the trigger, but he don't raise the gun.

I have a chance, I think, to do something. And I have to try.

"Listen," I say to Paul. "You can leave under one condition." He picks up his head. "Answer a question."

Paul snaps, "Fine."

I ask, "Do you feel bad about what you did to me?"

The HVAC hums. The refrigerated cooler room at the back of the garage clanks mechanically. And Paul thinks for a moment, sucking on his front teeth as he considers his words. Can't blame him. We're the one with a gun.

He says, "Can't feel bad when it's just how things are."

All the scripts I got in my head say that this is an unacceptable answer. This is the answer that should make me fly into a rage or break down in tears; *How dare you, What did I do to deserve this*, that kind of thing. And sure, there's a telltale pit in my stomach, the only thing I can rely on to let me know I'm upset. I'd know that sudden gut sickness anywhere. But what gets me is that I don't think I'm mad at *him*.

Because he's right. He didn't choose to be here and neither did I. It's just how the world's shaken out. If I wanted a real answer, I'd have to go to the questions that take up whole books. Once you start asking, *Why has human history created an economic system that loves profit and power more than people, which will always lead to disasters like the mine collapse and the violence that followed?*—once you start asking, *What went so wrong in society that bastards like Sheriff Davies are allowed to exist in the first place?*—the answers taste like sand in your mouth. It's all so far back that the only response becomes "Because that's how it is."

I ain't mad at Paul; I'm mad at the world that put us here.

I've been mad at the world for a long time. It's hard not to be mad at the world when you're eleven years old and everyone you know is suffering, when your mother cries herself to sleep and you can recognize your father's hospital room by the smell of his blood. But the summer before my sophomore year, I learned my great-great-grandfather was a socialist, and suddenly I had the words for why I wanted to burn it all down. Because none of this is real. It's real but it ain't *real*, it ain't real the way mountains or the rings inside a tree are real. You can't open a book on the laws of physics and find a chapter labeled "Exploiting Workers for Profit and Killing Them When They Ask You to Stop." It's *fake*! Someone made it up! Workers are exploited, rent is astronomical, the cost of healthcare is life-destroying not because they are the path a river carves through a canyon, but because some capitalist fuckers decided they wanted it this way.

And then who put them in power in the first place? What gives them the right to do this to us? Why do CEOs and governments get to make decisions that hurt people—cost-cutting safety measures in the mines, dumping chemicals in a water supply—but *we're* the ones deemed a threat? You can't call a cop on your boss for shorting you on your paycheck, but your boss can sure get you arrested for stealing from the till. You know what, open a history book. Show me a list of presidents and kings, show me a list of senators and lawmakers and Carnegies, and I will show you a list of who did this. I can show you who put Paul and I across from each other. And what is that if not politics, Saint would tell us. The fact that you're poor and scared and covered in blood is politics, and don't let no one convince you otherwise.

So of course I'm mad. I'm mad that this is the shape the world takes, I'm mad that we've both been put here, I'm mad because it don't got to be this way.

But it is.

I think Paul's answer was the only answer I was ever gonna get.

I gesture to the door behind me. "Get out."

Paul opens his mouth, stops, and then nods. He puts down his beer without breaking his line of sight. "I'll—" he starts. His low, slow voice starts to shiver. "I'll need to grab a bag. Some things. Can I—"

Bang.

Cooper must've found his guts.

Paul's jaw shatters.

CHAPTER
THiRTY-THREE

Paul stays standing.

Blood sprays in a bloom across the carcass behind him, the bullet going right through his face and clear into the muscle of the deer's spine. I see the entry wound in the animal's body, the little puckered hole, lining up perfectly. A tooth falls from the mess of Paul's face and hits the floor. Its roots are sharp, like a fang.

Paul blinks like he's surprised and tries to open his mouth, only to discover that his lower jaw has been turned into a mess of loose meat.

He retches. He tries to scream, or maybe he does and my ears are ringing too much to hear it. Near-black blood streams down Paul's throat and soaks the apron, splattering onto his shoes.

Cooper, still holding the gun up, shaking and pale, says, "Shit."

Paul stumbles for the workbench and tries to put his

weight against it while he gathers up the shattered mess of his face, but ends up losing his balance and thumping helplessly onto the floor. He looks like a zombie movie, how Bobby Abernathy's head must have looked shattered in the cab of his truck. Just tongue and gums and teeth. There's so much blood. I didn't think the human body had that much blood in it.

He was going to—

We didn't have to—

When my next words come out, I think I'm screaming. *"What the fuck."*

"He was gonna leave," Cooper says. The ringing fades, and his voice cuts above it, unsure and shaky. "He was gonna leave. You were gonna let him."

Of *course* I was gonna let him leave. It would have worked. Paul would've gotten away from Noah, and we wouldn't have this hanging on our conscience. It would have worked, it would have *worked*.

Paul tries to scream again and it comes out more like a gurgle.

Oh my god. Oh my god.

"He was lying," Cooper continues. He sounds hysterical. "He was going to get right in his truck and call Noah. Or go right to him. He was lying, man, come on, you know he was lying."

I'm not listening no more. I'm going to Paul. Kneeling on the floor with him. My stomach churns and I taste stinging vomit on the back of my tongue. He smells like copper and bile. He's sobbing, trying to hold everything together and failing. This close, I can see every piece of the damage, every splinter of enamel and fleck of marrow. Part of his jaw has straight-up disintegrated. Saliva drips from the mess. It's no different from a deer, I tell myself. No different than the squirrels Lady mauls sometimes.

It's taking so long, though. I thought dying happened quick.

"Cooper," I say. "Shoot him again. Please."

"He'll bleed out," Cooper says.

Paul shakes his head. Pieces of his face drip through his fingers. I don't know a hell of a lot about people, but he's barely a person right now. When you're dying, there's no more games. He's begging. *It hurts it hurts it hurts. Please make it stop.*

"Cooper," I say again, but he don't respond this time.

Paul reaches up, hand scrabbling for the workbench. I stand, try to see what he's reaching for. The knife. The one he used to skin the deer dangling right beside us. He can't reach it.

I pull it, gently, from the table. Out of his grasp.

I know what he wants it for. It'd be the kind thing to do, I think, to give it to him. But he stretches out his hand towards it, coughing desperately, fingers trembling with the strain, and I don't hand it over.

I don't want to watch him do it, so I'm going to take it from him and let him suffer. Because I'm afraid.

"We need to go," Cooper says. He reaches an arm around my shoulders to guide me away and I don't resist this time. I'm still holding the knife. "He'll bleed out. Let's go."

"But—"

"Come on," Cooper whispers, "come on, come on."

We leave Paul to die on the processing floor, the bullet still in the hanging deer, the doe's head watching us from the metal table as we back away. Paul tries to follow us, wheezing, but the blood is filling his throat, and it's getting harder and harder for him to move, to keep his eyes open, because that's what blood loss does to you.

He thumps against the floor, and we don't care that we had the tarp to wrap him up, that we were going to dump him in the mine, that we had a plan.

We run.

CHAPTER
THIRTY-FOUR

When I close my eyes, I see the broken jaw. Could count the pieces if I needed to. All the teeth, the flat slab of the tongue and palette, the bone and shreds of muscle. The dark hole that had been his mouth once, leading down to the throat.

The bullet must have hit at the right place that it tore through—I didn't know a bullet could do that—a caliber that small—

I thought—

I thought it was going to be a hole in the chest, like the easy wound in a deer. I've seen a hundred of those. But now I know what Papaw saw when he found his brother's corpse in the cab of the truck, what he had to clean up before his little boy saw, what he had to bury.

Beside me, Cooper stares stiffly out the windshield, white-knuckling the steering wheel. We ain't spoken since we left the Millers'. I'm not sure he's there, not entirely.

You're not supposed to feel bad for the person that tried to kill you.

Every half mile or so, on the main path through Twist Creek County, there's a gravel outcropping on the side of the road, fenced in with guardrails and boasting a faded plaque with a paragraph or two of sanitized historical context. They're the result of some tourism campaign in the eighties, the Twist Creek County Commission thinking they could capitalize on the neighboring Blackwater Falls and surrounding national parks to get people to spend their hard-earned, out-of-state money.

It didn't work, of course. Twist Creek has nothing; no stunning waterfalls, or ski slopes, or historical districts. All of its overlooks can be found anywhere else. We're drive-through country, or drive-around, considering that going *through* might not be worth the strain on your brakes. These days, the plaques are faded, almost impossible to read. I became obsessed with preserving them in middle school anyway and put together a plan to make Mom and Dad drive me to every single one, but the first I went to was so underwhelming that the plan collapsed immediately. They were old, and badly designed, and definitely approved by a Davies.

I pull out my phone. We're close to the outskirts of Pearson on the way to McLachlan, but the signal is still spotty. As I watch, the minute clicks over to midnight, and I hear the whistle and pop of a firework. Happy Fourth of July.

Google search: "how lojg does it take to die from.blood loss"

Result: Approximately one minute or less.

Paul probably died before we'd even gotten out on the road.

I grab Cooper by the sleeve. "Pull over."

"What? Here?"

"Pull over."

Cooper hits the brakes, swerving onto the last plaque outcropping on the road before the awkward Pearson "suburbs." I shove open the door and vomit into the gravel. It starts as a dry heave, with that ugly croaking noise, then acid comes up and my stomach clenches so hard it hurts. My eyes water and my nose runs and I yank open Cooper's glove box for napkins, desperately trying to clean off my face.

"Jesus," Cooper says, finding them for me. "Here."

I lean against the frame of the truck and gasp for air.

The truck's headlights reach a few branches before disappearing into the darkness. A little ways down the road, there's another bridge, a few shops, and eventually you'd run into Twist Creek County's only stoplight. The moon is three-quarters there, behind a wispy cloud. Nobody's out driving. It's the night before our favorite holiday, and we're all either resting up or pregaming, because that's what we do, even in the middle of the week. Another firework goes off.

It's just us out here.

The knife is sitting on the dirty truck carpet. The gun is in the bag I used to smuggle it out of the house and neither of us will touch it. I keep smelling my hands because I swear the stink of blood is still there. Bile too, but now that's gotten all mixed up and everything smells like it. I think it splattered on my shoes.

I spit into the gravel and press another napkin to my mouth like I'm gonna be sick again. "You *choked*."

Cooper says, "Don't."

"You were supposed—" My entire body is buzzing. My words are all jumbled up and I can't get them out right. It's so much work. It's always work, but usually I can do it, usually I have the space in my head to manage it. I don't right now. I have to fight for every syllable. "You were supposed to just do it. It wasn't supposed to—"

"What? It wasn't supposed to happen like that?" Cooper sneers. Any words I could manage disappear immediately. He takes off his seat belt, slides out into the gravel, comes around the bed to my side of the truck. "If you thought you could've done a better job, you should've done it then!"

I shake my head. We both know I couldn't have done it, we *know* that. He needs to lower his voice or I'm going to scream.

"You were gonna let him go," he says.

He keeps saying it and I don't know why. Most of the time when people do that, they want you to recognize the absurdity of what they're saying. The *stupidity* of it. But it wasn't absurd, or stupid. Paul wanted out. I'm not naive. I'm not a child. I'm . . .

What did Dallas call me? Honest?

Was Paul lying?

It don't matter no more. He's dead.

"It's," I manage, then I try again. "You wanted to hurt him." No, that ain't right. Cooper wouldn't have cared either way if he'd been the one to do it. I correct myself. "You wanted him to hurt."

Cooper coughs in a vague approximation of laughter. "Of course I did. Ain't that what we're trying to do?"

Hurting people for the sake of it? To make them hurt like I did? Revenge?

No. Hurting people was never the point. It happens to be an unfortunate side effect of what has to be done. Saint never *wanted* to dismember Joseph Davenport, but hell if it ain't what he needed to do. He was trying to protect his people. I'm trying to protect my people.

Cooper must not like my silence, or my expression, I don't know, I can't tell. He grabs me by the shirt. He drags me close and his teeth are so close to my face.

"Look at me," he says. I try to peel his hands off me but I can't. "*Look at me, Sadie.*"

I told him I don't like eye contact, he knows that.

"You don't get to back out of this now," he says. "Not after you dragged me into it."

I throw my weight against him and shove my shoulder right into his chest. He lets go with a grunt, stumbles back, catches himself on the truck bed. It don't do much, but it puts some space between us, leaves him sucking in air through his teeth as I grab the bag from the truck. The knife too.

He stares at the knife. "What are you doing?"

"Gonna call Dallas," I rasp. I don't bring up my old name. We're both fully aware of what he did. "You should go home."

"Dallas? Jesus Christ." When I don't reply to that, he continues. "I'm not leaving you here."

"Yes, you are."

In the quiet I realize that Cooper's got his turn signal on. It's blinking. Going *click click click*. He fidgets, grits his teeth, but I'm the one holding the knife. And the gun. He's got nothing except his size.

Cooper says, "If you talk—"

"I won't."

"I swear to god—"

"*I won't.*"

That must be enough. Cooper pushes past me. Gets into the truck. Drives off.

I don't dare move until his taillights disappear around the bend. Alone in the dark, I feel my teeth chatter. My throat seizes with nausea the way it did while I was going through withdrawal. Every time I blink, the blood and teeth are there. I need to call, but I'm not sure I can say enough to get my point across. Maybe I should text. Would Dallas be awake to see it? I jam the knife into the bag and tie the handles together.

Beside me, Saint leans against the faded plaque. He's got one hand at the base of his skull as if fidgeting with the point of the railroad spike sticking out of his head.

I say, flatly, "What."

But he don't say nothing, because of course he don't. He just slides his dead eyes to me, disappointed.

We really fucked up this time.

CHAPTER THIRTY-FIVE

Dallas answers the phone within two rings.

"Miles? You okay?" But I can't get out more than a few groggy syllables, so I take the phone from my ear and send a photo of my view. It's blurry but apparently it gets the point across. "Shit, man. Are you alone? You want us to come get you? You're close but—*what? No, it's Miles. Okay. Stay where you are.*"

In a few minutes, Amber is parked on the side of the road, getting out of her car with a blanket and bottle of water. Her pink cat-print pajamas clash with her dirty sneakers. I threw up again waiting for her, so I snatch the water, swish it around, and spit into the gravel before chugging as much as I can. Hadn't realized how dry my throat was or how badly I'd needed to get the taste of bile out of my mouth.

"Hey," she says softly. I gasp for air, water trickling down the sides of my mouth. "Dallas said you were having trouble speaking. Is that right?"

"I can—" *I can speak, I swear, it ain't usually this hard.* It's been hard before, but I've always pushed through, no matter how much I don't want to. I can't now. Pathetic.

Amber says, "That's going to be a yes. That's okay. You don't gotta if you don't want. Blanket?"

I nod and she wraps it around me, tucking the edges carefully under my hands. It's nice, even though it's too warm for it, even though it hurts to touch my left arm. That happens sometimes; touch or clothing feels like sandpaper. Nothing to do but put up with it.

Amber leads me to the car and bundles me in, helping buckle my seat belt. "Do you want me to take you home?"

I shake my head. No. Absolutely not. I can't go home after that. I know it don't make sense, but I'm convinced I'll leave bloody footprints on the floor, or my parents will take one look at me and realize exactly what we did.

Amber tries a different angle. "Should I call your parents, then?"

I shake my head again.

Amber offers the closest thing she can to a smile, a tight-lipped grimace, and closes the door for me before going around to the driver's side. Her car, of course, is packed with cats. A tabby plush on the dash, a calico ornament hanging from the rearview mirror, a little decal in the corner of the window. The engine is ticking. Probably an oil problem, or a worn-out belt. Bet I could fix it, if I called Dad to double-check.

"We know what it's like," Amber says carefully as she takes off the parking brake, "with bad shit." More fireworks crackle across town, and the light of them gets caught in the rearview mirror, white and gold and red. "If this has anything to do with Davies—"

"Don't call them."

Amber nods and turns on the AC full blast, making sure it's directed right at my face. "Okay. This helps when I'm sick." She's right. It does.

◆

Dallas shoulders open the front door to meet me halfway up the driveway, barefoot and shirtless, while Michael stands nervously on the threshold. Their house is a squat square built into a hill, a pride flag jammed into their little garden. The neighbor has a TRUMP PENCE 2016 lawn sign pointed directly at it. I'm clutching the bag tight enough it hurts.

"Christ," Dallas says, "what happened? Can I touch you?"

"Give him space," Amber chides, shooing them back.

Michael says, "Inside, let's go."

The inside of the house is dark and quiet and comforting. It reminds me a lot of Mamaw and Papaw's place: exposed brick, wood walls burnished orange, sturdy old appliances that ain't been replaced since the eighties. The only light is the dim fluorescent above the sink. I catch sight of a grey kitten hopping down from the cabinets and scampering into a dark hallway, collar jingling.

Amber gestures me to a stool by the breakfast bar. "Do you like music," she asks, "or silence?"

I point vaguely in the direction of the radio mounted by the fridge. Silence makes me uncomfortable. Amber dutifully turns it on and fiddles through the channels until she finds something acceptable; the stations around here play weirdly religious ads after dark. Michael leans against the counter and whispers something to her. She shakes her head. When I finish the bottle of water, Dallas fetches another from the crate of Deer Park on the floor and quietly relieves me of the empty one.

I feel disgusting. No matter how much water I drink, I can't get the acid taste out of my mouth. There's no blood under my nails, but I still want to scrub them clean.

"I didn't mean—" I start, but can't keep going.

"You're fine," Michael says. "If you don't want to talk, you don't have to."

They keep saying that. Staying silent's never been an option before, not without being called rude or antisocial. Or, no, Mom and Dad never said that, not to my face. They wouldn't dare. But when I translated their glances or frowns, that's what they meant.

It's easier, though. To be quiet.

The next time I look up, it's because Amber is handing me three things: a notepad, a pen, and a stack of little cards on a key ring. I clumsily turn over one card, then another. *I'm hungry. It's too loud. Leave me alone, please.* I'm suddenly smacked by shame. I don't need these. Right? My eyes burn. My leg bounces helplessly.

"If talking's too hard," Amber says, "you can use these."

A shower—I need a shower. I try to pick up the pen, but it's too heavy in my hand. Even writing it is insurmountably difficult. So I grab the ring of cards and flip through until I see the one that says *shower*, and shove it across the table, and then I start to think about actually *showering*, and I can't. I can't—I can't do the bright lights, or the humidity or the shock of cold air after hot water, or the struggle of putting on clothes while I'm still wet—but I have to, I have to, don't I? To get this off me?

I start to cry.

No, no—I jam the heels of my hands into my eyes. *Stop it, stop.* Paul is dead and I know what his blood smells like and all I can think of is my parents in the backyard, *Keep that up and we'll have to explain to our neighbors that our daughter is special.* They didn't mean it like that, I know they didn't, and it's awful because there's actually a disabled person in the room right now, but this is what they meant. Times like this, when I get upset and absolutely lose it. But I can't stop. It's just a shower, Miles. You can't handle a shower? What's wrong with you?

But then Amber is telling Dallas to do something. She's pushing Michael out of the room and telling him to stay out, and then she's talking to me.

It's nothing much at first. Her telling me that she's turning the light off above the sink, and turning the radio down a little bit since the high notes of the song are hurting her ears. She's sorry that the refrigerator hums, and she's brought me tissues. It's all her same perfect monotone. The cat's name is Smoky. Dallas missed you, and they're very happy you're back.

I'm shivering. Elbows on the table and trying to breathe. Eyes squeezed shut.

"I was fixing to be a teacher in Morgantown," Amber continues. "Wanted to work with disabled kids, autistic kids specifically. Thought it was my calling, being autistic myself, as it goes. Nobody better for the job than us." She's telling a story. I try to listen to her, focus on anything except myself. "Did the best I could, but school ain't friendly to people like me. Barely got through high school, so I never really had a shot at a bachelor's degree, let alone a teaching license."

I don't know why she's telling me this.

"When that didn't work," she says, "I switched to business admin. Much more technical, and I could knock it out in two years. But I still know a disabled kid when I see one. Take it your parents never took my advice to look into that, did they?"

The statement—as simple as it is—shocks me out of my crying.

Look into that.

I breathe in.

Shake my head no.

"Figures. You did fine in school. And at home too. But, you know, you have good parents, and a knack for covering up when you're hurting—lots of autistic kids get real handy at masking how upset they are." That word keeps rattling around. *Autistic.* She says it so easy, like it ain't the heaviest word I've ever heard. It reminds me how heavy the word *transgender* used to be for me, the weight of everything it meant. "I watched you get better at hiding it as you grew up. By the time we moved out of Twist Creek, you'd built that mask up strong. Had to, I figure, to survive all that."

There's no way she's saying what she's saying. I'm not— no. What? No.

"I ain't no doctor," Amber says, "but I think giving yourself a little grace might do you some good. It ain't your fault you're different."

I don't know what to think about that. I can barely think at all.

Dallas comes back with an armful of towels. "Done."

"Thank you." Amber puts the towels in front of me, along with a night-light and a set of ear plugs. "This is how I shower. Ain't as bright with the night-light. We've got a space heater going and the water running lukewarm, so the temperature shock won't be as bad neither. You'll need the fan running so it won't get muggy, but if that's too loud, that's what the earplugs are for." She puts her hands on her hips and inspects the pile of supplies. "Can't change that it ain't fun, or that getting through all the steps is hell and a half, but this makes it manageable."

Breathe in. Breathe out.

"But—" I whisper. "Putting on clothes after—"

"Because you're still wet?"

I nod.

"Then don't," Amber says plainly. "Sit in the towel until you're dry. You ain't gotta make yourself do something that sucks. You can do it the way that sucks less."

For some reason, my brain rejects that. *I can take a shower like anyone else*, it whines, ignoring that I put it off until I'm visibly greasy, that I used to sit on the bath mat with water running and swear to my parents that I'd gotten in, I swear. *I'm almost an adult and I am fully capable of washing myself normally.*

I'm not autistic. I'm weird and socially inept and a picky eater and had to be taught how to smile and made to stop chewing my hair and can't spend more than a few minutes around people before I want to crawl out of my skin and can't take a *shower* without losing my *shit* over it and I don't understand people at *all*.

I'm not autistic. I'm some unsocialized dog.

But I grab the towels and the night-light, and Dallas gestures for me to follow.

✦

In the basement bathroom—the bathroom connected to Dallas's room—I take a shower I don't hate for the first time in my life. The water is cool, I don't spend the whole time with my eyes closed to block out the light, I don't have to brace myself against the freezing air when I get out. And then I wrap myself in a towel and sit on the bath mat in silence.

It's . . . manageable.

And I don't feel as disgusting as I did. I don't keep mistaking shadows for blood, or catching the faint scent of vomit. It's bodywash and warm air now.

I don't deserve this. Not after what we did.

In my pile of clothes, my phone buzzes. My stomach drops. If Dad didn't fall for the decoy I built in my bed, I don't have an excuse. What would I say? I pull my phone from the pocket of my pants.

Cooper

Remember: keep your fucking mouth shut.

I put my phone on Do Not Disturb and bury it back under my clothes.

CHAPTER
THiRTY-SiX

Dallas gives me a pair of shorts and a too-big shirt—
"Sorry, laundry's tomorrow," they say when I realize
the shirt is Cannibal Corpse merch, complete with a
zombie doing weird shit to a woman's insides—and also
their bed for the night. Amber and Michael said they'll
take me home when they wake up for work. That's before
the sun rises. It ain't nearly enough time, but I don't say
so. Not sure I can.

Instead, I sit on the bed in silence while Dallas stands
in front of their full-length mirror, rubbing lotion into
their burns. Apparently my call interrupted them. I want
to say sorry, but Dallas can must smell the apology on me.
They shake their head. "Don't start."

I wrap Amber's blanket tighter around my shoulders.

They rub the lotion into what's left of their ear, up to
their temple, across their neck and jaw. Without their
shirt, I can see the expanse of the grafts across their chest,

the undersides of their arms, the lower back and shoulder blades. Their clothes must have caught fire. They must have tried to put themself out with their hands.

When they reach for their back, they struggle a little and laugh awkwardly. "Downsides of being a big bitch," they say, as if they need to explain themself. "The back is the hardest part."

I get down from the bed, plod over to them, and hold out a hand.

"I can manage," Dallas protests, but that don't stop me. They slump a little when I touch them, rubbing the lotion in right where the worst of the burns stretch from the small of their back halfway up their spine.

"Does it feel weird?" I whisper.

"Naw," Dallas says. "Used to it by now. It's mainly the upkeep—this, constant sunscreen, making sure they're healing okay." Hard to believe they ain't done healing yet. "Other people are the worst part. You know."

They gesture to my eye. I make a vague noise in acknowledgment. It ain't the same in my opinion, but that's up to them, not me.

Dallas's room is covered wall-to-wall with band posters and art prints. Goats, deer, two-headed sheep, Cannibal Corpse and Cattle Decapitation; the lyrics of "Forced Gender Reassignment" are written on the wall as a joke next to a re-creation of that famous medieval unicorn tapestry. A rainbow flag behind the headboard and the agender flag—the black and grey and muted green—pinned above the bed like a canopy. And there's a small print taped to the mirror: a human body stitching itself together, variously mangled but still alive, staring defiantly at the viewer with teeth bared. It's so *them*. So aggressively queer, so lived-in.

Once I finish, I straighten up and catch myself looking in the mirror over Dallas's shoulder. I barely recognize myself.

"Do you think I'm autistic?" I say.

"I—" They start. Hesitate. "Um. Did Amber bring it up?"

"Yeah."

Dallas sighs. "I mean, it'd make sense if you were. Not that I know a lot about it. I just know Amber. And you. But, you know, ADHD and autism are cousins, yeah? And we always did get on." They pick at their beard nervously. "You remind me a lot of her."

There's a long moment of quiet, and then they say, "Miles?"

I busy myself with getting lotion out from under my nails, even though there ain't nothing there.

"What happened?" Dallas asks.

"You know how it goes," I say, "around here."

Dallas thinks on that for a moment. They knew what they were getting into, moving back to Twist Creek. Just because Uncle Rodney said it in a nasty tone of voice don't make it untrue.

"Your parents all good?" they add.

"Yeah."

"Okay."

"Do you—" I rock from side to side, shifting my weight slowly. "You remember those sleepovers we used to have?"

Dallas laughs. "We didn't *sleep*."

It felt like every weekend we were packing overnight bags and setting up blankets on living room floors, accidentally calling Mrs. O'Brien *Mom* or giggling as Michael shouted down the hall to tell us to quiet down. Cooper would scrape together enough change to get a pizza, and Dallas would sneak in *The Texas Chainsaw Massacre*, and I'd clip a light to my book and read until the sun came up. When everyone came over to our house, we'd pile in my bed and sleep like Victorian children, curled up longways with our feet hanging off the side of the mattress. If you stayed up long enough, you could hear the grown-ups talking. They always sounded worried.

I feel like a small child saying it out loud, but it's the same impulse of crawling in my parents' bed after the accident, waking in the dead of night to check on them the way they do to me now. "You don't need to sleep on the couch," I say, "if you don't want."

Dallas says, "I dunno. Bed's a bit small, if that's what you're implying." I deflate, but they offer a smile. "I'm kidding."

Dallas takes the left side of the bed and I take the right. Their lotion smells vaguely like lavender. They snore a little bit, but I don't mind; it's covered up by the hum of the standing fan at the foot of the bed. They get warm easy, they explained.

Right before I fall asleep, I check my phone again.

Missed call: Cooper

Missed call: Cooper

Cooper

Pick up the phone.

Missed call: Cooper

Missed call: Cooper

Missed call: Cooper

My stomach drops. Did he run into Sheriff Davies somehow? Did we get caught already? I fumble to open my messages.

For some reason, what I find is worse.

Cooper

Shouldnt have let you leave

And you went to the Fosters??? The Fosters are cowards. They ran.

I did the hard part. You dont get to back out like this when I'm the one that did it

I did it. Not you.

My phone rings. Cooper. Again. My fingers shake when I dismiss the call.

Miles

stop

what is wrong with you??

Cooper

Oh THERE you are

The fuck are you talking about "what's wrong with me"?

I shouldn't have left you there. Tell them you're leaving. Go to
the road and I'll pick you up.

Miles

i didnt tell dallas shit! i said i wouldnt and i didnt!!

i'm not leaving

Cooper

You motherfucker

Another call. I reject it, open up settings, and block
Cooper's number.

There.

"Sleep," Dallas chides drowsily, reaching for my phone
as if to take it from me. I shove it under my pillow and roll
over so we're facing each other. I'm breathing heavy and I'm
shaking again. Dallas blinks as if they ain't quite awake.
"You need to sleep."

"It's bad," I tell Dallas.

Dallas says, "I know."

"Cooper—"

I stop. With only his name, I've said too much.

Dallas reaches across the bed until their knuckles touch
my arm, and we stay like that until we both fall asleep. It's
all broken bone and blood behind my eyelids. Don't think
that'll go away for a long time.

✦

When Michael wakes us up, my phone says it's four in the morning. We don't talk as I put on yesterday's clothes or chug the glass of orange juice Dallas gives me to keep my blood sugar up; they ask if they can hug me before Amber drives me home and I nod.

Then Amber drops me off a few houses away from home, and I make it back inside without anyone noticing—taking off my shoes on the porch, easing open the door, shushing Lady with a hand to the snout. My parents stay sound asleep as I ease the gun back into the safe. I hide the bag with the knife under my bed. The house is quiet and still.

But it's not enough.

I take the railroad spike from my bedside table and head back out. Just for a little bit. Just for a few minutes at most. Before McLachlan wakes up, I walk down to the burned remains of the theater and put the railroad spike in the same pile of rotten wood that Saint Abernathy pulled it from.

I saw the way he looked at me outside of Pearson. I know what he thinks of me—the fact he ain't here watching me is proof enough of that.

He put his faith in the wrong person.

Only then do I really go home. I fall asleep on my bedroom floor, using Lady as a pillow.

CHAPTER
THiRTY-SEVEN

hate the Fourth of July on principle. Which sucks because,
you know, it's the only day an Abernathy is allowed to
feel normal anymore, what with Sheriff Davies basking
n the glow of attention and all. But even ignoring the
social demands of the holiday—the whole family comes
over, and I can't get out of it since Mom caught on to me
playing sick a few years ago—there ain't nothing worth
celebrating. Not with this country.

But I have to be normal, because Paul is dead.

At least Mom lets me sleep in. When I wake up, it's the
afternoon and Mamaw and Papaw are here, hanging out in
the kitchen. Papaw scratches Lady's ears as Mamaw sits me
down, makes me eat lunch even though there's always food
at the festival, fusses over how short my hair is. I'm just glad
she ain't talking about my eye, or my broken tooth.

"Are you going to let it grow back out?" She tsks, plucking
my ear. "Hope you ain't planning on keeping it this length

Really, Sadie, I thought that pixie cut was short enough."
Dad opens his mouth, maybe to correct her on my name,
but Mom shakes her head.

Then Uncle Rodney shows up with Aunt Jill. Aunt
Jill hugs me tight, asks me a lot of questions about how
I'm doing, offers to give me her hat so my head don't get
sunburned. Mom's uncle wishes us a happy Fourth via text;
Mamaw's sister calls from Ohio and they spend an hour
chatting like schoolgirls. I try to keep up but I'm getting a
headache. There's too many people in the house, everyone's
talking, it's too warm in the kitchen. Before Mom can tell
me off, I grab a book and retreat to the living room.

I can't handle it.

Noah put a gun in Paul's mouth and threatened to kill
him, but we're the ones that actually did it.

I read the same page of this book five times but can't
retain a word. This is supposed to be a chapter about US
support of genocidal regimes abroad, the sort of thing I
soak up like a sponge, but my eyes keep slipping over the
timeline of war crimes.

You've done Twist Creek County a favor, Cooper said.

But Paul's tooth sounded like a piece of porcelain when
it hit the concrete floor, and I see it every time plates clink
against each other in the kitchen. I need to get that out of
my head somehow. I grab my phone and pull up Google
but stop, because what am I supposed to search for? "I
killed someone and can't handle it?" I didn't even kill him;
Cooper did. "I watched someone die"? Tough. Most of the
people in this house have been through so much worse.

A distraction will work for now.

Google search: "autism"

Result: "A serious developmental disorder that impairs the ability to communicate and interact. Symptoms include difficulty with communication and social interaction, obsessive interests, and repetitive behaviors." There are lots of pictures of little kids, and lots of resources for parents. "How to know if your child is autistic," one result says. "The challenges of a child with autism." Expensive therapists, antipsychotics, Autism Speaks. None of this is what I'm looking for.

Google search: "how do I know if I'm autistic"

Result: Autism tests. Signs and symptoms and checklists, YouTube videos with clickbait thumbnails. "Get diagnosed so you can get the support you need," it says.

I skim through the tests and try to pick one that don't seem too condescending, but apparently that's a big ask. The questions are too cut-and-dry, none of the available answers nuanced enough. Nobody's ever called me an eccentric professor. Antisocial and obsessive to the point of annoyance, sure, but never that exact wording. I can trick people into thinking I'm looking them in the eye, which is close enough to eye contact that it don't count as a problem. Yeah, I'd rather go to a museum than a musical, but I know what a *metaphor* is.

Still . . .

It's unnerving to see your entire personality reflected back at you under the symptom list of a developmental disorder. The more I read, the more I shrink back into the couch, clutching my phone. It's everything I tried to cover up, everything I thought was me being weird or weak, a cluster of quirks and failures coming together like a constellation. Chewing on my hair until Mom threatened to cut it off. Picking at my scalp until it bled. Rocking on my feet and bouncing my leg, studying other people because maybe then I'd be able to understand them. Crying about jeans and seams in socks, refusing to brush my teeth or change my clothes, bursting into tears at a change in routine or getting so upset I threw up. Few friends, if any. Feeling like an alien around others, no matter how hard I tried.

Anybody can have these traits, the research says. Autistic or not. But when there's so many, and there's a pattern, and it starts to *sting*?—when your existence is bent around it?

Google search: "advantages of autism"

Result: "Attention to detail and pattern recognition. Incredible wealth of knowledge in chosen interests. Resistance to social pressure. Disregard for hierarchy and strong sense of personal justice."

This reminds me of when I figured out I'm trans. It was like putting on glasses for the first time. The world comes into focus and you look back at the rest of your life and go, *Oh. That's why.* And now I'm holding glasses again. I've lifted them almost to my face and a small sliver of the world has unblurred, but I'm scared to put them all the way on.

Amber must have thought I'm autistic for a reason, right?

There's no time to think more about it though, because a knock sounds on the door. Dad jumps and Mamaw tells her sister that she's got to go. I freeze like a rabbit. Maybe if I stay still, whoever it is won't notice me.

And when Mom opens the door, it ain't Sheriff Davies standing there. It's worse.

"Afternoon, Mrs. Abernathy," Cooper says, a million kinds of sweet. Shit, shit, *shit*. Every face in the house beams at him; god, everybody loves Cooper O'Brien, don't they, the sweet boy just doing his best to take care of his father. "Is Sadie around?"

"Course she is," Aunt Jill says. She's getting some kind of idea, clear as day. "Sadie, honey, come here!"

"Be social," Mom chides.

But I don't move, so Cooper comes into the living room, sits in the armchair, and grins.

The smile don't reach his eyes.

"Who are you, then?" Aunt Jill calls from the kitchen.

"Her boyfriend," Cooper says back. Aunt Jill makes an excited noise.

"What do you want?" I rasp. My voice is drowned out by the TV, the white noise of the droning weatherman. The adults are right in the other room, but they ain't paying attention anymore, too busy with Aunt Jill's delighted questions directed to my parents because I obviously won't answer. We might as well be alone.

Cooper says, so quietly, "You blocked my number."

Obviously. I try to remember why people state things that are clearly true, but if he's asking *why*, that seems obvious too. When I remain silent, Cooper's face screws up. All the memories of sitting on the porch with popsicles, driving home after the hospital, his hand skimming the back of my neck as he shaved my head, they've all gone sour.

"Not gonna say nothing?" he asks.

"What do you want."

"You tell Dallas?"

"Of course I didn't."

Cooper scoffs. "Don't say it like that. Don't make me the bad guy here."

I thought I said it fine. And I don't think I'm making him the bad guy, neither. We *both* did it, didn't we? We've both done awful things this summer, right? "I'm not. I—" I stammer for a second before the words come out. "We never should've done this."

Cooper sneers.

"You're a coward too," he says. "Just like the rest of them."

Like my parents? Like Bobby and Lucille? Like the people that tried and ended up *dead*? He don't get to talk about my family like that. They ain't cowards—and you know what, neither are his parents. He don't get to talk about his dead momma and sick daddy like that, not around me. This son of a bitch.

Mom knocks on the doorframe to get our attention. I jump like I've been shocked. My heart is pounding and my vision is blurry and I've forgotten how to swallow.

Cooper turns with a pleasant smile.

"We're about to head down to the field," Mom says. "You want to come with us, Cooper? Only if you'd like. Don't mean to keep you if you need to be at work."

Cooper says, "I'd love to."

✦

Cooper chats with my family as we walk down to the old field for the Twist Creek County Fourth of July Festival—his knuckles brush my arm as he asks about work, the weather, the always-rising cost of gasoline. Dad refuses to use his cane, like always, and his jaw starts to tick with pain at the halfway mark. Beside me, Aunt Jill talks about her new favorite TV show while Uncle Rodney grunts disinterestedly. I'm tying the shoelace into knots again since it's the only thing keeping me from digging my nails into my scalp.

At least I get to bring Lady. She plods along beside me, leash looped casually around my wrist, tongue lolling out of her mouth.

You're a coward, Cooper said.

No, I'm protecting my family.

You can hear the festival grounds before you see them—shouting, music, the roar of truck engines. It's lower on the mountain, a baseball field in a bend of Twist Creek, red-white-and-blue everything. American flags on the back of every pickup, patriotic streamers and rocket pops. Even got a themed food truck with hamburgers and hot dogs and funnel cake. In previous years, I only ever came down for the food. Now the smell turns my stomach.

I scan for Sheriff Davies and Noah but don't see them. The DJ is playing "Born in the USA" like it ain't about a Vietnam vet bemoaning America's failures. Lady whines.

"You want a hot dog?" Papaw asks me, eyeing the food truck as he pulls a crisp twenty from his pocket. "I don't trust them burgers. Damn near shat my guts out last year."

"Roger!" Mamaw squawks, slapping his arm.

"I'm fine," I say, which is true enough. "Just—"

In the crowd, I spot Dallas. It's hard not to see them; they're big and queer and loud, all black nail polish and sleeveless denim vest to show off the scars, a stack of red flyers in hand.

Those flyers. The flyers Amber was talking about at the Red Holler. The ones that have the pictures of the accident.

I know I said it was okay for Amber to use them—I know damn well I weighed my options, considered the risks, and handed them over. Shoving them in Davies's face to piss him off, knock him unsteady, was the *point*. It was the right thing to do. Of course it was.

I'd kinda forgotten that, if everyone in Twist Creek County was going to see them, that includes Dad. And Cooper.

"Live music, cheap food, and a free drink with a ticket," Dallas says to the bearded dad in front of them. "Plus a true bastion of free speech. Don't get that much no more, do we?"

"What're you trying to say?" the man says, expression clouding over.

Dallas shrugs. "Just that cops don't get to be above the law, and apparently that's controversial to say now." The man takes the flyer and walks away, turning it over with wrinkle-nosed curiosity. Dallas lets out a sigh, rolls their shoulders—and sees us.

For some reason, it's like I've been caught doing something I shouldn't. I wave nervously.

Cooper stares.

"Oh," Mom says, "do you three want to catch up while Dad and I find a spot?"

"Sure," I say absently. Please get out of here; don't let Dad see the flyers. "I'll find you. I'm good."

So the grown-ups leave. Thank you, Fourth of July, for being the only time my parents would ever let me out of their sight.

Dallas comes over, bending a flyer to make it work as a fan. They smell like sunscreen, and their pins read *The Government's Boot Is on Your Throat* and *Both Parties Suck*. Perfect conversation starters in a place like this, gotta admit. Lady immediately starts sniffing their pants, nudging at the back of their knee as if trying to find something. Dallas reaches down to pet her.

"Hey, sweetie," they say. Then, as if in a business meeting, or not quite sure how they'll be received: "Cooper."

Cooper's empty expression does not change. "Dallas."

"I texted you, but—"

"I know."

Dallas skims the situation. Their eyes snap from me to Cooper to the people around us. Maybe trying to gauge how Cooper has changed in the years since they last spoke, comparing him to what I've said about him and the radio silence they've received.

The research I did before Cooper showed up at the house said that, sometimes, autistic people don't actually miss social cues. In fact, they might see every single one of them, but they've gotta decode them by hand, analyzing them quick as they can to avoid being left behind. And sometimes they get it wrong. No wonder interacting with people is so exhausting—it's twice the work for half the results.

I don't got to do a lot of analyzing to know this ain't gonna go well.

"Heard you're full time at the gas station now," Dallas attempts.

"You do what you have to." Cooper grabs a flyer. Inspects it. Grins nastily before handing it over to me. "Takes some balls, printing stuff like this."

Dallas shrugs. "This is America, right? We should be able to say whatever we want."

The brochure itself is dark red, an intentional choice, like the color of blood, with *F*CK THE FOURTH* in bold letters across the top. *The Red Holler, Pearson, WV, Wednesday the 5ᵗʰ, 8 p.m. Featuring Tennessee punk band Black Bloc.*

F*CK THE COAL MINES THAT WATCHED YOUR GRANDPARENTS DIE

F*CK THE COMPANIES THAT PROFITED FROM IT

AND F*CK SHERIFF DAVIES

PROTECT YOUR COMMUNITY FROM GOVERNMENT & CORPORATION OVERREACH

BRING BACK FREE SPEECH AND SAFETY

LEARN MORE

These smart bastards. Using conservatives' favorite words for a thing like this? I've seen this tactic before. It's how Michael talked to those contractors at the Red Holler. Starting where we agree—Democrats ain't never done a thing for us—and then pushing: Ain't it wrong that your boss makes so much more money than you? Don't you know it's 'cause he's stealing from you?

There's an arrow, so I turn the flyer over.

Gotta admit, I'm damn impressed.

An excerpt of Twist Creek County law, showing that Davies has been violating the office term limit for years. A security camera still of Davies shoving Michael in front of the Red Holler. The autopsy report for Deputy Steele, the cop that died a few years back, saying the wound lined up with a service weapon, and Davies's response of *Call it a fucking suicide*. And the photo of the crumpled car, Mr. O'Brien smeared in blood and Mrs. O'Brien burning, and Sheriff Davies standing by the guardrail, smiling.

YOU DESERVE TO SPEAK OUT
YOUR FAMILIES DESERVE BETTER
THAN THIS
WE'RE HERE TO HELP YOU DO THAT

I look up to Dallas, who gives me the shakiest, most unsure smile.

They're scared too. They're scared of what they're holding—the photo of the fire, the incriminating evidence, the target they're painting on their back. They're scared to be at the festival, in Twist Creek County at all. The cocky bullshit, the laughter and easy charm, it's all a cover. And I know because this is how they smiled at me the last time we saw each other *before*, in the hospital, tired and unsure how they'd survived and so, so terrified.

"Where'd you get that photo?" Cooper asks.

"Which one?" Dallas says, plastering over their fear as quick as they can. "The autopsy report? Steele's family got it to us, though we thought it'd be bad taste to print the crime scene photos. Guess Davies forgot he made that little note."

But Cooper don't take the bait. "You know what I'm talking about."

I cut in. I need Cooper to back off from Dallas right now. "I gave it to them. Okay? Stop. I gave it to them."

Cooper gets real quiet, real quick. All I can think is that this is a bad place to have an argument, when the air smells like hamburgers and the DJ has moved on to, what is this, "Party in the U.S.A."? A few yards away, Kara Simmonds and her brother are chatting with someone on the county commission, some old guy with old glasses. That should've been Dad, or Mrs. O'Brien. I wonder if they're talking zoning laws, or sponsorships for the next election all those years from now.

"Your dad know you got those photos?" Cooper asks me.

Dallas's face falls. "What?"

Cooper shrugs. "Miles stole those photos. His daddy probably don't know he's got them, let alone gave them to you. Kind of a shit move, you know, considering they got my dead mom in them."

Dallas freezes. Cooper needs to stop talking. I hold out a hand, try to push him back by the chest, muttering, "Not here, okay? Not here."

But Cooper barely budges. He points to Dallas over my shoulder. "You should've burned, not my mom. It should be you in those pictures. Not her."

Oh my *god*.

Dallas says, "Come on, man," and it tries to come out nonchalant but fails. The cocky facade shatters. "What?"

Cooper starts to laugh. Lady's ears pin back and a growl starts to rumble in her chest.

I say, "Cooper, shut up."

He grabs another flyer from Dallas's hands. "Fuck you." Immediately flings it in their face, crumples one up and pelts it at me. "*Fuck you.*" Someone in the crowd behind us yelps; people scatter like flies. They're staring. There's Kara Simmonds, and Claire Snyder, and Mrs. Amsler. "*FUCK YOU.*"

Lady lunges for him.

I catch her leash right before it slips off my wrist and haul her back, dragging her onto her back feet by the throat. She's barking loud enough my ears ring. Someone in the crowd screams. Cooper jolts back. She's heavy, and the rough fabric of the leash cuts my hand as I haul her away, shove my body into her shoulder to get her to *stop*. She plants all four feet on the ground and snarls.

"*You*—" I'm rasping in my throat and can't get a word out all over again. "Get away from us."

"Miles," Dallas says shakily.

"Get away from us," I say again, "or I'll let go of the dog."

Lady snaps her jaws, saliva gathering in the corner of her mouth, her barrel chest heaving with the effort. She's pushed herself in front of me, in front of Dallas, planting herself hard between us and Cooper. Daring him to get closer.

He stares at her.

And he nods.

"Okay," Cooper says. He's out of breath, almost exhilarated. "Okay. I see how it is. I get it. I'm the bad guy now, all right, okay." He's smiling again, and this time it reaches his eyes, but it's nasty. It ain't like any smile I've ever seen. "I'll do it myself."

And then he's gone. Storming off into the crowd.

Lady stops barking, coughing a few times to clear her throat. A bit of drool drips into the grass. Dallas makes a little noise, and I realize they're wiping their eyes, trying to pretend they ain't crying.

So many people are staring at us, and I hate it, but Dallas is more important. I stumble over to them. "You okay?"

"I'm fine." Dallas takes a deep breath. "I'm fine. I'm okay." They try to force a joke: "He really changed, huh?"

I manage, "I'm so sorry, I didn't think—"

Dallas shakes their head. "Don't. If he's unhinged, that's his own fault."

That don't make me feel better, though. Kids like Cooper don't snap like that. It's the world's fault. It's Davies's fault. And it's my fault too. I dragged him into this. I agreed to help him with something awful. I did this to him as much as everyone else.

Cooper was right about one thing: I didn't tell Dad about the pictures. I didn't tell Cooper. I gave Amber the photos to show to the whole county after I promised Davies he'd never see them again.

This is going to suck so bad.

"You sure you're okay?" I ask Dallas.

They hesitate, then say, "Does your dad really not know—"

But before they can finish, we're interrupted by the *tap tap tap* of someone testing a microphone. Dallas rubs their eyes to get a better look at who's standing on the stage.

It's Sheriff Davies. Noah stands perfectly beside him, a little toy soldier.

"Can I have everyone's attention, please?" Sheriff Davies says. His voice is slow and solemn. The field goes quiet in an instant. Even the DJ cuts the music. "Before we begin today's festivities, I have . . . an unfortunate announcement."

I know what he's going to say before the words leave his mouth.

"We have permission from the family of the deceased to inform you that, sadly, Paul Miller was found dead this morning."

CHAPTER
THiRTY-EiGHT

There's a long silence stretching out over the Twist Creek County Fourth of July Festival. Red flyers flutter in the hands of a good chunk of the crowd: people sitting on their blankets, paused in conversation with neighbors, halfway through an early dinner before it gets dark enough for fireworks. Noah's got a flyer too, folded carefully in his hand.

Twist Creek County knows Paul Miller is dead.

Sheriff Davies's hat is off, held to his chest like he's at a funeral. I wind the shoelace between my fingers and pull until it might snap.

"This has been a difficult summer," he says. "Edmund Ruckle, who still has not been found, and Paul Miller, God rest his soul, were both close friends of my son. The Ruckles and Millers are pillars of our community, and dearly important to many of us. We're saddened to pass along this news. If anyone has any information regarding either of these terrible situations, we urge you to come forward."

Of course there ain't a word about me. An Abernathy could never be a pillar of the community. The opinion piece I've preserved next to Lucille Abernathy's obituary called her *a damned nuisance.*

Dallas whispers, "Paul too? He was . . ."

They don't have to finish. I nod. Paul never caused too much trouble, not the way Eddie or Noah did, but he was always helping them. He was always doing the dirty work.

He wanted out, sure, but he still did it.

There's a thump on stage. Noah takes the mic from his father. He's casual, wearing a t-shirt from the 2015 Southern Memorial Hospital fundraiser like he ain't the nasty goddamn thing I know he is.

"Out of an abundance of respect," Noah says, "we will be delaying the annual Student of the Year and Twist Creek Princess awards. The prizes will be mailed to the recipients, and we will recognize the winners properly on Labor Day. However, there is still one award we'd like to give today, if you will allow us." He offers what's probably meant to be a soft, apologetic smile. "The Citizen of the Year Award. It's the least we can do to raise awareness and offer our support in a time that's been so hard for many of us."

What is he on about? The Citizen of the Year Award is usually for, like, the church janitor or a teacher. Not that they don't deserve it, because they do, but. Something's off.

Noah takes an envelope from his pocket. "In recognition of his bravery and strength, we recognize Miles Abernathy, a rising senior at Twist Creek County High and a member of the transgender community, who survived a terrible hate crime earlier this summer. Miles, if you could come up on stage, please?"

Oh.

No.

Shit, shit, shit. No. Fuck. *Fuck.*

Dallas turns to me, throat bobbing. I catch sight of my family—Mom, Dad, Mamaw, Papaw, Uncle Rodney, Aunt Jill—sitting with the picnic blankets a few hundred feet from the stage. Dad looks like he's going to be sick. Mom's gone pale. Everyone else is confused. Like they can't make heads or tails of why Noah Davies would say such a thing when there sure as hell ain't anyone named Miles in this family.

Thing is, I can't make heads or tails of it neither. That's my *name.* Coming out was supposed to be handled by my family, by me, by the people I care about. And this son of a bitch sneaks behind my back, finds out from god knows where, and takes it from me? This ain't how I wanted to do it. How does he even *know*?

And if I don't go up there, I make it clear to all of Twist Creek County that something's wrong. Too much attention. Too many unwanted questions. So I have to.

Good thing I was raised to grit my teeth.

I give Dallas the stack of flyers. "Be right back."

"Miles," Dallas starts, but I'm already walking towards the stage, wrapping the leash around my hand a few times so Lady don't slip through my fingers again. The folks around us are confused at first, but they catch on. People I grew up with stare at me and realize what's happening. Coworkers, classmates, teachers, everyone.

It'd be a walk of shame if I was ashamed of it. Instead, I'm pissed as hell.

When I reach the steps, Noah is smiling, or showing me his teeth. He claps my shoulder, walks me up, presses the envelope into my hand. He's crumpled the flyer. Behind him, his father watches. He's too close. I don't like it.

"You and O'Brien looked good together," Noah says as he guides me across the stage. "Shame what happened." He saw the fight, then—but who didn't? Too much is happening at once. My head is fuzzy. "And a shame about what's going on at that restaurant too. Where'd they get those pictures?"

"Go fuck yourself."

"Careful, Abernathy."

And then I'm in front of the microphone, and Noah is shaking my hand, and Sheriff Davies is telling me how glad he is that I'm healing okay. Lady pants uncomfortably, standing her ground between me and them.

"We're honored to have you up here with us today," Noah says to me, enunciating perfectly for the crowd to hear. "After everything you've been through, we wanted to give you a chance to speak your truth. You're a, uh, *beacon of resilience* for the transgender community, as it were."

He's done his research, then. Pretending he's an ally when he did this just to out me. In the crowd, Mom covers her mouth with her hand. People are moving their seats away from my family.

Noah raises an expectant eyebrow and gestures for me to speak. I can't feel my fingers.

Talk, Miles. Bark like a dog.

"I—" I start shakily. "I don't like the word *resilient*." The echo of my voice from the speaker confuses me. It's higher than it should be, different than it is in my head. "I guess it implies surviving something terrible is a, a moral issue. A reward for having a lot of willpower or inner strength or whatever. When it ain't. It's luck."

Being up here, I have a chance to do something, *say* something where all of Twist Creek County will hear it. But what? Do I tell all of Twist Creek County what Noah and Paul and Eddie did to me? Do I say I gave Cooper the gun that killed Paul, that Eddie's body is at the bottom of the sub-shaft in the mine? If I did, then at least there'd be no more lying. No more games. Just truth and the consequences of it. I could make sense of that.

"No need to be humble," Noah says, giving my shoulder a friendly shake. My teeth rattle. "We're proud of you, Miles. And we're all praying that the person who did this is caught and brought to justice. None of us are safe until all of us are safe. Ain't that right?"

There's an awkward smattering of applause as people in the crowd realize they're probably supposed to clap. I see more flyers now. Amber and Michael are carefully canvassing the crowd, handing them out, whispering.

"Is there anything else you'd like to say?" Noah asks.

"No," I say. "Thank you."

I leave the stage as fast as I can. Gasping for air, trying to calm my heartbeat. Lady whines, and my hands shake so badly as I rip open the envelope that I nearly tear what's inside, nearly drop it into the dirt. It's the typical cash for the award. A check for three hundred dollars, provided so kindly by the Rotary Club as it is every year. Sure, okay, because three hundred dollars is gonna put a dent in the astronomical amount we owe to Southern Memorial.

There's something else.

A note.

WE KNOW RUCKLE'S DEAD TOO.

It takes everything I have not to scream.

CHAPTER
THiRTY-NiNE

i grab Dallas in the crowd as they come to me. They open their
mouth to say something but I interrupt them. They *cannot be
here.* "Go home," I say. "I'm not kidding. Go home right now."

And then I find my parents. As the music starts back up
and people go back to getting food and chatting and waiting
for fireworks—this time quieter, an air of anxiety, looking at
the flyers in their hands—my family implodes. Dad is saying,
"That wasn't okay. They can't do that." I think Papaw is going
to kill someone again; he's staring at the stage, unblinking,
hand curling and uncurling. Mamaw says, "Why did they
call you Miles? What's going on?" Mom says, gathering me
up against her chest, "We're going home. Come on. Let's go."

◆

Dad and Uncle Rodney argue until Dad kicks him out of
the house. Uncle Rodney drags Aunt Jill with him, saying

over his shoulder at us, "We should've left years ago. I swear to god, I told you, you asked for this."

We asked for this by staying? By standing our ground? At what point did our simple refusal to leave Twist Creek County became an act of aggression in and of itself? At what point did it become something cruel to the next generation, to make them go through this?

But it shouldn't work like that. It's not our fault people want to hurt us. Even when we hurt them back, we're doing it because we have to. I have to tell myself that, otherwise the sound of dishes in the sink or a fork against a plate will make me think about Paul's tooth hitting the floor for the rest of my life.

Mom leans against the counter, pulling her hair strand by strand out of its bun.

I'm on the floor with Lady.

"Why would they say those things about you?" Mamaw is saying. Papaw stares out the window. "What do they mean, transgender? Is that like transsexual? Them cross-dressers?" She says every single one of those words like it's a language she don't speak.

I turn Lady's collar round and round her neck. She puts up with it.

I whisper, "This ain't how I wanted to tell y'all I'm a boy."

Boy is such a small word. Makes me sound like a little kid. But *guy* is too informal, and *man* makes me sound too grown and I'm not there yet, of course I'm not.

Mamaw blinks as if I told her the sky is green.

I have to admit, by tactical standards, this was a genius move on Noah's part. With all the eyes on me after the attack, he had to be careful with how he got back at me—and there's no better way than throwing a grenade into someone's house. If you out someone, there's a good bet that the family will devour itself, taking away every support system and leaving the victim exposed.

I'm a second away from begging my parents. *Don't let Noah be right.* I know my family, I love my family, they're good people, but *don't let his bullshit work, please.*

"I know you've never been real girly," Mamaw says, as if trying to rationalize a thing as irrational as gender, "but Sadie, I really don't—"

"His name is Miles," Mom says. It's her nurse voice; kind but no-nonsense, no room for argument because she knows best.

"Mom," I whisper.

"He told us a few weeks ago," she continues. "We thought it'd be best for him to tell everyone on his own time, but apparently that's not an option anymore."

"They outed him," Dad says, voice small. "Do you know what happens when you out someone? Sometimes their parents abandon them."

"Probably what they were banking on," Papaw says gruffly.

Nobody fights him on that, but it is what makes it click for Mamaw. This was a violation. This was something taken from me. She don't need to get it; she needs to be kind. She gets down on the floor to wrap her arms around me and hugs me tight. She smells like old perfume.

"It's okay, baby," she says, and I lean my head against her frail shoulder and breathe.

Noah had it wrong. We're a better family than he thinks we are.

But it just means he's going to find another way to hurt us.

Everyone is talking again. Papaw says he'll get his shotgun out of the Jeep, pulling a cigarette from his shirt pocket. Mom is telling him not to but Dad considers it. I should feel better, right? Now that it's out? Now that everyone knows I'm trans? I don't know. I'm tired. They found Paul's body, they know Eddie's dead, the Fosters have a target on their backs, Cooper's gone off the deep end—

Mom crouches in front of me. I sit up, pulling away from Mamaw who is still smoothing out a bit of the awkward stubble on my scalp.

"What all did they give you in that envelope?" Mom asks.

"Three hundred bucks." I laugh coldly. "For medical bills."

She snorts. "We don't accept blood money in this house."

"Don't be precious, Linda," Mamaw chides. "You can default on medical debt all you want, but you always gotta keep them lights on."

The two of them start to chatter, Mamaw insisting that you can't be too proud to take money from a bastard, but Dad catches my attention and nods me out to the porch. I get up carefully, click for Lady to follow, and kiss Mamaw on the forehead before stepping outside.

It's starting to get dark. From the porch, we can kind of see the light from the festival grounds, the world continuing without us. I guess that's how it works. There's a warm breeze and Lady stands at the end of the rickety wood, sniffing the air.

I figure I'll be the one to break the ice. "I think Cooper and me broke up."

Dad says, "Was it because of—"

"Gender stuff? No." I shrug. "He's just not doing good. And also Lady almost bit him."

Dad glances down at Lady. She's a smart-as-hell dog, and I can almost see Dad doing the math, trusting the mutt's instincts, what that says about Cooper or me or both of us.

"Poor kid," Dad says. "He's going through a lot."

"I know."

"Can I ask a question?"

"Depends on what."

Dad laughs a little. "Nothing about that. Lord knows I don't need the details. I remember being sixteen."

I groan. Not that Cooper and I ever did anything like that; couldn't bring ourselves to, given everything. Still, I say, "Eww," because going with the joke is a form of bonding and Dad's good with that. Dad flashes a smile and hunkers down on the porch steps with Lady, gestures me down with him. Her nose twitches.

Dad takes a *F*CK THE FOURTH* flyer out of his pocket.

I know where this is going.

He turns it over to the side crammed full of evidence. Looks it up and down, like he's somewhere between proud and terrified.

"Where'd you get the photo?" he asks.

Ain't nothing to do but tell the truth. "Found the key to the lockbox." He sighs. "You left it out on your desk. C'mon, man, I've been digging up our medical bills and reading our insurance policies for fun since middle school. You really thought I wasn't going to stumble across those eventually?"

"You been reading our insurance policies?"

"There are some interesting clauses. You know we're insured if the water comes from above, but not if it comes from below? *Below* is flood insurance, which is different."

Dad shakes his head. "Not the point." I can't help but snort. He turns the flyer over one more time, and then back again. "And you gave it to Amber and Michael?"

"Thought it was the right thing to do."

"Should've told me."

"I know. Sorry."

He leans back a little bit, folding the flyer over and over in his hands. He does stuff like that—fidgets, bounces his leg, taps over and over. "It's getting bad again, ain't it?"

"Yeah."

"Probably just gonna keep getting worse."

I should tell him everything, but I stop myself. For some reason, I'm convinced I can spare them the worst of the horrors if I keep my mouth shut. I don't want them to know what we did to Eddie, what we did to Paul. I can't handle them thinking of me any different.

Instead, I say, "Don't it always?"

"I think," he says, "your mom and I should drop by this event of theirs tomorrow. See if we can't chat with the Fosters, see what all we can do about this whole Davies situation." He nudges me. "If you want to come."

I smile. "Hell yeah, I do."

CHAPTER FORTY

Twenty-four hours after the festival—the night of Fuck the Fourth—I try to dress for the occasion: all black, one of Dad's caps, work boots only a little too big for me. I even reach back between the bookcase and the wall to dig out my handmade Redneck Revolt tee with the sleeves cut off. And then the bandana, tied tight around my wrist.

"I'm trying," I tell Saint, alone in my room, talking to the empty air. "We'll figure it out."

Mom and Dad ain't doing nothing fancy, but that's fine. They've never been the type. I tell Lady to keep an eye on the house while we're gone.

"Remind me," Mom says as we drive. It's getting dark and the moon is already out. It's a beautiful evening. "Dallas is a, uh, *they*?"

"Uses they/them pronouns," I say, leaning up to the front seat, "yeah."

"That's their book," Dad practices. "That book belongs to them."

I assure my parents, "You'll get there."

The flyers must have worked, because parking at the Red Holler is crammed full, spilling over into the church lot. String lights are hung up around the door, and I can hear the distant hum of noise, of some kind of loud music. Dad gets out of the car and leans on his cane; Mom only agreed to come if he used it for the evening.

"Y'all good?" I ask them. I'm a few paces ahead, almost buzzing out of my skin. I've never been to anything like this before. I know I said to Dallas that big gatherings ain't my scene, and that's true, but my excitement—or nervousness, they're the same to me—for something like *this* overrides my hatred of social interaction.

Mom clicks her tongue. "Easy, easy. Give us a second."

And when we open the door . . .

There's *so* many people, and I recognize everyone. My middle school PE teacher. Some of Mom's coworkers from the nursing home. The mailman, truck drivers, cashiers from the Dollar General. The lights are dim and the band on the janky stage sets up, running through a riff to test the sound system. The vibe is what I imagine a basement show is like: chairs and tables spread out scattershot, people standing by the stage to chat, a few old couches pressed up against the outer walls.

Next to the kitchen door, Dallas collects drink tickets while Amber restocks flyers at the counter and Michael pours liquor, hands out beer, slides a shot across the counter.

They're the only ones working. Dallas said the staff got the day off today, full pay.

As soon as my parents are in, I grab Mom's hand and start to pull. I gotta raise my voice to be heard over the noise. "Come on, they're over here."

Dallas is the first one to spot me. They're jittery, packed full of nervous energy they don't know what to do with. It's still weird to see them some kind of upset—when we were little, it felt like nothing could scare them, let alone make them cry—but yeah, I guess trauma will do that to a person. I'm proud of them for being here.

"Evening, Mr. and Mrs. Abernathy," they say. "Here for a drink?"

Michael snorts. "Abernathys don't drink nothing but moonshine, and we ain't got that in today." He flashes us a smile. "What can we do for y'all?"

"I thought we could talk," Mom says. "As long as you aren't too busy."

"We can manage," Michael says. "Dallas, git, go hang out."

Dallas and I glance at each other, hesitating. It's jarring to be dismissed, being kept out of adults' business—but if we're gonna be honest, we both need it. They look over-whelmed as hell. "Take a break," I tell them, and they come out from behind the counter to wrap me in a hug before leading me towards the couches along the back.

"That was so bad yesterday," they say, immediately falling into a ramble, collecting bottles from a FREE WATER cooler as they pass by it. Their pins today: *Defund*

Police, *Fund Abortions*, and *Come Back with a Warrant*. "Why would Noah say that? How did he know that? Did someone tell him? And then what happened with Cooper? Oh my god, I'm so sorry."

"I'm fine," I say, which is all I can really say since there's nothing we can do about the situation now. "Are *you* okay?"

"Yeah. It's just." They start a few more sentences and don't finish any of them. "Ugh."

We settle ourselves on an open couch with broken springs and saggy cushions. From here, I can see the messy underbelly of a punk show: all the wires and the edge of the stage, the back of the drummer's setup and the bassist's shoes scuffing on the cheap carpet. Cheap standing fans blow at their backs and flutter the banners. Dallas slings an arm around my shoulders, easy as anything, like we ain't spent half a decade missing each other.

Around us, people talk. They argue over the flyers. "If you ask me, this is a reach," they say about Deputy Steele's autopsy report, but then, "You heard what happened to the Snyders, right? Then that poor girl Nancy and her dog. And those Abernathys . . . ," "Oh, don't talk about the Abernathys, don't start."

"It'll be years before we can vote him out," Dallas says. "If the vote even works."

I shrug. "I think we're past voting at this point."

Then the band on stage whistles, taps the microphone, starts to get everyone's attention. The lead singer grins, and says, "Evening, folks." The words BLACK BLOC hang from a banner behind them in janky, hand-painted letters. "Thank you for inviting us down. Let me tell you, it's an honor to play somewhere like this. Home of the Twist Creek Calamity? Y'all, we love you."

The band is all torn-up jeans and camo jackets, like a younger version of Papaw's hunting buddies. The guitarist's got THIS MACHINE KILLS FASCISTS written on the body of the instrument, right next to the strings, and I can smell the beer and work dirt from here.

"And I hope," the lead says, "y'all are as sick of this shit as I am. This country and all the fuckers that run it. What's in it for us? We work and die for rich pigs, and for what? Because that's what my family did. My daddy got black lung in the mines, and his daddy, and his daddy before him. And what did we get? Three dead men and *nothing*."

It surprises me how many people roar in response to that. How many people here lost family members to jobs that killed their workers or beat their grandparents down to dust.

The music, when they play, is almost country, almost punk, somewhere in the middle—angry and loud, acoustic guitars and hard drums. I'm rocking back and forth a little bit, because it's what my body wants to do. Dallas cracks open a water bottle and drains half of it in one go. At the back of the room, our grown-ups are chatting in the door to the kitchen; arms are folded, expressions are grim. Makes me feel like a kid again.

Dallas and I talk.

✦

"Sometimes I wonder if I should go back to using he/him pronouns," Dallas says. "You can still be nonbinary if you use binary pronouns. Or maybe he/they."

"Do you want to?" I ask.

"I mean," Dallas says, "of course not. If anything, if you made me pick a binary pronoun, I'd probably go with she/her. But, like, I don't want to go on estrogen or anything. And, I don't know, you spend enough time on the internet, you start to think that maybe if I want to look like this, I need to suck it up and let people call me a man."

"Fuck that," I say. "You're gonna listen to people on Twitter?"

Dallas laughs. "I walked into the middle of a class war, and I'm worrying about validity politics."

✦

"Amber calling me autistic was life-changing, sure," I say, "but I don't want to call myself that." Dallas glances over at me. "And not because I don't want to be autistic, or I don't want people to know I am, if I am. But I need a diagnosis. Aren't they stupid expensive?"

"You don't need a diagnosis," Dallas says.

"What?"

"If you think you are," Dallas says, "you probably are."

That's the logic that got me to accept I'm trans. I press the heels of my hands into my eyes.

Dallas explains, "That's what Amber tells me. She didn't get a diagnosis until, like, last January, but she's known she is for years. Because where are you supposed to get a psychiatrist around here? Where are you supposed to get that kind of money? And none of the doctors know how to diagnose anybody who ain't, like, a five-year-old boy, and if you don't want it on your medical record . . ."

"But I feel bad," I admit.

"You're in the middle of a class war," Dallas repeats, "and you're worrying about validity politics!"

"Fine," I say. "I'm autistic. Fine. Fine."

The lead singer dissolves into coughing laughter, and while it's part of the song, it sounds so real—the anger, the rage, the urge to burn whatever we can get our hands on. I wonder if Saint is in the crowd now, if he's seeing this the same way I am. He'd love something like this. The drummer has a trans flag patch on her jacket and her blonde hair is held back with a clip, her eyeshadow the color of blood.

✦

"Michael gets real uncomfortable when I call myself disfigured," Dallas says.

"What? Why?"

"Dunno. When he's talking about me, he uses all the soft words, the dance-around-it stuff. *Burn survivor, facial difference*, whatever." Dallas sniffs. "Like, I kind of get it. He don't get to call me a faggot because I call myself that.

But it's kind of like the word *fat*, right? *Disfigured* is—that's what I want him to call me. It's a loaded word, sure, but it's true."

"This is a little out of my wheelhouse," I admit.

"Technically," they say, grabbing the side of my head in their big hand, their thumb on the pitted skin running from my scalp to my eye, "you get to have an opinion on that now."

"It's just a few scars," I protest, ignoring the fact that my left eye is lopsided now, my nose will always be a little crooked, my teeth always broken, my ribs always full of metal. My cheeks and forehead will always, always remind me of what happened that night.

"A few scars right on your noggin that'll get you looked at funny for the rest of your life," Dallas says. "You count, man. You're in the club."

✦

"And the more I think about it" —I'm rambling now—"I don't know how much of Cooper and I was because . . . I *wanted* to have a crush on him. Because it felt like it was supposed to happen and I was following a script or something." I scrub my face. "And sure, I didn't hate it, but—I don't know. It was only the physical stuff that I was cool with, if that makes sense? I know that's weird. He said he was my boyfriend once and I almost lost it, and . . ."

I stare at my water bottle as my words trail off.

"Wait," I say, grabbing for my phone, "hold on."

Dallas says, "If you're looking up what I think you are—"

Google search: "aromantic spectrum"

Results: Oh, you can probably guess by this point.

I show my phone screen to Dallas, and they immediately burst into giggles, wiping tears from their eyes. I throw a pillow at them.

"Sorry!" they gasp, even though they're still laughing. "This is a big moment for you!"

But I'm laughing too and reading through the massive list of flags and sub-identities under the wiki page, and Dallas helps me sort through them all—not that one, not that one either, maybe that one? I don't have enough experience to actually *know*, but I bookmark the page so I can come back to it one day and really figure it out. It's nice to have a place to start. An explanation, or something almost like it.

As the second song fades out and the lead singer of Black Bloc starts to talk again, I lean against Dallas, settling my head into the crook of their arm. We watch as Claire Synder gets up on stage. She talks about her daddy bleeding in the back of the patrol car, the way he can't close his mouth right no more, the fear that's caused her family to start planning their move out to Keyser. Deputy Steele's momma, a grey-haired mamaw in a black tee, says her son was so, so scared in the days leading up to his death, and now she knows that good cops either quit or die.

And there's Saint in the dark corner by the couch. Arms crossed. Watching like he's been waiting a century for this.

I wonder if this is how the union started. Workers huddling around drinks and food, snarling about how they'd been wronged, how their families had been hurt, how the world could be better. Knowing they'd be smoked out and shot if they did something, but knowing just as well that they couldn't sit and do nothing. They couldn't make a difference alone, but they could damn well do it together. Even if it got hard. Even if it got violent.

Across the Red Holler, Saint catches my eye and gives an approving nod.

Maybe, when he gave me the railroad spike, he wasn't telling me to get revenge? He wasn't telling Cooper and I to do what we did. He never meant it like that, because why would he? America loves a lone wolf, but lord, it never works, does it? *This* is what he wanted. Community. Collective strength. The Fosters had the right idea from the start. Black Bloc circles around Steele's momma, holds Claire's hand, gestures the crowd closer.

I stand, grab Dallas's hand, and pull them onto their feet. "I'm gonna get up there. Come with me. Come on."

Dallas hesitates.

"I don't know," they whisper. Their free hand skims the side of their face that has—what's the right word? *Melted*, I guess? "Man, I'm gonna be honest, I just stopped hating myself over all this. I can't . . ."

There are a few ways a conversation could go. If this were a movie, some inspirational moment, I could tell them to put their nerves aside, we've got bigger things to tackle. Their injuries *mean* something. They're living proof of what a monster Davies is. Get up there and drive home the point: Look what this man did to a child, look what he did.

But this ain't no movie, and their burns ain't some kind of political statement if Dallas says they ain't. Right now, they're just scars.

I squeeze their hand and let go.

The drummer, the trans girl with the bloodred eyeshadow, sees me coming to the stage and reaches down to help me up. The stage ain't that much taller, not really, but it still gives me a vantage point of the Red Holler, so that I can see every soul in the building—Mom and Dad, Michael and Amber, everyone I've grown up with and lived with all my life. It's warm up here and we're surrounded by banners: strung along the instruments, between the rafters, red and white and black. Hissing cats. Hands holding hammers and wrenches. Burning cars and red bandanas.

COPS AREN'T SUPPOSED TO KILL GUILTY PEOPLE EITHER

WE DO NOT DREAM OF LABOR

HERE PIGGIE PIGGIE

YOUR SENATOR IS A LITTLE BITCH

The lead singer says, "Jesus, kid, you're busted. What happened to you?"

He holds the microphone to me.

And I laugh. I can't help it. It comes out before I can stop it, and I must sound hysterical, but at this point, dear god, can you blame me?

"The sheriff's kid!" I pull up my shirt to show the scar from my surgery drawn across my ribs, still a nasty color even if it's almost done healing, a sharp puckered line. And then there's my broken face. My crooked fingers. The scar ripping across my scalp and hairline. "Noah Davies tried to *kill me* because my dad wanted to run for office, because we wanted to make things *better* round here, and the sheriff of Twist Creek County made sure I stayed *quiet*."

And like that, it's gone. The lie is shattered. The shared reality of my amnesia, that I couldn't quite remember my attackers' faces, is in pieces.

It's so good to finally say it.

The crowd reacts like a den of rabid animals. It's been building, I think, between Claire and Mamaw Steele, the cruelty that Davies has enacted on this town. The awful things they've been living through. The fear. The surveillance. Because, fuck, this ain't freedom.

I look to my parents at the back of the Red Holler, who are watching in . . . I don't know. I don't know what their expression is. Hurt. Anger. Pain. Not at me, but for me. Because I didn't tell them everything, because I couldn't risk it. And sure, we may not have Twist Creek County, but we have the Red Holler, and ain't that enough? Whatever that means?

Ain't this what Saint Abernathy was trying to do?

It's funny, then.

That I'm the one who sees Sheriff Davies by the door.

CHAPTER
FORTY-ONE

He's right inside the Red Holler, half-illuminated by the string lights, cast in harsh enough shadow that it takes me a moment to recognize him. But Christ, there he is. Sheriff Davies holding a red flyer, watching the crowd like a dad waiting for his misbehaving kids to realize they've been caught.

The Sheriff of Twist Creek County made sure I stayed quiet.

There's no way he didn't hear that. All of it.

I take a step back. The heel of my slightly-too-big boot catches on a wire and I stumble. The drummer catches me, her eyeliner smeared a little with sweat.

"Shit," she says, "you all right?"

But I don't have to say a damn word. In that moment, it's like everyone in the Red Holler knows something's happened; the air's gone rotten. The sound of the crowd dies like a deer dropped by a hunting rifle.

Every head turns.

And Sheriff Davies has the gall to be *surprised* that we've noticed him.

"Hey now," he says, nonchalant as all get out. "No need to stop on my account."

A smile creeps up his face. It ain't right. Unnatural. And I hate that it reminds me of myself, smiling because I know I have to, smiling because I'm using it to communicate. Does it look like that on my face? I hope it don't.

"Honestly," Sheriff Davies continues, "I think all this is fascinating. Heard about it on the news, actually. Antifa, right? Those nasty little rats?" He holds up the flyer. The one with all the evidence collected against him, the photo of him standing over the fire. "Shitty little liars, the lot of you. Or do you actually believe all this? Really?"

And there's that collective agreement again. The false idea of the world we have to stick to in the name of safety. If everyone accepts that the Fosters and the Abernathys are liars, then everyone else can go on living their lives. Some people are considering it. Folks glance between each other, weighing the options. Short-term safety for themselves and their families means a lot around here. Sometimes it's all you can ask for.

Two people, a young couple—I think they graduated from Twist Creek High a few years ago—get up from their table in the corner and leave. Their drinks sit half-empty by the window. The bell above the door rings when they leave. It echoes.

That's the moment a hand touches mine from the side of the stage. I flinch but it's just Mom. Oh thank god,

Mom. She's gesturing me down, holding Dallas by the sleeve of their shirt. I glance out over the crowd again, try to find Dad, Amber, Michael, but the faces are blurring together.

"Come on, baby," Mom says. "Come on, we need to go."

My voice comes out in a whimper. "Where's Dad?"

"By the kitchen, come on, come on."

"Those are some reasonable folk," Sheriff Davies calls, gesturing the way the young couple had gone. "Don't like mess any more than I do. I respect that."

Wait. There's Amber. She's going up to Sheriff Davies with a rag to wipe off her hands, but more likely giving herself something to fiddle with. With the beaded glasses chain, bright pink makeup, and lavender nails, she should be completely nonthreatening. By the kitchen door at the back of the room, Michael holds a broom next to Dad like he might use it in self-defense, gesturing Mom to him.

"Can we help you with something, officer?" Amber says.

"Actually," Davies says, "I think you can. You the one who made these flyers?"

Amber's face remains perfectly placid. "I sure am. Was there anything you'd like to add? Researching this was difficult."

I grab Mom's hand and slide off the stage, the drummer helping me down. Mom crushes me to her side, kisses my temple, starts to drag Dallas and me through the crowd.

"Awful gutsy," Sheriff Davies says. "What's that say on your shirt? *All Cops Are Bastards*?" It's baby pink, decorated with angelic cats and daisies; I hadn't noticed the words until he said them out loud. "Where's your sense of respect, Mrs. Foster?"

Amber don't back down. "Respect is earned, not given, officer."

Now, it's important to note that, at one of the tables next to Amber, there's a big ol' construction worker. That's Terry. I don't know much about Terry, besides him being one of the few people who ever comes by Uncle Rodney's garage even though he knows damn well who we are. He ain't said much this whole time; just watched all us on stage and nursed a half-empty glass of water, because he quit drinking last year. Good for him.

And sure, I don't know what Sheriff Davies expected with all this. Maybe he expected people to flinch from him. To shuffle out, like we sometimes do. Trying to keep our families safe, backing away from the mess that's about to happen.

"I think," Sheriff Davies says, "you should tell all the folks in your establishment the party's over."

Amber says, "No. It runs until ten. Says so on the flyer."

Sheriff Davies laughs. "You're funny." His voice raises to a snap. "Everyone, *out*."

Nobody moves. Except Mom, bringing us to the kitchen door. As soon as I get close enough, Dad grabs me to his side. Michael puts a hand on Dallas's shoulder, breathes in, tries to get them to do to the same because they ain't breathing at all. As soon as Michael touches them, the block dislodges, and they're gulping for oxygen like they've been held underwater.

Davies says, "This gathering is disrupting the peace. You have five minutes to leave."

Amber says, "We have the proper permits for an entertainment venue. Would you like to see them? They're right in the office, I can grab them for you."

"Fuck your permits." His voice raises to a roar. *"OUT!"*

When nobody moves, I'm proud. I'm *proud*. It's a collective stance. What right does he have to tell us what to do? The way it works, in a town like this, and in the most basic form when it comes to government, is that we decide to give authority to someone because it helps us. We've built up a social contract around it—we give them power because we get something in return, be it safety or what have you.

But if it ain't worth it, we can revoke that authority. We don't got to listen to this son of a bitch.

Terry takes one last drink of his water and sighs into the rim of his glass.

Then he hands the glass to Amber.

"What's the best way out of here?" Mom is asking Michael.

"Through the kitchen," Michael says. "Into the alley."

Amber throws the water in Sheriff Davies's face.

A gunshot goes off.

The Red Holler erupts—and Mom shoves Dallas and I through the swinging doors into the kitchen, screams, *"Run!"* and slams the doors shut, barring them with Michael's broom with a finality that feels a hell of a lot like a grave.

CHAPTER
FORTY-TWO

From behind the door, it sounds like a riot. But muffled. If we're gonna stick with the metaphor, sure, grave dirt will do that.

CHAPTER
FORTY-THREE

Ain't no way in hell we're running. My parents are in there. The Fosters are in there. But the door to the front of the restaurant won't budge—Dallas rams themself against it but the broom handle holds fast, and they only manage to hurt themself. I have to stop them because they probably won't stop unless I make them. I grab their arms to hold them still.

"Hey," I say. "Hey hey hey."

They gasp for air, wild-eyed.

Through the doors, we can hear everything. Screaming. Something shattering. The drum of feet and, I don't know, the sounds of—a stampede? What's happening in there?

"Hey," I say again. "Breathe."

They do.

It's dark in the kitchen. There's only a single emergency light flickering above the office door, and even that thing's about to die. It's all turned-off stovetops, the packed-up prep counter, the dish pit unnervingly empty, and looming shelves packed with supplies. Behind me, there's the door to the alley, where Dallas and I met for the first time. The door to outside. To safety.

Dallas says, "Did he shoot Amber?" Their voice cracks, then shatters. "Did you see? Is she okay?"

"She's fine," I say, even though I've got no idea if I'm lying. It comes out on instinct, the first thing I can think of to get Dallas to calm down. But also, logically, of course Sheriff Davies wouldn't shoot Amber in front of everybody. That ain't his style. It was probably—probably a warning shot. Into the ceiling. Or something like that. "He didn't get her. She's fine. She's okay."

"Shit." They reach up to pull on their hair. "Okay."

That heroic instinct, *Stand your ground, don't run*, crumbles in the face of a locked door and Dallas's panic. What would we even do that wouldn't make things worse than they already are? I grab Dallas's hand, start to lead them to the back door. "We'll go to your house," I'm saying, talking to keep them with me. "Everyone can find us there. We can lock the doors, keep an eye on things, we'll be okay. Sound good?"

I'm good at keeping it together when other people need me to. Like when Dad got hurt. I kept it together as long as Mom and Dad needed me to. I can collapse and scream or go silent or whatever *after* it's over, when people ain't relying on me no more. I can do that. I'm good at that. Just don't think about the fact that Dad can't move quick anymore, that Davies might consider Mom a perfect target. My parents are tougher than Davies. They'll be fine.

"Okay," Dallas says. I hear the howl of a police siren—shit, Davies must have called the other officers. The ones he ain't killed, at least. "Okay."

Dallas is looking at me like *I'm* the one who knows what to do. Like I'm the grown-up here.

Am I? I thought I was. I thought when we threw Eddie down the mine shaft, or left Paul there to bleed out, we'd done something to make us distinctly *adult*. We'd seen death. We'd caused it. If that didn't make us grown, what did?

And then someone says, "Announcing your next move ain't a good idea. Someone might be listening."

Standing in the doorway of the dry storage where the Red Holler stores its liquor, Noah Davies—splattered in blood—clicks a lighter to spark the fabric end of a Molotov cocktail, a dish rag stuffed into a bottle of Absolut.

CHAPTER
FORTY-FOUR

The dish rag burns beautifully, lighting up Noah's face the same way the stage illuminated his father. This picture-perfect motherfucker, Sears catalog son of a bitch. Jaw chiseled, hair swooped back, teeth too perfect for how much dip he goes through.

The blood is the only thing that makes him even halfway real: up to the elbows, dried and flaking off at the joints. Some of it is smeared across his face and hair, the way it'd be if he'd forgotten the mess and tried to wipe sweat from his forehead. He's leaving fingerprints across the Absolut bottle, bits of red on the cloth where he'd stuffed it into the bottle's neck.

The fire crackles. Dallas squeezes my hand so hard it hurts.

What was it like, to burn alive? After Dallas ended up in the hospital, I became obsessed with researching it. I scoured interviews with survivors, Reddit threads, anything *human* and not the stiff, unapproachable WebMD descriptions of one of the most horrible things a person can experience. What always stood out most to me was how, after the fire is put out, it's not all that unusual to succumb to hypothermia. How you get cold because you no longer have skin to keep you warm, and all your insides are open to the outside.

I reach over and put my other hand on top of theirs, trying to pretend I'm not about to lose it too. And I know it's nothing—in the grand scheme of things, it is truly nothing, maybe even childish—but the only thing I can think of, seeing all that blood, is the video of Nancy Adams's dog.

If Noah Davies killed my goddamn dog, gutted her because she had the misfortune to be *mine*—

I say, "What did you do."

Noah inspects the fire, and for a second I think he's ignoring us entirely. But then he says, "What do you mean, *what did I do*? I defended myself." He shrugs. "Self-defense is legal, Abernathy. Especially against a murderer. Which makes Foster here an accomplice."

Dallas says, "What?"

"Oh, she didn't tell you?" Noah says. "Abernathy and O'Brien killed Eddie. And Paul. Both of 'em. Threw Ruckle in the mine and shot Miller in the face." His eyes flick to Dallas's. Dallas flinches. "Even commies know that's a bad idea."

"Miles," Dallas says, "what is he talking about?"

I don't take the bait. "Whose blood is that."

Noah hums. He's done explaining himself. Instead, he raises the Molotov cocktail, which has burned down closer to the neck, to the anarcho-communist flag hanging on the kitchen wall behind him. It catches hungrily. The kitchen immediately smells like burning plastic, and flames streak towards the ceiling.

Noah says, "Why would I ruin the surprise?"

And he throws the bottle.

We run.

CHAPTER
FORTY-FIVE

We erupt into the alleyway. The warm night air tastes bitter. Lights in every building are starting to come on, *click click click*, around us. Police sirens wail. I pull Dallas away from the restaurant, towards the church parking lot. People scramble out of the Red Holler, filling the street and sidewalk, fleeing to their cars to get the hell out. I see Mamaw Steele clutching Claire Snyder on the sidewalk, trying to find the girl's momma. A cop car's parked in the middle of the road, lights turning everything cold blue and bloodred.

"Fuck," Dallas is whispering, "fuck, fuck." They pull their hand out of mine and stop in the mouth of the alleyway, staring at me. "Fuck, man."

"What are you—we need to *go*."

Dallas looks around them, at the mess, at the lights, at the people. The smell of smoke is getting thicker and their eyes are blown.

I need to get them away from the fire.

"Was Noah lying?" Dallas says.

Of course he was lying, I want to say, not because it's true but because it'll get Dallas to move. *Of course he was.* But—I remember the weight of Eddie's head lolling against my chest as I dragged him into the dumpster corral, the smell of Paul's blood and bile. I remember Eddie hitting the bottom of the sub-shaft and leaving Paul on the processing floor.

None of that made us grown, did it? It made us kids that did awful things.

"I—" I start.

But my words catch, because I see them in the crowd: Mom and Dad. Michael and Amber. Amber is hunched over, clutching a rag to her shoulder, Michael and Dad keeping her upright.

Mom sees us too and breaks into a sprint, grabbing us both in a hug. She's crying.

"Are you okay?" she says. She inspects Dallas's face and then mine, checking that we're still breathing even as we're standing in front of her. "Oh god."

I should say it. It ain't the time, not here, not now, but the urge comes up like vomit, to spill everything. *Fix this,* I'd beg my parents, *please fix this. I'm a little kid and I don't want to do this anymore. Noah wasn't lying, Dallas, I'm sorry.* But even if I wrote myself a script, my voice would fail a few traitorous sentences in. If I told them, I'd write it out and leave it on the table and wait. Or email it so I didn't have to see anyone's face as they read it.

How would I say it, though? Where would I start? When I went to the party—no, not there.

When Sheriff Davies sat down with me in the hospital—
no. Not there either.

When Eddie hit his head on the wheel stop and died—

When Saint showed up with that railroad spike jammed
in his throat, when Cooper ran his hand over my scalp and
said we should get rid of the rest of them—

Or do I rewind all the way back to Dad's accident,
to Saint's body rotting on the stage of the burned-down
theater, to the worker's strike that put him there?

It don't matter where I start. It's the same story all the way
through. It leads to Paul's jaw shattered in the processing
plant, me in Dallas's bed staring up at the ceiling, my new
name crackling through the festival microphones, Noah
covered in blood with a Molotov cocktail.

"We're okay," is what I say instead, my words almost
muffled by Mom's palm.

She sighs in relief and pushes her car keys into my grasp.
"Good. Take Dad home. Now. We'll be right behind you."

"Wait, what—"

"We've got Amber. She'll be okay."

"What happened?" Dallas says.

"Looks like some deep tissue damage," Mom rattles off.
"Don't know about bone, won't be able to tell until I get a
closer look." Oh god, Davies did shoot her. Dallas's face
falls. "She'll live but it'll hurt. Don't worry about her right
now, okay? Take the long way back home so you don't run
into anyone. Speed if you have to."

I start to protest—*I want to stay with you*—but Mom
squeezes my wrist. She's trusting me with this.

I nod.

She kisses my forehead, and then Dallas's.

At least Dallas still trusts me enough to follow when I break for the car.

✦

I take the long way around, like Mom said. Dallas is in the back seat with Dad. They keep watching me in the rear-view mirror, and I can't meet their gaze because of course I can't, and I have to keep myself from shaking because I have to *drive*.

Keep it together, Miles. Lady ain't dead until I see her body.

Dad takes a call from Mom, then leans forward to tell me, quietly, that the Red Holler has burned. The fire almost reached the church. The cop cars were positioned in just a way that the volunteer fire department—what little we have—couldn't get close enough until the fire truck mowed down the offending vehicle like roadkill.

✦

This is how it happened with the North Mountain Coal Company union here in Twist Creek County a hundred years ago. When the Baldwin-Felts agents and that damned sheriff couldn't get the union to break—when Saint Abernathy took Joseph Davenport down into the mines and started sending up severed fingers—they retaliated. They burned the theater.

They razed houses and shops. They left McLachlan in ruins. Guess it's Pearson's turn now.

Did you know that, even though the official count of the dead at the Paint Creek mine war was about fifty, so many more died because of starvation and malnutrition in the worker camps?

Did you know that, at the Battle of Blair Mountain, strikebreakers dropped leftover World War I bombs onto the miners from planes?

Though I hate to admit it, I'm almost jealous of those miners a century ago. Even without cell phones and recording devices, without 911 and modern antibiotics— at Paint Creek and Blair Mountain, I'm pretty sure their sheriffs were on their side.

Not ours.

✦

By the time we get home, it's dark. Mom left the kitchen light on, and our cockeyed porch is lined with golden rectangles. When I cut the engine, I hear Lady barking. Oh my god, she's alive, she's okay. I nearly crumple against the steering wheel. My hands are numb. Dad is still on the phone with Mom. Dallas can't move.

And Cooper lays slumped against the porch stairs.

There's no more panic. I don't got any words. There's just the cold finality of, *Oh*. This is what Noah was talking about.

As Michael pulls into the driveway behind us, I pop open the car door and step outside to the familiar smell of death.

CHAPTER
FORTY-SiX

"Oh my god," Michael says. Mom helps Amber from the back seat, holding the rag steady over her shoulder wound. Dallas braces themself against the car door, Dad trying to keep them upright. "Who is that?"

Inside, Lady bays. Throws herself against the front door. Sounds like she's going hoarse.

I stand at the bottom of the stairs, looking at Cooper's body.

He's been taken apart like a deer. Field dressed and half-butchered. The bullet hole sits neatly at the chest, a good hit from a decent rifle; the cut goes from pelvis to breastbone, stopping at the base of the throat like the killer planned to mount the head. Ribs cracked apart, insides scooped clean, his heart and liver packed inside cleanly as if left to be eaten. His jeans are tacky and stiff, stained red, and his bare chest is deformed like a surgical patient abandoned halfway.

What draws my attention though, ain't none of that. It's the ring of keys peeking out from his pocket.

He had his keys. The keys to his truck, the keys to the Sunoco up on the hill and the one in Pearson. His house key too. They're hanging out of his pocket the way he always had them, because he liked to hear them jingle when he walked.

"It's Cooper," I say finally. "Noah got him."

Cooper said he was gonna do something. He left the Fourth of July festival red-faced, screaming at me, shattered somewhere in his head.

Guess that whatever that *something* was, it didn't work.

His eyes are open. I lean over his body to close them because I don't like it, and he's warm. If I feel anything about it besides *I think I saw this coming*, I can't tell. Michael throws up. Dallas is staring at the tree line, trying so hard not to stare but they can't not, because this is Cooper and we'd all been friends when we were little and yeah, I know. I know.

Dad says, "Alan."

Alan. Mr. O'Brien. The man that had been Dad's best friend once, the man whose wife he didn't have time to save.

"Back door," Mom says quietly. "Now."

But there's no key to the back door, so while Mom shepherds everyone around the house, I'm the one who steps over Cooper's body to go in the front and let everyone in the other way. Lady won't get out from under the kitchen table. Her hackles are raised and there's spit gathering in the corners of her mouth.

There's no time for panic. We're a family that gets shit done.

Mom calls Mamaw as she brings Amber into the kitchen, grabs her medical kit, and starts laying out sterile supplies on the kitchen table—*Can y'all come down?* she says. *We've got a bit of a situation.* Dad disappears into the bedroom, reappears with the handgun, says he's going to get Alan. Dallas sinks onto the floor next to Amber and she puts a hand in their hair, smoothing the rough patch next to their temple.

"Are you okay?" Michael whispers to her.

"Could be worse," Amber says.

Mom says, "Michael, scoot. I need to get to that shoulder. And Miles, can you make the dog be quiet? *Please.*"

But I don't hear her. I'm looking to the front porch again.

For a moment, Saint is there too. Crouching over Cooper, arms braced on his knees, head tilted. The yellow light from the house shines dully on the dry texture of his old eyeballs.

With his ring finger, the rest of his hand held lazily, he traces the pattern of Cooper's wounds.

I should have said something to Cooper. Texted him to be careful, or not to do whatever he thought he was gonna do to Noah. No telling whether or not he would've listened. Probably not. But it reminds me of Cooper telling me he'd hit my dad, lashed out at one of the only adults who'd been able to do anything for him, was willing to get close enough anymore. What are you really doing when you do something like that? Expressing anger in the only way you know how, towards someone safe enough to weather it? What's really going on when you snap?

Maybe he was searching for someone who'd care enough to reach out to him anyway.

Saint watches me, waiting for what I'm going to do next. I don't got a clue. I say, "Lady, c'mere. It's okay."

✦

When Mr. O'Brien sees Cooper on our porch—when he recognizes the dark form slumped against the stairs, a few yards down the driveway—he collapses against my father's chest, falls to his knees, wails like the world is ending. It's the same kind of scream I heard all those years ago from all the way up the mountain.

Dad picks him up under the arms as best he can, still struggling with his own limp, whispering to him the whole time they walk. The bags under Mr. O'Brien's eyes are near black and his hair sticks to his face, plastered to his forehead. Once he gets Cooper's body in his arms, lighter now that the insides are gone, he starts screaming at Dad. Michael goes to stop him, but Dad holds out a hand.

"Let him," Dad whispers. "It's okay."

In the kitchen, I help Mom with Amber. Mamaw and Papaw are on their way, so Mom is on the phone with Amanda now, my favorite nurse from Southern Memorial, and Amanda is walking her through bullet-wound treatment. Amanda says we need to go to the hospital, and Mom responds that it ain't safe for us to be on the road right now. I bring washcloths from the linen closet and throw bloody ones in the sink to soak.

"Should I pull the bullet out?" Mom asks, reaching for a pair of tweezers. Amber groans.

"Depends on where it's at," Amanda replies. Her voice crackles on speaker phone. "How close it is to the joint. Can't have the metal grinding up against it every time she moves."

Mom tells me to come over here with a flashlight and shine it into the bullet hole, please.

It's funny how much I see myself in both of them, Mom and Dad. Mom's no-bullshit attitude, speaking bluntly and plainly, the tips she's given me to cover up what might be a developmental disorder, what might be autism. And then Dad's gaze sliding away at every opportunity, the way he works with his hands, his fixations and the million things in his head. I want to ask Amber—if this is genetic, where did I get it from? Which one passed it down? But Mom is busy pressing gauze to a wound, and I need to hold the light, so I don't.

✦

Mamaw and Papaw arrive around nine thirty, as Mom is walking Amber through how to care for an open wound and the removed bullet sits on a folded paper towel. Papaw brings in his shotgun with a Ziploc bag of shells and Mamaw says she's been calling Uncle Rodney and Aunt Jill all the way down, but neither of them will answer.

"Figured as much," Mom mutters. She's trying to be angry but she can't. Hard to be angry when people are only trying to survive. "Well, then, I hope they're okay."

Papaw takes his shotgun to the porch, sits with Dad and Mr. O'Brien, talks them both through what they'll need to do with Cooper's body. Asking if Mr. O'Brien wants to try a funeral home or bury the poor boy with Uncle Bobby, wondering if Sheriff Davies has enough control over Twist Creek County to determine whether or not we can get a death certificate. Lady paces the house restlessly. Dallas is doing dishes and won't talk.

Mamaw finds me anxiously fumbling for something to do. "Sit your butt down," she says. "You're a mess."

"I'm fine," I say instinctively.

Mamaw ain't having it. She leads me to the couch and settles herself next to me before pulling my hand into her lap. Her fingers are small and cold.

"Your momma told me what you did at the Holler," she says. "Brave. Stupid, sure, but brave."

"I get that a lot."

Mamaw tuts, as if she knows I'm deflecting the emotions of the situation and ain't too happy about it. "Why didn't you tell us? Baby, we could've helped. We been dealing with these sons of bitches for so much longer than you've been alive."

Believe me, I know. Mamaw was born and raised here, and damn if she didn't marry an Abernathy despite her parents threatening to disown her for good. She knew what she was getting herself into. Everyone knows what it means to be one of us. Everyone would have understood if I'd said something, if I'd panicked and broke my "deal" with Davies.

"I didn't—" My brain rifles through all the ways I've learned to fake eye contact but I can't bring myself to do any of them. It's too much work. "I didn't want to drag y'all into this. Mom and Dad are dealing with enough, and Davies ain't messed with you and Papaw for a while, so I didn't want him to—" I sniffle and wipe my nose on the hem of my shirt. It's the handmade Redneck Revolt one, with the old fabric paint and hand-measured words across my shoulder blades. It seems odd that I'm still wearing the clothes I started the evening in. Could've sworn I was getting ready for Fuck the Fourth days ago. "This is my fault. If I hadn't gone out that night—"

What? If I hadn't gone to that party, Eddie would still be alive? Paul? Cooper? Amber wouldn't have gotten hurt? The Red Holler wouldn't have burned?

"Shh," Mamaw says. "Absolutely not. Don't talk like that."

I nod weakly.

She carefully holds the back of my head. "I have something for you. Your daddy told me about your interest in our family history, how much it means to you, and it— it reminded me of something we got from your great-grandmother, Lucille. I made sure to grab it before we left."

She bustles into the kitchen to grab her purse, leaving me on the couch alone. I wipe my eyes and watch everybody else. Dad and Papaw guide Mr. O'Brien into the house, bringing him water and tissues. Michael helps Amber up from her seat. Mom cleans her medical supplies. Dallas finishes the dishes and sheepishly lingers in the kitchen as Lady tries to herd everyone together. She's still stressed out; I can tell by the way her eyes are showing the whites at the edges, so I whistle to get her back to my side. She trots over to sit at my feet.

Mamaw comes back with a bag, a small piece of paper inside.

"Here," she says, setting it carefully in my lap.

It's an old, old photo. Another one of Saint Abernathy and Lucille and that dark-haired miner he loved. Looks like it was taken at the same time as the one I have in my photo album, but far less stiff, less posed. They're laughing, the image blurry thanks to the longer exposure times of a hundred years ago.

Mamaw says, "Check the back."

I hold it carefully, afraid if I move too fast that the delicate photo paper will crumble in my hands—and turn it over.

Saint Abernathy, it reads in perfect old-timey hand-writing. *Lucille Abernathy.*

And, right beside those names: *Billy Hawk.*

A name. Finally. Saint's lover, Lucille's other father. William, his full name must have been, but I imagine Saint never called him that. I roll the words over in my head. William Hawk. Where have I heard that before?

A few months ago, while I was searching for scraps of reporting that a Davies had forgotten to destroy, I came across a list of miners who died in the cave-in. It was written almost carelessly, as if taking stock of inventory instead of transcribing the names of the dead. William Hawk was on that list. The North Mountain Coal Company killed him. And a few days later, the ramshackle union—cut off from the world by the coal operators, struggling to get word out to the United Mine Workers of America, all returning correspondence seized and burned—would give a rifle to every man that wanted one. They would turn to violence because everything else had failed.

My hands shake enough that I have to put the bag down.

"Saint, he—" I have to collect myself. "He was probably trans. None of his documents line up the way they should, which is weird, because West Virginia usually keeps *really* good records. It's like he appeared out of thin air. Plus he disappeared for seven months right before Lucille was born, which is telling if you ask me."

Imagine going back to the mines right after giving birth. I don't know a thing about having babies, and if it all goes right, I never will, but I know it rips you up. Even when it goes well. Try suiting up, grabbing your tools, packing yourself in with the coal dust and canaries while you're still aching and bleeding.

Dad is standing in the entryway to the living room now. Papaw too, and Dallas. Mom. Amber. Michael. Mr. O'Brien. All in the room, or watching from the kitchen. I'm rocking a little bit too, I notice, just my head and my shoulders but enough to calm me down. It's the sort of thing Mom used to tell me to stop when I was younger. She don't now.

"He was a socialist. Loud about it too, because you could be loud about it back before the Red Scare." Dad laughs a little. I turn the photo back around so I can see Billy's face. "And the mine disaster killed this guy, his daughter's father, so can you really blame him for doing what he did to Joseph Davenport?"

Wouldn't everyone in this room do the same?

"But the strike failed, and he died."

I hear it sometimes, even when Saint's not here: the railroad spike in his throat, clicking against his teeth, the muscles of his throat contracting around it like it's something he's trying to choke down.

"It was a Davies that did it," Dad says.

I nod weakly. "Yeah."

I breathe in.

"Eddie and Paul," I try, then start over. "Cooper and I . . ."

And I'm about to say it. I'm about to say everything. *I killed them. We killed them. The first one was an accident, but Christ, Dad, we used your gun for the second. Noah wasn't lying.*

But Papaw interrupts. "Could've guessed that was you."

Everyone turns to look at him.

"What?" he says, though it comes out more like a grunt. He don't even bother to shrug. "You're an Abernathy. S'just how it goes."

Nobody in the room seems all that surprised. Mainly varying shades of tired, or sad, or heartbroken that it's come to this. Dallas, of all people, the one who begged me to say Noah was lying, only takes a deep breath and stares at the ceiling.

Mr. O'Brien says, "Did they deserve it?"

Ain't no good way to respond to that. I think they did. I think, in the grand scheme of things, they didn't.

✦

The night is divided into shifts—someone needs to be awake at all times, just in case—but nobody will let me take one, and Dallas ain't in the kitchen while the adults decide. I find them on the back porch. They've got a long, skinny cigarette, and they're struggling to light it.

"Today sucked," I say. "We should probably go to bed."

Dallas ignores me. Every time they click the lighter, they falter. It won't spark.

This time, I say, "Thought you quit."

"I was trying," Dallas corrects. Their voice trembles. "I think I'm done trying this month."

But they still can't get the lighter to work so they fling it into the grass and drop their head into their hands. I'm not sure what to do. My instinct is to say, *You didn't get hurt again, you're okay*, but that don't seem right. Mom says that sometimes trying to fix a problem instead of being a kind ear can come across as rude.

"Sorry," I say. "For all of this."

Dallas shakes their head. "This is what I get, being friends with you."

"What, a class war?" I hesitate on my next words, then creep forward anyway. I know the answer, but I want to get them out of their rut. "*Is* it a class thing? Davies don't got that much more money than most people around here, and he ain't much of a capitalist."

My attempt to reach out with the minutia of political bullshit works. Dallas laughs. Thank god.

"If you want to get into whether or not cops count as working class," they muse with a half smile, "be my guest. I've got all night." They think for a second. "Plus, don't he technically own the processing plant?"

"Oh, I forgot about that." I hold out a hand. "Come on."

Dallas comes inside. We distract ourselves the way we used to when we were younger, talking/debating/arguing about whatever—I insist you can't call law enforcement *class traitors* since you can't betray the working class if you're not part of it (*"What value do they create?"*), but Dallas says the semantics matter less than the message, though if we want to get into the idea of *value*—until we cram ourselves onto my twin-sized mattress facing each other. Dallas gets the outside, so they have room to stretch. Lady ends up at our feet.

"Bad day, huh?" Dallas whispers.

They've lost a lot today. The Red Holler. A sense of safety. An old friend, even if Cooper wasn't doing okay for the little bit they'd reconnected.

"Yeah," I reply, and I am not prepared for either of us—for both of us—to collapse into a mess of ugly sobs, fumbling for tissues on the dresser, for Lady to crawl up between us, both of us apologizing to the other for crumbling so suddenly. Our faces are puffy and tissues litter the bed and neither of us can breathe.

"Bad day," I repeat between hiccupping breaths, and Dallas pulls me into a hug.

They fall asleep that way.

I don't. I can't.

Which works out, because my phone dings.

CHAPTER
FORTY-SEVEN

Cooper

I take it you found him?

Seeing Cooper's name in my text messages is like coming face to face with a zombie, a reanimated corpse puppeted around by something else.

Miles

you motherfucker

you took his phone

~~Cooper~~ **Noah**

Nice work, Sherlock.

You want this over with?

You want this done?

Because I can make that happen. Just the two of us.

◆

Dad is on first watch. He's trying not to doze off in the kitchen, gun on the table in front of him.

I grab him and show him the messages. "It's Noah."

He says, "Shit."

CHAPTER
FORTY-EiGHT

It's a few minutes past midnight, and we're all huddled around our wobbly kitchen table. Lights off except for that awful florescent above the sink, shutters drawn, everyone drinking coffee or ice-cold water to wake up. Lady paces restlessly.

I have an idea. It ain't that I came up with it—I couldn't come up with something like this. But Saint did, a hundred years ago, and I think we could pull it off this time.

Trap Noah Davies in the mine, and we'd have one hell of a bargaining chip on the sheriff's table.

Miles

sure, just the two of us, and your fucking father

Noah

My dad don't have to get involved. This belongs to me, not him.

Thought you'd get that.

"Watch your language," Dad hisses as he reads my texts over my shoulder.

I wave him away. It's hard to talk, but I force myself through it because that's what I've always done. "I know what I'm doing."

Miles

i don't give a shit anymore as long as this stops

"It's too dangerous," Michael says. "Absolutely not. We're not about to lose another kid to this."

Across from me, Mr. O'Brien's shoulders crumple like wet paper. Dallas holds my hand under the table. I try to squeeze comfortingly but I ain't sure it gets the point across. Also it's hard to text with one hand. There are nine people in the kitchen and that's too many. I'm already overwhelmed.

"I know the mines better than the Davieses do," I say firmly. "Better than anyone in this room. I can do it."

"You shouldn't have to," Michael says.

"*None* of us should have to do *any* of this," Amber retorts. She's got herself a makeshift sling now so she don't move her shoulder too much, but the handful of cheap painkillers we've got ain't working and it's showing on her face. "But here we are."

"And Noah certainly ain't gonna talk to none of y'all," I add. "Let me do it."

No dissent. It's decided. I thought it would be more difficult than this, but we're all at the ends of our ropes. A bad idea is better than no idea at this point.

Mom reaches across the table and takes my face in her hands. Her voice cracks. "When did you get so big?"

Papaw says, "Best start getting ready."

Mamaw brings a backpack from the hall closet and rattles off what she's putting inside. A bundle of rope. A roll of duct tape. A bottle of water and matches too, because you can never be too safe. I change into black clothes, more suited for the inky darkness of the mines, and snag Paul's knife from under my bed. Mamaw takes my phone so it can charge in the meantime.

"We've done this before," she says with an unsteady smile. "We can do it again."

The adults talk about what they're gonna demand from Sheriff Davies once they have the leverage—the child captive—to do so. Mom suggests forcing Davies to abdicate the office. Amber offers the idea of exile, forcing him out of the county, but that can't really be enforced, can it? Papaw suggests killing him. Amber sighs, "I was hoping we could avoid another murder charge," but Mr. O'Brien shakes his head. An eye for an eye, the way he sees it.

Dad sets the handgun on the kitchen table in front of me.

"Here," he says. "Figure you already know how to use this, then." I blink at him, and Dad gives a wry smile. "We keep a piece of dog hair in the safe lock—lets us know it's been tampered with."

For some reason, I laugh, even if it's just to keep me from losing it. "Jesus," I say. "But for your information, no, I don't know."

When Dad shakes my shoulder, his touch lingers. "Shit. Let's get your papaw over here."

Noah

When and where?

The goal is to be out of the house and headed down to the mine by one thirty in the morning. In the meantime, the house is alive with whispers and the creaking of wooden floors under bare feet. Nobody can come with me in case Noah catches on and backs out. My phone is at 76 percent battery, which is good enough. Papaw shows me how the gun works, even though I'm terrified to hold it. I have explicit instructions to track down cell service and call as soon as I have Noah because, Mamaw says, what happens after that ain't my problem no more.

When Dallas hugs me, they don't want to let go.

"If you die," they say, sounding like they're about to cry, "I'll kill you."

I nudge them playfully so I don't have to face the horrific weight of the situation. "I expect nothing less."

I drink one more glass of water, try to get sensation back into my fingertips, and lean down to kiss Lady's head. Mom won't stop fretting and Dad might be on the verge of some kind of meltdown. And Mr. O'Brien . . .

He's got the yellow cast of someone about to be ill. I can't exactly blame him, considering everything he's been through. If nothing else, I'm glad he's still alive.

"Hey," he says quietly. "I—"

His bottom lip wobbles.

"Thank you for being there," he says. "For my boy. Even when he wasn't doing good."

I don't deserve those words. Cooper spent a whole lot of time not doing good, and I was barely there for a fraction of it. I walk away from big feelings instead of *feeling* them, because they scare me, because I don't know what they are or how to show them. Apparently, it's an autism thing. Jumbling up my emotions, not understanding them, expressing them for the benefit of others instead of myself.

And now that I know that, I can start—I don't know. Unpacking it. Teaching myself to exist without running it through the filter of what I'm *supposed* to do.

I wish Cooper had gotten to know the version of me that's going to exist one day.

I smile the best I can. "He was a good kid."

And then I raise a hand to everyone who has ever loved me—"If I don't call in an hour, burn this place to the ground," I say—and step out into the warm summer night, with the crickets chirping and the wind and the mountains. The gun is in my bag. The knife is wrapped in leather and pushed into my hiking boot. A family of deer at the edge of the property perks up, ears twitching and grass hanging from their nervous mouths.

I take the bandana off my wrist and tie it proper around my neck.

Lady barks once, then stops.

Miles

meet me @ the mine. half an hour

nobody but you

Noah

Nobody but you.

CHAPTER
FORTY-NiNE

It's dead silent in McLachlan.

I walk down the road to Main Street. I pass Cooper's apartment, the pizza parlor, the burned-down theater. Then it's across the bridge over Twist Creek, where I hesitate for a moment, looking down over the edge.

Twist Creek is less a creek and more a strangled river. The water is rough and gets deeper than you'd think. I peer into the trees separating it from McLachlan, trying to pinpoint where my body had been. Where Cooper had picked me up off the forest floor. After he dropped me off at the hospital, did he have to lug the tarp into his yard and hose it off? Or did he throw it out and buy a new one?

It ain't worth thinking about. I taste copper on the back of my tongue.

I keep going, holding up my phone flashlight to find the path to the mine. Alone in the dark, you can't help but think about how the trees are so much younger and the mountains are so much older than you'd expect. A fire wiped out a lot of these forests a long time ago, so the trees are still infants in the grand scheme of things. In contrast, remember, the Appalachian Mountains are literally older than bones.

Saint Abernathy falls into step beside me. He's less rotten now, the blood fresh and his open wounds new. The railroad spike was just recently wrenched into his body, so he's still bleeding into that new bandana, ruining the complex designs. I'm wearing it the same way he is.

"I'm sorry about what happened to Billy," I tell him. "He looked like a nice guy. Probably a good dad too."

Saint don't say anything to that.

"You miss him?"

Saint nods. I wonder if he sees Lucille in us.

Or, fine, if we're wondering. What would it have been like if I'd gotten to live my whole life knowing my great-great-grandfather was trans? If he'd been able to talk openly about it, if I'd gotten every artifact of his life instead of the scraps the Davieses hadn't burned? In another version of the world, Saint Abernathy wouldn't come to save us. He'd come visit his great-great-grandson in excitement. He'd come to see how much different life is for trans people these days, to pass along our history, to *tell me* without a railroad spike jammed into his throat.

Instead, the mines murdered his lover, and law enforcement murdered him. Instead, we have to do this. And I could wrap this all back around to politics like I always do, right? Because that's how it goes. The union, the company, the workers, and the strikebreakers. Power and money and control; who gets to get away with murder.

At the mouth of the mine, pulling the metal grate from the adit and throwing it into the leaves, I try to picture it all—to keep from losing it, to keep my mind in one piece. The rumbling of the mountain as the cave-in crushed a dozen men to death, trapping them in a stone grave. Miners gathering outside the theater to listen to a grieving mamaw holding a Bible aloft, asking her community what they were gonna do about it. Picking up rifles and wiping sweat off their necks with old rags. Aiming for the whites of the strikebreakers' eyes.

Saint Abernathy wrenching a rope around Joseph Davenport's neck. *Scream and I'll cut your throat.* Taking him into the mine: down, down, down.

I crawl through the gap and leave it open for Noah Davies to follow.

Stand.

Breathe in the wet, stale air.

I check the time on my phone. In this gaping maw, what little signal I have flickers in and out. I make note of where it reaches, where it don't. Together, Saint and I walk to the room at the end of the mine, the one with the sub-shaft holding Eddie's body. If you go all the way to the back and inspect the rocks piled there, you can almost see the edges of the cave-in, track where the stone is still loose if you're the nervous type. It's boarded up and closed off with chain-link and barbed wire.

Saint hesitates here, looking at the collapsed tunnel, and he won't move. I leave him to it.

There's lanterns down here, old as hell. Oil lamps? I find one or two that have candles inside and fumble with the book of matches from Mamaw's supplies, light them so I don't have to rely on my phone flashlight. There's also bullet casings. Old shovels and axes. At the barrier to the sub-shaft, I see a pair of dulled, rusty shears. Probably easier to cut off fingers with that than a knife.

And then I take the gun out of the bag and weigh it in my hand. It's as heavy as I remember; heavier than you'd think it should be. It's uncomfortably warm in my clammy hands.

When the clock ticks over, half an hour after my final text, I put my fingers in my mouth and whistle. The sound echoes, echoes, echoes—telling Noah Davies exactly where the fuck I am.

✦

If Saint Abernathy could talk, what would I ask him?

How did you meet Billy Hawk? What was he like? Was he a mean son of a bitch like you, or was he softer? Did you plan for Lucille? When did you figure out you were pregnant? Were you scared?

When you realized you were a man, were you scared? When you learned the mine had killed Billy, were you scared? When you knew you had to do something, were you scared?

Because I'm scared.

This is the first time in weeks I've thought to question if he's real; whether the mistake that lets me see him is outside my brain or inside it. The weak candlelight don't land on him correctly. He don't throw a shadow, neither. The hand holding the gun has gone sweaty, and I wipe off the grip with the hem of my shirt.

✦

When Noah arrives—

He shows up in work clothes and slicked-back hair, smiling like he's stuck in rigor mortis. Like he smiled at the gas station, at the festival, at the Red Holler. Like he had to carve it into himself because his face don't know how to do it otherwise.

Saint Abernathy's teeth click on his iron spike. *Click click click.*

"You brought a gun," Noah says. "Gotta admit, didn't think you had it in you."

I raise it.

I ain't Cooper. I pull the trigger.

CHAPTER
FiFTY

The bullet hits where I'd aimed—the rock a few feet from Noah's shoulder—but I'd forgotten that bullets ricochet. It rapid-fire pings twice, then goes suddenly silent.

I can't hear nothing except a high-pitched tinnitus scream.

Noah and I freeze, looking in the direction we think the bullet went. We stare down the throat of the mine, then at each other. Waiting for some sort of pain to tell us we've been hit. Waiting for the other to say it first.

Then Noah starts to laugh. It's the first thing I hear as the ringing fades. Tiny, hysterical giggles, a sort of *I thought I was dead* noise.

"Jesus Christ," he says. "You missed."

I wasn't trying to hit him. Just trying to imply that I *could*, if I wanted. If I'd messed up and hit him—shit. There'd go our leverage.

You can't blame a person for not being able to hurt someone else. Humans can accept a hell of a lot of terrible things as long as they never have to see the bone and gristle. But as soon as the gun gets put in your hand? As soon as you gotta do it yourself? Hell, most people I know couldn't handle the stress of slaughtering their own meat.

"O'Brien told me everything," Noah says between barks of laughter. This is so damn funny to him that he's tearing up, a hand on his stomach like it hurts. "I said if he started talking, I'd put his intestines back in his stomach and sew him up fine, and I'd meant it as a joke but—"

No. I don't want to think about Cooper laid out on the same kind of grassy hill hunters use to field dress their deer. I don't want to think about Noah standing over him with a knife, slitting his belly while Cooper begged and pleaded. I don't want to think about Cooper awake while Noah reached in and started scooping out piles of innards. Just as he did with Nancy Adams's dog. I can't, I can't do it.

I say, "Stop."

"Or what?" Noah giggles. "You'll shoot the wall again?" He meets my eyes and leans forward. "You won't do it. O'Brien said you couldn't. Ain't that right? Ruckle was an accident, and you couldn't stomach handling Miller yourself. What'd he call you? A coward?"

"*Stop.*"

"I came down to give you a chance, you know. To *prove* you ain't a coward like he said. All you'd have to do is come on home to my dad. Easy, right? I think he'd leave y'all alone if you did."

His smile cracks at the edges, the skin peeling just a little.

I don't believe him.

"Think about it, Abernathy," he nudges. "You'd be a good deterrent, even as a dead body, and my dad would—"

His voice cracks at the mention of Sheriff Davies.

"My dad would have that stupid car crash," Noah says. "And I'd have *you*."

He ain't smiling no more. He's showing his teeth. All those perfect white teeth crammed into his mouth.

I think about it. Letting Noah take me back to Davies. Giving myself up completely, letting Davies do what he wanted in exchange for my family's safety. If Davies gave me this choice on stage on the Fourth of July, I don't know what I would've said. Would I have said yes? I'd do anything to keep him from going after Mom and Dad again, but . . .

It wouldn't be safety, though, not really. I'd be another knife in their back, another point of pain for Davies to hold over them.

And Noah wants this so bad. I don't got to interpret that. He wants this. He wants me. He wants to leave a bigger gouge in Twist Creek County than some car crash and a burned-down building.

"But if you're here to lure him into a trap," Noah says, "it won't work."

He says, "You think he cares about me?"

He says, "That's funny, Abernathy."

No, he's right, it is funny. It don't matter whether Sheriff Davies cares about Noah. Sheriff Davies could be the worst father in the world and none of this would change.

What matters is that one of *us* hurting one of *them* makes Sheriff Davies look weak.

"So?" Noah says. "What's it gonna be? You got an answer? Or are we gonna sit here forever since you're too much of a pussy to use that gun?"

It must be something on my face—something in the way I'm standing, maybe, that tells him I'm unsteady, stuck between words like I always am. That I ain't gonna give him the answer he wants.

Because, in that moment, Noah drops all this bullshit about deals and safety, and throws himself at me.

Fights happen fast. Everything you see in movies and on TV—the choreography, the trading blows, the drawn-out back-and-forth—is a lie. It's the same way medical shows leave out how good CPR breaks ribs. They bend the truth because reality is terrifying, because real violence happens quick and there's nothing you can do about it. The gunshot that took out Paul's jaw, Eddie's head hitting the wheel stop, Noah's boot coming down on my rib. The second it takes for the sledge to come down on the railroad spike. *That's* how it goes. In a snap. When you grow up in a family like mine, you know that.

Real fights are measured in seconds, and they always end with someone fucked up or dead.

Noah hits me. Takes us both to the ground. My head knocks the dirt and my vision swims and it's suddenly dark, a lantern kicked over and spluttering out in the dust. I'm not holding the gun. I dropped it. Noah rolls off me, hands scrabbling to find it before me.

He grabs the gun before I can get up. Fumbles it into his hand.

But I have a knife in my boot.

✦

I didn't mean to kill him.

I didn't want to. I only wanted to hurt him enough to make him stop. Not enough to *do* anything. I swear. I swear to god, I didn't mean it.

But when the blade of Paul's knife ends up in the soft spot between the jaw and the throat, that's what happens.

CHAPTER
FiFTY-ONE

Noah's eyes bulge. Blood streams over my hand and it's hot and sticky and I panic. I rip the knife out of his neck. As soon as I do it, I remember I shouldn't—you're supposed to keep the blade in the wound if you want the person to survive, or at least have a better chance, that's literally the *first* thing you learn about injuries—but god, I think I severed something important, I think he was dead either way. He tries to say something but only manages to gurgle. He reaches for his neck and sticks his fingers in the wound to figure out what it is, what I did to him, then his arm gives out.

He collapses on top of me. It pushes the breath out of his lungs one last time and he wheezes against my neck. I dry heave. No no no get *off*, get *off* me—I jam my shoulder into his face and shove him away, throwing him limply into the dirt and stumbling to my feet. I drop the knife. My knees threaten to buckle.

He ain't moving. He's gone.

I clamp my hands over my mouth and scream.

Noah's dead.

I cough, splutter, realize I'm crying. I try to wipe my face but only smear blood across my cheeks; I try to clean off my mouth but accidentally swallow some. Sheriff Davies is going to—he's gonna hunt us down and kill us. We have to get out of Twist Creek County. We have to get out now. I fumble my phone from my pocket and my fingers leave red smears on the screen, making it hard to see a thing. No signal. According to the clock, it's still fifteen minutes before I told everyone to raise the alarm. Fifteen minutes is more than enough time for Sheriff Davies to wipe out a bloodline, right?

I look up one last time, over my shoulder, towards the cave-in. Where Saint Abernathy had been clicking his teeth against the railroad spike.

He ain't there. Of course—of course he ain't. Of course I'm alone.

One last gasping sob as I force my body to work with me. No time to have a breakdown. No time to think too hard. I have to warn everyone.

I leave Noah's corpse on the floor and stumble into the mineshaft. It's pitch-black and I barely remember my phone flashlight. I've left the backpack. The gun and the knife and everything. What am I supposed to tell my parents? What am I supposed to tell Dallas, what am I supposed to tell Mr. O'Brien? *Sorry* won't cut it. I check my phone again. All the places I found a signal on the way in, none of them work. I don't got my shoelace, so I drum my hand against my mouth over and over and over, try to keep pace with my heartbeat, do anything to calm myself down enough to think.

I hit the metal grate in front of the mine after I don't know how long and have to crawl through the small opening, bracing myself on the rock to stand up. My phone gets a single bar. Then loses it. Then gets it again.

The first contact I find is Dad. I press *call*. It rings once before the signal shits out.

I swallow down another dry heave. Try again. Call fails.

I take one step away from the mouth of the mine, then another. I can't see the buttons because my eyes are blurring with tears. There's too much blood on the screen protector.

We can find another way to do this. Right? We have to. I press the button one more time, or where I think the button should be under the mess.

For a single second, it rings.

Bang.

CHAPTER
FiFTY-TWO

The force first: a fist with sharp knuckles right below the eye.

Then the heat and cold, both at once. Like the skin's been peeled away and exposed to the night air, or the aftermath of a burn. From the corner of my orbital socket to the temple, a straight line ripped out of my skull.

I can't open my eye. I can't see anything out of it.

Then the pain.

CHAPTER
FIFTY-THREE

Sheriff Davies lowers his deer rifle and walks to my side, feet crunching in the old leaves and underbrush.

He crouches just enough to get a good look.

"Damn," he says with a proud bent to his voice. I'm on my knees. Wheezing. Gasping for air. If I press hard enough on my face, if I hold it all in, maybe the bleeding will stop. Pieces of bone grind together and the raw muscle feels like mud packed onto the skull. "Thought I missed."

He grabs my jaw and tilts my head up with a smile. My heartbeat pounds in the open wound: *thump-thump, thump-thump.* My phone lies in the leaf litter, shining against the ground like a halo.

I want Mom and Dad. I want Lady. I want Mamaw and Papaw, anybody. Even Saint. But he ain't there. It's just empty woods.

The worst part is—underneath the pain and fear, the part of my brain that's still working despite it all—is that I

350 Andrew Joseph White

can't figure out how much of Saint was ever real. Accepting a ghost would've been so much easier than facing a traumatic brain injury and the full-body sickness of withdrawal. Maybe I'd wandered to the burned-down theater on my own. I'd imagined him standing there in the backyard. Was he really trans, or was I reaching for a splinter of history to hold on to, cobbling together a theory from wishful thinking?

I can't keep myself up on my hands and knees. Sheriff Davies catches me.

"There we go," he says. He takes the strap of the deer rifle and slings it over his shoulder so he can prop me up. I want to fight, but my hands won't make fists, only hold on weakly to his shirt. I can't scream, only breathe out hard. "Atta girl. I don't feel good about killing kids, you know. I don't like this any more than you do."

He takes my hand and touches the blood cooling between my fingers. He don't need to see Noah's corpse to know what I did.

He says, "But that was mine."

Not *That was my son*. Not *That was my boy, you son of a bitch*.

Just *You took something that belonged to me*.

You made me look weak.

I manage to scoop up my phone before Sheriff Davies rolls me against his chest, tucks me against him, lifts me off the ground. I bury the light in my shirt, clutching it tight.

"Should we invite your parents?" he whispers against my shattered face. "So they can watch?"

✦

Sheriff Davies carries me to the squad car he's parked at the mouth of the road. Packs me in the back seat. Jams a piece of cloth against my face and tells me to hold it there. I cradle the phone against my belly to smother the glow. It's still on for some reason.

He slams the door and it hurts.

As soon as he starts driving, I peel the phone from my stomach. The screen is too bright even on the lowest setting, and that hurts too. There's blood all over my hands, dripping onto the screen and the car seat. It hits the old vinyl of the police cruiser in errant little drops, sometimes streaming like drool. It's in my mouth. My vision blurs and I struggle to focus; of course I can't figure out what's on the screen when I have to remind myself to breathe. I hear some animal keening noise and I think it's me.

"Should've done this a long time ago," Sheriff Davies mutters.

We hit a bump and the phone falls from my hands. It hits the floor of the car, facedown, and in the blurry mess of my vision, disappears.

"I wonder if y'all ever got the impression I was doing this for fun," Sheriff Davies says. "Or that I've spent so much time fucking with you because it's a family pastime." In the rearview mirror, I see the glint of his teeth. "I dunno, kid. It's funny. You folks love playing the victim. You mess with my county, you hurt people, and then go pitch a fit when there's consequences for your actions."

Playing the victim. We ain't playing at a damn thing. We're defending ourselves or breaking under the pressure. For a hundred years, the Davieses have pushed us until we snapped, then put us down like rabid dogs. We try to make the world better for the next generation and we're punished for it. Is he really as scared of us as we are of him? Is he as afraid of losing his power as we are of dying?

I think he is. That's how the strikebreakers felt. And the Baldwin-Felts agents, and the coal operators. The people who killed Saint Abernathy and Billy Hawk and the rest of my family.

It hurts it hurts it hurts.

✦

The car comes to a stop. My breathing is slowing down; it's so much harder to drag air into my lungs, it's so much work, I don't want to do it no more. I'm tired.

Sheriff Davies pulls me out of the car and hefts me against his chest. It smells like grass and old wood and night air and Sheriff Davies's police uniform. He leaves the gun. Only takes me.

And he steps into the grass surrounding the burned-down theater.

CHAPTER
FiFTY-FOUR

When the Baldwin-Felts agents—picture them, in three-piece suits and bow ties and old-timey hats perched on their heads—brought Saint Abernathy to the stage of the burned-down theater, I never actually imagined him resisting. There'd be no thrashing as he stepped through the ruins and still-hot ashes. He'd be so still as he faced his executioner, the sheriff holding the iron spike and gesturing him up, a magician calling a child volunteer for his next trick.

Saint Abernathy wasn't going to fight, because they'd go after Lucille if he did. But he'd smile, vicious and on the verge of martyrdom, and spread his bloody hands.

There's no record of Saint's final words. I've tried to imagine them several times over the past couple years; if he quoted Marx or John Brown, or if he called into the crowd to look after Lucille, reminding them of a will he'd written on scrap paper.

Knowing him, though, he probably said, "Fuck you."

Sheriff Davies hefts me onto what's left of the stage and climbs up beside me, steps over me into the dark mess of wood and ash, all the rotted remains of the theater. I roll over onto my stomach and drop the bloody cloth I'm holding to my face. I think a piece of my skin comes off with it. For some reason, I don't puke. I note, distantly, that I'm in shock.

Davies is digging in the ruins. His hands turn black in the mess.

He finds the railroad spike.

I put it back because I wasn't fit to have it, and here he is. Picking it up. Inspecting it in the moonlight.

It ain't his. He don't get to have it. He don't get to—

I bet he loves this. I bet he's so proud of himself, bringing me here. It must be pretty, going all back around in a circle.

I reach for the edge of the stage. Grab it. Drag myself closer. But Davies laughs and snatches me by my shirt, pulling me back, popping stitches in the fabric. "No, you don't," he says. He hooks a boot under me, shoves me onto my back, pins me down. I'm crying. Did you know that tears, being salty, hurt when they touch an open wound?

He takes his weight off me just enough to crouch down and grab my face. Pushes his bitter fingers into my mouth. I bite and he yelps, but it don't stop him. He grabs my jaw and presses his fingers in like opening a dog's maw to get it to take a pill. When I try to bite him again, I only get the inside of my cheek.

He jams the railroad spike between my teeth.

"Come on, Sadie," Sheriff Davies mutters. "Bite down if it helps."

What was it I said? We're not grown, we're some kids that did some terrible shit.

That lived through some terrible shit.

I forgot to tell my parents I loved them before I left.

My vision is going dark at the corners. I want to stop. Maybe if I fall asleep now, let my eyes fall closed, maybe I won't feel it when he puts the railroad spike through me. I don't want to feel it. Sheriff Davies don't got a hammer. He tries to find something that'll work but comes up with nothing. So he puts a hand on the flat driving end, so he can put all his weight on it instead. Rusted metal touches the back of my tongue. My throat spasms and gags.

It's so dark outside, what with the dim streetlamps starting to give out around here, and the stars are beautiful.

I watch them instead of him.

But above me . . .

✦

I think I would've liked to grow up into Saint Abernathy. Or something like him. If I'd gotten the chance. Sandy blond hair gone wild in death, the rebellious red fabric tied around his neck, hard work-callused hands. If he took off his stained linen shirt, there'd be stretch marks and narrow hipbones and that cobbled-together chest binder, scars and bruises and patches of sunburned skin.

He ain't pretty. He's got crooked teeth and bags under his eyes and busted knuckles, and coal dust in his lungs that would've eventually killed him if the railroad spike hadn't.

But he's perfect if you ask me.

✦

Saint Abernathy reaches into his throat and rips out his own railroad spike.

He says through phlegm and blood: "Remember me?"

Sheriff Davies looks up. Because Sheriff Davies hears him—

And the baying of a hunting dog. Lady howls in from stage left. Crashes into Sheriff Davies. Sends them both off the stage, into the mess of rotted wood and grass and dirt. I lurch to the side and vomit up the railroad spike. It hits the stage hard and a string of spit connects it to my lip. My stomach heaves. Lady is *screaming*. So is Sheriff Davies. The wet sound of meat, the ripping of fabric.

"*Miles!*"

Voices. People.

I shove myself up onto my elbows. Sobbing with the strain of it. Mom runs up the broken stairs to the stage, Dallas following. Dad hauls Lady back, yanking her off Sheriff Davies. Moonlight reflects in the gore trapped between her teeth, blood across her muzzle and chest. She's still shrieking. I didn't know a dog could make that noise unless it was dying.

Dallas pulls me into their lap, lifts my head up. Mom crouches in front of us and gasps.

"Is he okay?" Dallas whispers.

Mom barely pays attention to them. Her eyes are locked on me as she presses an old Mountaineers shirt to my face. "Hi, baby," she's saying. "You're alive. It's okay. Look at me, look at me. You're alive."

"He—" I reach for her. "He was going to—"

Mom says, "I know, baby, I'm so sorry. I'm so sorry. Look at me."

Below us, Mamaw hands Papaw his gun. Dad's crouched, holding Lady against his chest, one hand tight around her collar and the other fisted into her scruff. Sheriff Davies looks like he'd fallen face-first into a grinder. It's hard to see in the dim light, but I think his shoulder's been ripped open, his throat shining black like his son's. His nose is missing. His face is mess of skin flaps and glints of bone.

Sheriff Davies wheezes. His hand twitches as his head lolls to the side, fingers outstretched like he's begging for mercy.

Papaw racks the shotgun.

"You don't have to watch," Mom says. "It's okay."

I think there are lights turning on in the apartments above Main Street.

I think there are people wandering out to see.

None of them try to stop us.

It's the merciful thing to do.

CHAPTER
FiFTY-FiVE

He's gone.

CHAPTER
FiFTY-SiX

I'm tired.

"Don't sleep," Dallas whispers on the ground with me. Their eyes keep flicking to Sheriff Davies's body in the soft grass. Around us, people step out of their homes with tarps. Flashlights. Shovels. Dad drags Lady away from the mess and limps up the stairs, whispering my name. Lady tears out of his hands to run to me.

"Keep looking at me," Dallas says. "Michael and Amber are bringing the car around. We're getting you to the hospital. Okay? Nod if you can hear me."

CHAPTER
FiFTY-SEVEN

Lady curls up beside me. She's whining. Her bloody nose nudges my cheek.

Dad's bad leg gives out. He stumbles to the ground, his phone clattering to the stage. He's in the middle of a call. To me. My call went through. It's been going this whole time.

He heard the gunshot. He heard everything.

"Oh," Dad sobs, "you're alive, you're alive."

CHAPTER
FIFTY-EIGHT

"I get it," Saint says, lighting a cigarette with a match. Nobody sees him but me. His voice is softer than I'd expected—raspy from smoking and the years he forced it down to pass as male, but still gentle. This is how I imagined he spoke to Lucille, to soothe her when she cried. "I'm tired too. But I get to sleep. Not you."

CHAPTER
FiFTY-NiNE

The official cause of injury, if anyone asks, is a hunting accident.

The bullet hit my eye socket—the one already weakened by the orbital fracture—and destroyed it completely, sending shards into the surrounding tissue. I burned through a lot of blood. "Not as much as you needed last time, at least," Amanda tells me. "Be grateful nothing hit the brain."

The cover story is useless, because nobody asks.

Claire Snyder brings flowers to the hospital. So does Eddie's stepsister. Mr. O'Brien sits by my bedside and talks a lot about Cooper, and I leave the hospital for an afternoon to attend his funeral. It's small and held on the riverbank because Mr. O'Brien don't go to church these days.

There's another funeral for Noah, because he was a child, and if you want my opinion, he was a victim of this as much as I was. I don't go to that one, though. I don't ask who does.

There's no funeral for Davies.

Nobody asks.

CHAPTER SiXTY

My face heals rough. Southern Memorial cleans up what they can, but rural hospitals can only do so much. The eye has to go; the surgeon attempts to salvage the socket in hopes that a prosthetic might fit, but it's such a mess that nobody can give me a straight answer as to whether or not it'd be possible. Once I'm discharged, I'm left with a big weeping wound packed with gauze, the remains of my eye socket and cheekbone smothered with bandages. It'll take forever to heal, but I'm used to that by now.

My senior year of high school starts in two weeks. My legal name change should go through soon—Miles Elizabeth Saint Abernathy, keeping my old middle name and adding a new one. Dallas's smoking habit has regressed, and I can see them getting pissed at themself for being afraid of fire all over again, for quitting being harder the fifth, sixth, seventh time. It hurts but we're okay. We're all doing okay, or as okay as we can.

I ain't seen Saint, but that's okay too. He deserves the rest.

CHAPTER
SiXTY-ONE

In the parking lot of the Pearson Methodist church, the gravel patch it shares with the Red Holler (or what's left of it), I sit with Dallas on milk crates as people gather between the cars, and say, "I think I'm gonna drop out of school."

Dallas makes a somewhat-but-not-too-shocked noise. Lady, whose head is in my lap, cocks an ear curiously. She ain't left my side since I got out of the hospital, but I don't mind. After what she did to Sheriff Davies, she's been spoiled rotten.

"Not sure I can go back," I offer by way of an explanation. "After that."

Dallas considers it.

Mr. O'Brien, Mom, Dad, Amber, and Michael are here, and so are Mamaw and Papaw. There's Claire Snyder, and Mamaw Steele, and most of Twist Creek. Okay, maybe not most of the county, but it sure seems like it with how packed this place is. The contractors Michael had been arguing with are now inspecting the Red Holler's scorched exoskeleton—shattered glass where the windows broke, the blackened mess where the flames went up—and chatting about the damage, the cost and timeline of repairs. Mom and Mr. O'Brien are setting up tents for shade while Amber hands out water the best she can without using her right arm.

We've been doing okay. Amber's healing fine. Mr. O'Brien's been sleeping on our couch. And there's been no arrests, no questions, no retaliation. I would say we got away with it, but that don't seem correct.

Twist Creek County simply, quietly, decided we'd done the right thing, and that's that.

As for Dallas and I? We ain't dating, not exactly. We're . . . I dunno. Turns out, in aromantic circles, there's something called a "queerplatonic partnership," which is a relationship that ain't exactly romantic but don't hold up under *platonic* neither. I brought this up at the hospital, and Dallas laughed, "Is this a roundabout way to ask if I want to hook up?" I threw my bag of cheap cookies at them before saying, "Maybe," then, "but only if you want to." We haven't yet, but we've talked about it. We'll see.

"Think your parents will let you?" Dallas says about the dropping-out thing.

I shrug. "Dunno. Do you regret it?"

"Nah." They reach out and skim part of my freshly shaved head. "If you want to back out and go for your GED, we can do that together."

Taking some time off sounds nice. I put my new black shoelace in my mouth and start peeling apart the aglet. I think I deserve a break.

The clock must hit eleven, because Amber gets up on a table to get everyone's attention. There's a lot to do in Twist Creek County now—a lot of decisions to make. Will we allow anyone to take over the sheriff's office; can the position be saved, or do we have to scrap it and start over? What about the county commission that allowed every Davies to stay in office so long? We can't recall elections, so what's the next step? How do we get everyone in the county on board in the first place?

"Fuck it all," Claire Snyder says on the topic of the Twist Creek County Police Department. Her momma sits beside her, fiddling with her hand. "You saw what they did to my daddy. You can't save that."

Mrs. Amsler ain't sold on the idea of police abolition, apparently. "I wouldn't go that far. An office is only as corrupt as the person that holds it, right?"

"Mm," Mamaw Steele says. "Depends on the office."

I did a lot of reading in the hospital, and I gotta say, I agree with Claire and Mamaw Steele. What's law enforcement except a group of people legally allowed to hurt you without cause? I don't trust no one with that kind of power.

Terry, then, suggests abolishing the county commission and instituting a direct democracy; we don't got a whole lot of people, so we might be able to pull it off. Mr. Simmonds says there ain't no way that'll work, and that devolves enough that Dad has to break it up. Amber reminds everyone that a complete and utter reworking of local governance is a big task, and we can't just throw it around without fully understanding it.

It's a lot of talk, and I'm tired. I lean against Dallas's shoulder, eyes heavy, and sigh into the crook of their neck. Their fingers twitch. We're on try eight of quitting now, and this one has lasted a lot longer than the others, but I don't say so in case that jinxes it. I just pull a pack of gum from my pocket and pass it over.

A few days ago, I'd asked Dad if there was anyone else we should be worried about. If Sheriff Davies had any cousins that would come back pissed, any siblings, anyone. Dad sighed, and said, "I'm sorry you have to think about this," but finally replied no, not that he knew of. We'd have to be vigilant, of course—we're Abernathys, we always have to watch our backs—but we're okay for now.

Dallas is popping a stick of gum in their mouth when their eyes dart over to the end of the alleyway. They nudge me and I sit up with a groan before seeing what they're nodding to.

Shit. Cop car. West Virginia State Police, the big blue cruiser with the gold stripe. It sits there idling for a moment, parked up on the sidewalk because there's never enough room, before someone steps out. A state trooper, all dark green and metal badges.

I stick my fingers in my mouth and whistle.

The crowd goes quiet. Papaw is still putting up a tent, so it's Mamaw that picks up his shotgun.

When that cop comes over here, none of us are gonna know a thing. Even Mrs. Amsler and Mr. Simmonds. No, sir; no, ma'am; we ain't seen the sheriff in a while. He was a right son of a bitch, though. We're all doing better without him. Ain't that right? And if that cop comes over to *me*, I'll hold Dallas's hand and say, *Look what he did to us*. No, sir; no, ma'am; we don't miss him at all. No, we won't tell you where he's buried. No, we won't tell you which of us killed him.

But while you're here, officer, why don't you hold this railroad spike for me? Hold it in your hand and tell me how heavy it is. Tell me which one of us you'd use it on.

See what happens if you try.

END

ACKNOWLEDGMENTS

start this acknowledgments page with an awkward smile towards the family members who made it this far, or at least weren't scared off by the dedication. Thank you for reading it anyway! If you recognized yourself in any of the characters, I hope my version of you was fair. (And if I had to cut you for space, or replace you for plot reasons, I hope you're more relieved than disappointed. Hey, at least I didn't kill you!) But for what it's worth—

Mom and Dad, while Miles's parents aren't perfect re-creations of you, they come close where it matters. It's rare for a YA novel to feature living, good, and competent parents, especially ones that grow alongside the protagonist. I'm glad I got to use y'all as the basis.

Mamaw, I knew that a book like this would always have to be a little about you. I tell people that, when folks in our family talk about going "home," they always mean West

Virginia, no matter if they were raised there or not—but maybe I heard you say it so often it stuck.

And Papaw, I wish you could have been around to see this one. You would've gotten a kick out of it. Miss you.

Then, thank you to the usual teams:

To Jennifer, Ashley, Barbara, Gordon, Marissa, Wylie, Wes, and the little one. I adore you all, and I'm very lucky to have you in my corner, even if I am a strange little possum that only sometimes remembers to reply to a message. (Special shout-out to Sam, who suggested that Miles might be aromantic and lost his shit when I said, "Yeah, that makes sense. Let me work that in real quick.")

To my day job, and especially my bosses, for giving me the many, *many* days off for tours and festivals. Y'all have been so very forgiving about my schedule, and very encouraging of my second full-time job. (Sorry about the back-to-back events in 2023; you hired me and I immediately disappeared for weeks at a time.)

To my design and editing team, and my readers, and everyone that's made this book a reality. I've been sitting on this idea for eight years, and seeing it come together with your help has been better than my wildest teenage daydream. I can't believe I get to do this as a career? Unreal. (I am, admittedly, glad to get it off my plate, but the point still stands.)

And to Ally. When this comes out, we'll have been married for almost a year. Your wedding ring is opal instead of diamond, because you hate diamonds. Mine is antler, because of course it is. Do you think about when we visited West Virginia together? When we spent the night in a strange city so I could start testosterone without telling anyone else? When you explained your gender for the first time and showed me your flag? When we were teenagers making out in the back seat of my truck, when we spent hours trying on dresses in the same Forever 21 changing room, when I got too excited to propose and gave you the ring in the parking lot of a gas station?

Because I do. I think about it all the time.

ENDPAPER PHOTO CREDITS

"A striking miner." September 2, 2014. *Libcom.org*. https://libcom.org/article/battle-blair -mountain-1921-photo-gallery. Submitted by Steven.

"Mine Guards at Paint Creek, W. Va." *West Virginia University History OnView*. West Virginia University, n.d. https://wvhistoryonview.org/catalog/004201. Acquired from H.B. Lee.

"Miners surrender their arms after the battle (I)." September 2, 2014. *Libcom.org*. https://libcom.org/article/battle-blair-mountain-1921-photo-gallery. Submitted by Steven.

"Miners surrender their arms after the battle (II)." September 2, 2014. *Libcom.org*. https://libcom.org/article/battle-blair-mountain-1921-photo-gallery. Submitted by Steven.

"Mother Jones rallying the miner at Eskdale." December 5, 2014. *The Register-Herald Reporter*. https://www.register-herald.com/news/remembering-the-violent-coal-wars/ article_8f70204b-634f-5df0-b065-6f5c721deec6.html.

"Some miners surrender their arms after the battle." September 2, 2014. *Libcom.org*. https://libcom.org/article/battle-blair-mountain-1921-photo-gallery. Submitted by Steven.

"Striking miners at the town of Eskdale on Cabin Creek." December 5, 2014. *The Register- Herald Reporter*. https://www.register-herald.com/news/remembering-the-violent-coal-wars /article_8f70204b-634f-5df0-b065-6f5c721deec6.html.

Hine, Lewis Wickes, photographer. "Monongah, W. Va. Nola McKinney, Secretary, 1910, West Virginia Child Labor Committee. Frank P......., whose legs were cut off by a motor car in a coal mine in West Virginia when he was 14 years 10 months of age. Location: Monongah, West Virginia." United States Monongah West Virginia, 1910. March. Photograph. https://www.loc.gov/item/2018675569/.

Hine, Lewis Wickes, photographer. "Young Driver in Mine, (W. Va.) Over 10 hours a day, underground. Sept. 1908. Location: West Virginia." United States West Virginia, 1908. Sept. Photograph. https://www.loc.gov/item/2018673773/.

United States Resettlement Administration, Shahn, Ben, photographer. "Abandoned mine, Dobra, West Virginia." United States Dobra West Virginia, 1935. Oct. Photograph. https://www.loc.gov/item/2017730514/.

United States Resettlement Administration, Shahn, Ben, photographer. "'Black Fury' a movie about a strike, Scotts Run, West Virginia." United States Scotts Run West Virginia, 1935. Oct. Photograph. https://www.loc.gov/item/2017730382/.

United States Resettlement Administration, Shahn, Ben, photographer. "'Black Fury' poster, a movie about a strike, Scotts Run, West Virginia." United States Scotts Run West Virginia, 1935. Oct. Photograph. https://www.loc.gov/item/2017730374/.

United States Resettlement Administration, Shahn, Ben, photographer. "Children of coal miners, Sunbeam Mines, Scotts Run, West Virginia." United States Scotts Run West Virginia, 1935. Oct. Photograph. https://www.loc.gov/item/2017730438/.

United States Resettlement Administration, Shahn, Ben, photographer. "Hernshaw, West Virginia." United States Hernshaw West Virginia, 1935. Oct. Photograph. https://www.loc.gov/item/2017730504/.

United States Resettlement Administration, Shahn, Ben, photographer. "Kimball, West Virginia." United States Kimball West Virginia, 1935. Oct. Photograph. https://www.loc.gov/item/2017730741/.

United States Resettlement Administration, Shahn, Ben, photographer. "Omar, West Virginia." United States Omar West Virginia, 1935. Oct. Photograph. https://www.loc. gov/item/2017730441/.

United States Resettlement Administration, Shahn, Ben, photographer. "Payoff at Pursglove Mine, Scotts Run, West Virginia." United States Scotts Run West Virginia, 1935. Oct. Photograph. https://www.loc.gov/item/2017730387/.

United States Resettlement Administration, Shahn, Ben, photographer. "Untitled photo, possibly related to: A deputy with a gun on his hip during the September 1935 strike in Morgantown, West Virginia." United States Morgantown West Virginia, 1935. Sept. Photograph. https://www.loc.gov/item/2017730381/.

Vachon, John, photographer. "Coal miner. Kempton, West Virginia." United States Kempton Preston County West Virginia, 1939. May. Photograph. https://www.loc.gov/item/2017809446/.

Vachon, John, photographer. "Coal miners playing cards during May 1939 strike." United States Kempton West Virginia, 1939. May. Photograph. https://www.loc.gov/item/2017718015/.

Vachon, John, photographer. "Mine tipple, Kempton, West Virginia." United States Kempton West Virginia, 1939. May. Photograph. https://www.loc.gov/item/2017718006/.

Vachon, John, photographer. "Miner's sons salvaging coal during May 1939 strike, Kempton, West Virginia." United States Kempton West Virginia, 1939. May. Photograph. https://www.loc.gov/item/2017718014/.

Vachon, John, photographer. "Miners playing cards during May 1939 coal strike. Kempton, West Virginia." United States Kempton West Virginia, 1939. May. Photograph. https://www.loc.gov/item/2017718016/.

Vachon, John, photographer. "Sign at entrance to mine, Kempton, West Virginia." United States Kempton West Virginia, 1939. May. Photograph. https://www.loc.gov/item/2017717898/.

Vachon, John, photographer. "Signs at entrance to mine, Kempton, West Virginia." United States Kempton West Virginia, 1939. May. Photograph. https://www.loc.gov/item/2017717909/.

Wolcott, Marion Post, photographer. "Abandoned mine tipple. Scotts Run, West Virginia." Monongalia County United States Scotts Run West Virginia, 1938. Sept. Photograph. https://www.loc.gov/item/2017799479/.

Wolcott, Marion Post, photographer. "Burning slag near coal mine, Scotts Run, West Virginia." United States Maidsville West Virginia, 1938. Sept. Photograph. https://www.loc.gov/item/2017753590/.

Wolcott, Marion Post, photographer. "Caples, West Virginia. With coal mine tipple in foreground." United States Caples West Virginia, 1938. Sept. Photograph. https://www.loc.gov/item/2017752554/.

Wolcott, Marion Post, photographer. "Change of shift, coal mine, Maidsville, West Virginia." United States Maidsville West Virginia, 1938. Sept. Photograph. https://www.loc.gov/item/2017753593/.

Wolcott, Marion Post, photographer. "Children's favorite playground, around coal mine tipples. Pursglove, Scotts Run, West Virginia." United States Pursglove West Virginia, 1938. Sept. Photograph. https://www.loc.gov/item/2017753567/.

Wolcott, Marion Post, photographer. "Hauling coal up the hill, picked up near mines, to his home. Chaplin, West Virginia." United States Chaplin West Virginia, 1938. Sept. Photograph. https://www.loc.gov/item/2017799311/.

Wolcott, Marion Post, photographer. "Old and sick, mine foreman's wife does washings in front yard. South Charleston, West Virginia." United States South Charleston West Virginia, 1938. Sept. Photograph. https://www.loc.gov/item/2017752557/.

Wolcott, Marion Post, photographer. "Untitled photo, possibly related to: Abandoned mine tipple. Scotts Run, West Virginia." Monongalia County United States Scotts Run West Virginia, 1938. Sept. Photograph. https://www.loc.gov/item/2017799480/.

Wolcott, Marion Post, photographer. "Untitled photo, possibly related to: Coal miners waiting for next trip into the mine, Maidsville, West Virginia." United States Maidsville West Virginia, 1938. Sept. Photograph. https://www.loc.gov/item/2017753191/.

ABOUT THE AUTHOR

Andrew Joseph White is a queer, trans, *New York Times* bestselling author from Virginia, where he grew up falling in love with monsters and wishing he could be one too. He earned his MFA in creative writing from George Mason University in 2022. Andrew writes about trans kids with claws and fangs, and what happens when they bite back. Find him at *AndrewJosephWhite.com* or on Instagram and X @AJWhiteAuthor.

West Virginia Regional History Center